LETHAL GROUND

ALSO BY RONN MUNSTERMAN

FICTION

SGT. DUNN NOVELS

Raid on Hitler's Dam
Sword of Ice
Castle Breach
Rangers Betrayed
Capture
Saving Paris
Brutal Enemy
Behind German Lines
Operation Devil's Fire

NONFICTION

Chess Handbook for Parents and Coaches

LETHAL GROUND

A SGT. DUNN NOVEL

RONN MUNSTERMAN

LETHAL GROUND – A SGT. DUNN NOVEL

Copyright © 2018 by Ronn Munsterman
www.ronnmunsterman.com

Published in the United States

Cover Design by David M. Jones
www.triarete.com

Printed in the United States of America
10 9 8 7 6 5 4 3 2 1

ISBN-13: 978-1725900493
ISBN-10: 1725900491

BISAC: Fiction / War & Military

Acknowledgments

Thank you readers. Here we are together again, this time for Tom Dunn's book number ten!

I was thinking about the characters in these books, especially, of course Dunn and Saunders, and I realized these men have been alive in my imagination since about September, 2003, fifteen years! As many writers do, I feel close to these imaginary friends. I guess in many ways they are alive to me. When good things happen to them I feel happiness. When they are hurt I feel pain. When I write chapters that are particularly emotional, I deeply feel what is happening. I hope that emotion carries into the story for you. The truth is, I owe everything to you, my readers. Thanks to your support since 2011, I was encouraged to continue writing the Dunn stories. So you are responsible!

This book's story line covers the war time period from 9 November 1944 to 20 November (which is Pamela's 23rd birthday). There is a prologue that is on 9 October, the month previous. *Operation Devil's Fire* began on 25 May 1944, so we have been following Dunn and friends for almost six months of story time, and seven years in real time. Dunn has been adamant about not accepting a commission, but you'll recall from *Raid on Hitler's Dam* that he took a platoon with him for the first time. He'll do it again in this book and our excellent British friend, Saunders, will do the same. The tasks they've accepted are daunting. There is much at risk.

We have from late November 1944 through May 1945 to reach the end of the war. I already have the story line for book eleven, but I don't know what the future will bring for Dunn and friends. I do plan to keep on researching, and dreaming up fun and challenging events through the end of the war.

This book focuses on Dunn's and Saunders' missions, so we don't see Gertrude or Mr. Finch. They'll be back sometime in the future, don't worry. I know you love Gertrude, and so do I. Reggie Shepston and Eileen Lansford from Bletchley Park are with us for a chapter, providing crucial intelligence, as they'd done before (*Saving Paris*).

The beautiful, haunting cover is by my longtime friend, Jonesy (David M. Jones). This is his ninth cover for the Sgt. Dunn Novels. I tell him what I "see" and he makes it real. Thanks, Jonesy! His website is on the copyright page.

Thank you to my FIRST READERS. They read the book after edit one, which is always pretty ugly. Their help with the manuscript and their insightful suggestions always make the book better.

Dave Cross
Steven B. Barltrop
David M. Jones (Jonesy)
Zander Jones (Jonesy II)
Nathan Munsterman
Robert (Bob) A. Schneider II
John Skelton
Steven D. White

And please welcome two new FIRST READERS:

Gordon Cotton, a longtime reader
Jackson Cross (Dave's son)

There are three father-son pairs who work on the Dunn books:

Cross
Jones
Munsterman

My friend Derek Williams deserves a thanks for his friendship and support all these years. Thank you to my wife for her wonderful help with the manuscript. Her red pen is ruthless, but so valuable.

Thank you to all the servicemen and women of the Greatest Generation. Your courage and willingness to do "what had to be done" will never be forgotten.

For my wonderful granddaughter Julia.
You bless audiences with
your beautiful performing arts talents.

One seldom recognizes the devil when he is putting his hand on your shoulder.

Albert Speer, Nazi Germany Minister of Armaments

What are the bastards up to now?

Technical Sergeant Tom Dunn, U.S. Army

LETHAL GROUND

Prologue

Office of Albert Speer, Nazi Minister of Armaments
Former Academy of the Arts Building
Berlin
9 October 1944, 1500 Hours

Two men who had worked on Germany's Project Dante, the atomic bomb program, entered the former Academy of the Arts building. The irony of destructive men entering what had been the haven of creative men was not lost on either physicist. Albert Speer had seized the building in 1938, forcing the academy to move. It was here as Chief Architect of the Third Reich he had begun his work on Hitler's dream: a World Capital Germania in Berlin, a city more resplendent than Paris, London, and Rome.

The two PHDs stared in wonder at the building's entry hall, with its magnificent marble floor and columns supporting a ceiling ten meters over their heads. They stamped their feet on a large rug and shook the water from their umbrellas.

The *click-clack* of shoes on the marble floor came their way. They looked toward the sound and were surprised to see the Minister himself coming to meet them. They'd assumed some assistant would do that. He had descended a staircase on the right side of the lobby.

Speer approached the men quickly and stopped a meter from them. A handsome man with a high forehead and swept back brown hair, he grinned in apparent real pleasure at seeing the men.

The two men glanced at each other and turned back to Speer, their arms raised in the Hitler salute.

"*Heil* Hitler!" they said.

"*Heil* Hitler!" Speer returned the salute, and offered his hand to the shorter of the two.

"Dr. Bauer, I'm pleased you could make it."

Volker Bauer couldn't help but smile in return.

"Dr. Gerber. Good to see you. I'm very pleased you both are here."

Rudolph Gerber shook hands and smiled, too.

A regular happy fest.

"Follow me to my office. It's on the second floor toward the front of the building where I have a beautiful view."

Speer turned and strode off without bothering to check whether the men were keeping up with him. Of course they would. Their careers were at stake.

Speer led the way up the wide staircase. Half way to the second floor, they reached a landing. From there, the stairs split so you could go right or left and walk up the last segment to the next floor. Speer chose the right, which was closer to the front of the building. At the second floor, a walkway went left, with a bannister supported by many small columns surrounding the open space of the entry hall below. Following the walkway a short distance, Speer turned right at its corner and marched down a longer walkway. At the midpoint, he opened a door with his name and title tacked to it in a brass engraved nameplate.

He stepped through and made his way across the enormous room to his desk. The two men followed him inside. Their eyes widened at the opulence and size of the room. It was a good ten meters long by five wide. Various work tables were spread around the space, each with different models of stunning buildings and memorials. They glanced at each other clearly thinking they wished they had an office like this.

Stepping behind his two-meter-wide oak desk, he motioned for the men to be seated in a couple of rather comfortable looking stuffed chairs. They sat and he did, too.

Born in Mannheim, Speer and his family moved to Heidelberg when he was thirteen. He later attended the Technical University of Munich where he studied architecture. This was the same school his predecessor, the late Dr. Fritz Todt, had attended years earlier. Speer eventually passed his exams at the University of Berlin. After helping renovate the Nazi Party's Berlin headquarters in 1932, he was asked to submit plans for the 1933 Nuremberg Rally, which was where he first met Hitler. Following the huge success of the rally, Hitler awarded him the impossible title of Commissioner for the Artistic and Technical Presentation of Party Rallies and Demonstrations.

Speer, at thirty-nine, was eleven years younger than Todt. They had been at Hitler's eastern headquarters, the Wolf's Lair, in February, 1942. One evening, Todt invited Speer to return to Berlin on Todt's aircraft at seven a.m. the next morning, February 8th, and Speer accepted. But fate intervened. Hitler invited Speer for a late night meeting which ran from one to three a.m. Following the meeting, exhausted from a week-long trip to Russia, Speer begged off the flight, knowing he would have to take a miserably long train ride to Berlin. He was awakened early the next morning by Dr. Karl Brandt, one of two personal physicians to Hitler, who excitedly told him that Todt's plane had crashed shortly after takeoff and Todt had been killed.

Speer was summoned to Hitler's office at one p.m. where the *Führer* simply said, "*Herr* Speer, I appoint you the successor to Minister Todt in all his capacities."

When Speer objected because he knew nothing of managing armaments production, Hitler had cut him off and told him he had confidence in him and besides, there was no one else. Speer had proven Hitler's trust in his abilities and had increased war production capabilities within six months.

Bauer and Gerber sat upright, their feet squarely on the floor. Worry was written in their body language and on their faces. Speer was accustomed to seeing worry and dread on faces during meetings with Hitler. He himself had shown it many times over the past few years as Hitler's rampages seemed to get worse by the minute.

Speer considered himself to be a thoughtful man. A considerate man. A man who was merely doing his job to the best of his remarkable abilities. He saw no reason to exacerbate these men's problems. He did however, need their sharp intellect to solve a problem brought to him by Hitler.

"Gentlemen. I'm grateful you were able to come see me today." He glanced over his shoulder at the large windows behind him where the rain was beating a staccato rhythm on the panes. "Especially in miserable October weather like this."

Gerber, acting as the spokesman, said, "We're happy to meet with you, Minister."

Bauer nodded.

Speer decided to dispense with what was worrying the men first so they would relax and be able to fully engage their intellect.

"The investigation into the explosion at the Project Dante lab has been completed by the Gestapo."

Bauer and Gerber immediately sat up even straighter and froze in place, only their eyes and rasping fearful breaths giving away that they were indeed alive.

"You have both been cleared of any wrongdoing."

Bauer let out a breath that was on the border of a sob. Gerber placed a hand over his eyes and rubbed them like a little boy with a scratched up knee.

The men recovered enough to look at Speer.

"Thank you, Minister," both said.

"You're welcome. To be honest, it's very fortunate you were both having breakfast at your hotel's restaurant at the moment of the explosion. As you know, it was impossible for the investigators to get anywhere near the site due to the dangers of the radiation. Nevertheless, they've concluded either Dr. Franz Herbert or Dr. Gunther Winkel, or the two together, somehow set off the explosion. Neither has been found and it's believed they expired in the atomic blast."

Herbert was the project lead and Winkel was one of the other physicists. Bauer and Gerber glanced at each other briefly. They knew Winkel hated Herbert and thought he himself should have been in charge. The two men had had a showdown when Winkel had threatened to go over Herbert's head and obtain enriched plutonium to use in place of the uranium. Herbert laid into the man and made it clear he would be off the project if he did that. Winkel backed down, but his anger grew day by day.

"The explosion site has been covered by a hundred feet of dirt. Concrete would have been preferable, but we can't spare it."

To Speer's eyes, Bauer and Gerber had relaxed, at least to some degree. They were ready for the questions.

"I understand you experienced a radiation poisoning death on the project."

Bauer blanched. They had seen the result of someone getting a fatal exposure to uranium-235. It had been a horrifying painful death. The man's face and hands were filled with red blisters and eventually the skin had begun to slough off like snow from a mountain during an avalanche.

"We did, sir," Gerber replied.

"Were there any cases of non-fatal exposure?"

Bauer frowned. Where was the Minister going?

"Yes, sir. One. The man's exposure was extremely brief. He experienced severe nausea and vomiting, and for several weeks afterwards he suffered complete weakness and fatigue. He recovered fully some time later."

"You seem well versed in this, Dr. Gerber."

"Oh, well, we all were. We had to be to make sure everyone on the project understood the dangers."

Speer cleared his throat. "How would you go about causing radiation poisoning?"

Bauer frowned. "You mean expose people on purpose?"

"Yes. Exactly."

"I don't understand, sir. Why . . . would . . . you want to do that?"

Speer's eyes seemed to bore straight into Bauer's.

"The *Führer* is asking."

Bauer's eyes widened.

Gerber said, "He wants to weaponize the uranium we still have."

Speer turned to Gerber. "Correct."

"I see," Bauer said. He turned to Gerber, who gazed back unperturbed. "What do you think?"

This was Bauer's way of asking Gerber to explain it to the minister.

Gerber nodded acceptance of Bauer's request.

"Minister, there is one major problem with weaponizing a radioactive material."

Speer nodded. "Go on."

"Radioactive material remains dangerous for many years. Any material left exposed to the world would make that place radioactive far beyond our own lifetimes. It's on the order of millions of years."

Speer sat back. "You're saying it would render a location exposed to radiation uninhabitable, in essence, forever?"

"It would depend on the amount of radiation we would use. It would take some calculations to determine how much material would work. Are we seeking to kill enemy soldiers or merely incapacitate them?"

"Either or. How long would a soldier be incapacitated?"

"The man I mentioned who was briefly exposed was unable to work for about a month."

"How long will it take you to work out the calculations on the quantity of the material?"

Gerber gave Bauer a questioning look.

"We would need to have the medical staff from the lab where we worked available to us. They would be better able to provide us with dosage numbers. That would allow us to move ahead with the quantity calculations," Bauer said.

"I'll arrange that. How would we dispense the material?"

Bauer rubbed his upper lip absentmindedly as he thought about that.

"We could grind the uranium into a fine powder. This could be sprayed from an airplane like a pesticide," Bauer replied. "Or we could pack it in artillery shells and deliver it that way."

"Are you confident you can find the right quantity so it'll kill or sicken the enemy but not ruin the landscape?"

"Possibly, sir," Gerber said.

Bauer cleared his throat. Speer looked at him.

"Since we're discussing powder, there's another consideration. Depending on the terrain, if it rains after we deliver the powder, it could be possible for the powder to run off, make its way into streams and rivers. There could be serious ramifications to German civilians if this happens."

Speer nodded. "I'll find another team who will focus on how best to detect the uranium if it does get into the waterways, as well as how best to protect the citizenry."

"Thank you, Minister."

Speer nodded again, a 'you're welcome' kind. "Good. I'll find a suitable workplace for you and your team. Closer to the French border, of course."

"Of course," Gerber said.

"Whomever you need, you just give me a list and I'll get them there. Let me know how much uranium you'll need. We have a substantial supply still."

Speer stood. "I'll contact you both soon. Send me the list of staff quickly."

Bauer and Gerber understood the meeting was over and jumped to their feet.

Speer reached across the desk and shook hands solemnly with each physicist.

"You can find your way out?"

"Yes, sir," both men replied.

"Thank you for this opportunity, Minister," Bauer remembered to say.

"I have high hopes, gentlemen. This project is a top priority for my office. You have my, and the *Führer's*, full support."

Bauer reflexively swallowed.

"Yes, sir," Gerber replied.

The two men walked to the building's front door, where they stopped long enough to button their overcoats and get their umbrellas ready.

Once out on the rainy street they walked south toward their car.

They felt free to speak out in the open.

"When he said we were cleared, I felt happy for the first time in months," Bauer said.

"And then he gave us this horrible task," Gerber said.

"Yes. When we were working on the atomic bomb, I felt it was . . . fair. Just a bigger explosion. If we were ready to kill hundreds of thousands of American civilians, we shouldn't have any compunction over killing thousands of combatants." Bauer paused to look around the street. "But it feels wrong. Dirty."

"Yes. And if we miscalculate, we may doom parts of Europe to a lingering death."

"What choice have we?"

Gerber shook his head. "None. If we refuse, Speer will arrange a trip to a concentration camp, I'm sure."

"Or he'll have us shot."

"There's no chance of escaping Speer, is there?"

"No. None at all."

Chapter 1

Bletchley Park, England
9 November 1944, 0924 Hours, 1 month later

A frigid north wind blew rain almost horizontally as a young woman ran across the open ground toward Bletchley Park's hut number three. Her coat was wrapped tight around her lithe form. She carried a leather satchel of the same style popular for decades with British barristers. There was no umbrella; what was the use when it would invert itself in the first five seconds? She stumbled a few yards from hut three's door, but somehow regained her balance before she would have landed face first in the mud. She gripped the door knob with a gloved hand, twisted and yanked. She darted through the doorway and slammed the door shut behind her.

She stood in the doorway, dripping on the piece of old carpet placed there a week ago when the bad weather was predicted. Setting down the satchel, she removed her soaked blue knit hat, which she put on the coatrack by the door. She took off the gloves and stuffed them in the coat pockets, and peeled off the coat. She wore a blue blouse and black slacks. Pulling a handkerchief from her pocket, she dabbed her face dry. She pocketed the cloth and ran her fingers through her damp hair in a feeble attempt to make it presentable. Finally ready, she looked around the hut's small space. There were ten men scattered about, each with his own paper-covered desk. No one was watching her. Their eyes were focused on the papers atop their desks.

Her lip curled into a half smile as she watched one handsome man in particular. He was the one she'd come to see, which was something she always completely enjoyed. They'd been dating more or less on the quiet since August.

She picked up the satchel and wound her way past a couple of desks and seated herself in front of him.

"Hello, Mr. Shepston."

Reginald Shepston, an MI6 analyst, looked up in surprise. He hadn't even heard the door when she slammed it shut. His face broke into a wide grin and his eyes crinkled in pleasure at seeing Eileen Lansford. Her wet brown hair was up and away from her lovely oval-shaped face. Her eyes, somewhere between green and hazel, regarded him in a way that always made his heart jump.

"Good morning, Miss Lansford."

They'd agreed to keep things formal around the others. They remembered most of the time, not that the others were paying any attention.

She opened the satchel, which was sitting on the floor next to her, and removed a sheaf of papers, a common occurrence for her visits. She worked in the hut that reviewed messages after translation and collated those that were possibly connected, and drew initial conclusions to help the analysts save time. She had proven herself to be an astute analyst in her own right, and had shown considerable initiative. She had discovered the Nazis were making biological weapons at a facility at Insel Reims, Germany. Her work, and Shepston's, led to the destruction of the facility and the capture of the bioweapon canisters in Paris just as they were about to be released during the celebration of the city's liberation. Sergeant Tom Dunn and his Rangers had accomplished that with the help of a platoon of Sherman tanks.

She handed over the papers. Shepston laid them on the desk and began reading. Eileen's work style was to provide him with a summary of her conclusions followed by a summary of the details in the papers. It was always orderly and logical. She took the reader from A to Z smoothly and concisely.

He finished reading the two summaries and sat back. "You've got to be kidding me. They're at it again?"

"They're getting desperate."

"Let me see if I have this right. The messages are from Speer to Hitler and from Speer to two physicists. Speer met the physicists at his office. At this meeting, they discussed the use of raw uranium as a weapon? Bloody hell."

"Yes. You have it. There's also a message trail from Speer to Göring and back."

"Why does Speer need Göring?" This last question was more to himself, which Eileen recognized, so she just waited. Shepston stared at the papers and picked up his ever-present pencil. He tapped a drumbeat on the desk with the eraser end. Eileen thought this one was to a Glen Miller song, "In the Mood." They'd danced to it a few weekends ago.

Göring was nominally Speer's boss under the so-called Four-Year Plan. This was an economic and rearmament plan Hitler had dreamed up. He'd put Göring in charge at the beginning, in 1936. Although the plan was set to expire in 1940, Hitler extended it indefinitely due to the war. Göring remained in charge, in spite of his inability to truly work with the industrialists. This was where Speer came in because he had learned quickly how to get agreement from those same men who hated Göring.

Speer was also able to work with the increasingly peculiar Göring, a real challenge. Göring was known to have become addicted to morphine following his being shot at the Beer Hall Putsch in Munich twenty-one years ago. He'd been certified a dangerous drug addict in 1925 and committed to Langbro Asylum in Sweden, where he was weaned off the drug by 1927. However, it was a short-lived success and he'd returned to using some years later.

"Speer must believe he needed Göring's support, perhaps to convince Hitler?" Eileen asked.

He raised his head and looked at her. "Or he wants Göring to have foreknowledge and be involved in the decision to share the blame."

She lifted her eyebrows. "They really think like that?"

"They are a duplicitous lot, that's known for sure."

She shook her head in disgust. "That's just beyond belief."

"Believe it, Miss Lansford."

"Right."

"We need to put a stop to the whole endeavor."

"Mr. Finch?"

Shepston had introduced Eileen to his friend, Alan Finch, when they were working on the bioweapon problem. Finch was a former MI5 analyst who worked directly for the Prime Minister, Winston Churchill.

"Yes, indeed." He picked up his phone and dialed the number from memory. While it rang, he said to Eileen, "I haven't talked to him for quite a while."

"Mr. Finch's office," a male voice said.

"Hello, this is Reginald Shepston, may I speak with him, please?"

"Sorry, sir, he's unavailable at the moment."

"When do you expect him?"

"I can't say, sir."

"Will he be back today?"

"I can't say, sir."

"I see. Listen, I work at Bletchley Park and I have something that must be handled urgently. Is there someone helping Mr. Finch."

"One moment, sir."

The phone went dead and he thought the connection was broken.

Another, quite gravelly male voice suddenly came on the line. "How may I assist you, Mr. Shepston?"

Shepston's mouth seemed to have stopped working and it hung open. It was a voice he'd heard many times over the wireless.

Eileen stared at him and whispered, "What's wrong?"

He managed to say, "Mr. Prime Minister. Hello."

Eileen sat up perfectly straight, her eyes wide.

"I . . . wasn't expecting to speak to you, Mr. Prime Minister."

"Oh, I know. Alan told me about you, so I'm familiar with your work. Alan is on assignment overseas, so I thought I could give you some assistance. What is it that's so urgent?"

"I should really see you in person, sir." Shepston heard the rustling sound of papers being moved around.

"Oh, bloody hell, where is it?" Churchill cried. "Simon!" This last was at the top of his lungs and Shepston had to move the receiver from his ear. He glanced at Eileen and shrugged.

A few seconds passed. "Simon, do I have anyone at lunch?"

Simon, Churchill's assistant, replied in a calm voice, "No, sir. You are free during that time."

"Humpf. Can you come to my place at noon?"

Shepston figured Churchill was talking to him and answered, "Yes, sir. I can be there."

"Good. Bring that young woman with you. Lansford. Eileen? She helped you on this, correct?"

Shepston looked across the desk at Eileen. She'd been upset when she learned she was supposed to meet Alan Finch, who only *worked* for the Prime Minister.

"I will do that, sir. Yes, her name is Eileen Lansford."

"See you then."

The line disconnected and Shepston turned the phone in his hand and stared at it. He hung it up gingerly.

Eileen's expression was one of shock. "He knows my name?"

Shepston grinned. "He sure does." He leaned across the desk and said, "I have to go meet him at lunch time to talk about this."

She nodded.

"He asked me to bring you along."

"Oh no he did not. Stop it."

"Oh yes he did."

Eileen closed her eyes and muttered, "Not again."

"Face it, young lady, you're making a name for yourself in the upper circles."

"I just want to do my job!" she complained, her voice strident and loud.

A couple of the other men glanced her way and frowned at the interruption.

"Part of the job is meeting the Prime Minister. You should be excited."

Eileen's eyes narrowed and Shepston had time to think, *uh oh.*

In a dangerously low voice, barely a whisper, she snapped, "You do not get to tell me how I should feel, *Mr. Shepston.*"

Shepston sat motionless for a moment, doing a frozen bunny impersonation. Maybe if he didn't move she would forget he was there. Finally, he remembered to take a breath, and cleared his throat.

"Yes, of course, Miss Lansford. My apologies."

Her eyes still flashing in anger, Eileen said, "I guess we'd better get going."

"Yes, right."

"I'll tell my supervisor, Miss Woodhouse."

Shepston imagined Woodhouse's expression upon hearing the news, pinched lips and a frowny face. He smiled at the image. He knew better than to offer to call on Eileen's behalf. The first time had been fine, but after Eileen's last trip to 10 Downing Street, word got around and she became a bit of a hero for all the women working at Bletchley Park.

"Of course," was all he prudently said.

Chapter 2

Sgt. Tom Dunn's private quarters
Camp Barton Stacey
60 miles southwest of London
10 November, 0602 Hours

Technical Sergeant Tom Dunn jumped out of his bunk and bounded toward his desk by the window. The phone was ringing. He'd been awake exactly two minutes. He snatched the black handset off the phone's body on the second ring and held it to his ear.

"Dunn here."

"Took you long enough to answer, Dunn," Colonel Jim Cole snapped, his voice dripping with irritation.

"Good morning, Colonel."

"We'll see about that. I want your men ready for inspection by oh six twenty-five. Class B service uniform, and M1s."

Dunn gripped the handset so hard his knuckles turned white.

"Inspection at oh six twenty-five with Class B service uniforms, and M1s. We'll be ready, sir."

"See that you are." This was followed by a loud click as Cole hung up on Dunn.

Dunn calmed himself and hung up the phone without slamming it. He leaned on the desk with both hands. A sigh escaped. *Get well soon, Colonel Kenton. Please.*

Ten days ago, Colonel Mark Kenton, Dunn's commander, had been seriously injured when the C-47 he was aboard crashed on takeoff at Hampstead Airbase. Two other officers, both doctors, had been killed because they'd chosen the wrong place to sit. The crew survived. Kenton was still in the camp hospital. The last Dunn had heard, which was the day before, he might get out next week.

He didn't know how much more of Colonel Cole he could take. Following their first post-mission meeting, the man had reamed out Dunn for choosing British Commando Sergeant Malcolm Saunders to go along on the successful raid on Hitler's Dam. Cole had warned Dunn to never do that again. Dunn had told Kenton he thought Cole was planning on somehow getting his spot as commander of the special mission Rangers company. Kenton hadn't been surprised because he'd known Cole at West Point where he'd undercut just about everybody at one time or another. That he hadn't been found out was a blemish on the army in his opinion.

Dunn threw on a pair of pants and went to the main barracks area. Some men were getting dressed while others were still sacked out.

"Everyone up! Get up!"

This woke up the sleeping men and stopped the others in their tracks. Dunn never came into the barracks without a shirt and he never shouted.

When everyone looked his way, he said in a normal voice, "Colonel Cole just called for an inspection at oh six twenty-five. Service uniforms, class B, and M1s. You have twenty one minutes to get outside in formation."

There were a few 'oh shits' and some 'son of a bitches,' but the men scrambled into action.

Dunn ran back into his quarters and quickly washed his face, and shaved. He combed his brown hair after wetting it down some to help control it. He dressed in his class B uniform as fast as possible, making sure his tie was snug against his throat. Otherwise Cole would gig him, a demerit. His shoes were already shined, thank goodness he and his men kept them that way. He checked himself in the mirror one more time and left his quarters.

The men were finishing getting dressed.

He unlocked the rifle rack and prepared to hand out the weapons. As each man completed dressing, he ran over to Dunn, who handed him a Garand M1. Dunn's process was to clean the weapons after each use, whether on a mission or at the firing range, so he knew they were clean. However, it had been two days since the last trip to the firing range. This meant there would normally be some dust motes in the barrels. However, Dave Jones, Dunn's sniper, had come up with a wooden plug that fit right into the end of the barrel. With the breech closed, there was no way dust could find a way inside. At the moment, Dunn was thinking that had been one of the smartest things they'd done related to inspections. Colonel Kenton never called inspections, believing they were a colossal waste of time for Rangers, who knew how the hell to take care of their weapons. Dunn removed the plugs as he handed the rifles over and dropped them in a small cup attached to the rack. Jonesy had thought of everything, bless his heart.

Dunn checked his watch: 6:20 am. "Five minutes, men."

Dave Cross, Dunn's second in command, was last. He'd spent time checking each Ranger over before letting him go outside, correcting a few ties and collars.

"Damn it, Tom. What's the deal?"

Dunn shook his head. "Who knows? Colonel Brilliant is just trying to make sure we know he's boss."

Cross sighed. "Swell. Do you think he'll screw up our weekend passes? I was going to go to London."

Dunn shrugged. "No way to tell, Dave."

"Well, shit."

Dunn handed over Cross's weapon and grabbed one for himself. He locked the rack and pocketed the key. Both men removed the plugs and dropped them in the cup. They slid back the bolts and locked them in place. Dunn inserted his left thumb in the breech with the nail facing the barrel. He looked into the barrel and held the rifle so light reflected off his thumbnail. It was like a small spotlight shining inside the barrel. It was perfectly clean, just as he'd expected. Cross had done the same thing. When they were done, they closed the bolt with a snap and ran out of the barracks.

The day was cloudy, something that had become a regular occurrence lately, but it was not raining. A north wind blew across the camp.

The men were in inspection formation facing away from the barracks. Cross took his spot on the right of the line, checking his interval by extending his left arm until his fingertips touched Stanley Wickham's right shoulder. Dunn stood front and center. He checked his watch: 6:24 am.

The sound of a jeep's roaring engine came their way and soon it appeared, coming from the south. Colonel Jim Cole sat in the passenger seat and the driver was Captain Samuel Adams, his temporary aide. Adams pulled the jeep to a stop just off the road and shut off the engine.

Cole climbed out, grabbed the bottom hem of his own uniform jacket and snapped it. Adams, who was carrying a clipboard on which demerits would be noted for each man, joined Cole following to the left. Cole marched stiffly over to Dunn, who was at order arms. Dunn saluted by bringing his flattened left hand over sharply to a point just in front of the tip of the barrel.

Cole returned the salute and Dunn placed his left hand by his left leg.

"First Ranger squad ready for inspection, sir," Dunn said formally. He performed a perfect and smooth inspection arms by raising the rifle to port arms, sliding open the bolt with his left hand, and snapping his head down to ensure the breech was clear. He snapped his head back up and stared into Cole's mean eyes.

Cole stared at Dunn. He examined the brass on the lapels, the tie's knot, and the rows of ribbons over the left breast, including the light blue one for the Medal of Honor, which was centered above all the rest by itself. Everything was in exactly the right spot.

Dunn was taller than Cole by a few inches, reaching six-two and weighing about a hundred eighty. He had brown hair and dark brown eyes over a slim, almost regal, nose, as his wife liked to call it.

Cole snatched the rifle out of Dunn's hands. He peered into the breech and was disappointed because he could see no dirt. He checked the round rear sight aperture, which was infamous for collecting dirt. Clean. Like Dunn, he inserted a thumb and checked the cleanliness of the barrel. Another disappointment. He handed the rifle back to Dunn. As Dunn closed the bolt with his right forefinger and went back to order arms, Cole looked at Dunn's shoes. He thought he could have shaved using Dunn's shoes as a mirror. Damn it.

While staring at Dunn's tie, Cole muttered, "Zero."

Adams wrote that down next to Dunn's name, which he had already written on the page.

Dunn right-faced, drew his weapon to port arms, and marched toward Cross at an angle.

Cole followed and took a position in front of Cross.

Cross performed inspection arms as soon as Cole arrived, as would all the rest of the men.

Adams was to the colonel's left, and Dunn was to Adam's left.

Technical Sergeant Dave Cross was a native of Winter Harbor, Maine, a fishing village about forty-five miles southeast of Bangor. At six-two, he was the same height as Dunn, but was about fifteen pounds heavier. They'd met at Ranger school in Scotland where they became best friends. Not long before Pearl Harbor, he'd moved to New York City hoping to find a life different from fishing, which he'd grown tired of. He wanted to expand his world. While his parents had been understanding about it, he knew deep down he'd broken his dad's heart. After seeing combat in North Africa, Italy, France, and many other European countries, he was ready to go back to Winter Harbor and go fishing with his dad. He longed for that day. At Dunn's wife's suggestion, he sent a letter to his dad saying just that. His dad had written back quickly saying he was looking forward to that day. As Dunn's second in command, he made sure everything that needed to be done got done and was done properly.

Cole finished his inspection of Cross with a terse, "Zero," to Adams, who wrote it down next to Cross's name.

When Cole moved to stand in front of Sergeant Stanley Wickham, Adams took position in front of Cross.

The two men stared at each other impassively. Adams suddenly winked at Cross, using his left eye so the colonel couldn't see it. The unexpected familiarity almost threw Cross, but he kept his face stony and his mouth shut. He blinked slowly once in return.

Captain Samuel Adams had been Colonel Kenton's aide for quite some time. He'd recently been promoted and was awaiting Kenton's return to duty so he could move on to his next assignment as a training company commander at a base north of London. That had been placed on hold so he could assist Cole during his stay as commander. Adams had made the request himself of Brigadier General Hopkins, Colonel Kenton's boss. Adams was a Florida boy, growing up in Pensacola and watching the navy pilots work their magic with aircraft. An Officer Training School graduate, he'd led an infantry platoon in Italy, and later was selected by Kenton as his aide.

Cole snatched Wickham's rifle and inspected it. Wickham stared straight ahead. He was from Longview, Texas, a two-hour drive east of Dallas, and had a considerable Texan drawl, which had mysteriously blended with a British accent creating a Brit-Tex sound the women loved. A big man at six-three and two-twenty, he had a dimple in his chin like Kirk Douglas. The women loved that, too. He'd played high school football in Longview, an oversized running back instead of being on the offensive line. He'd broken records for the most touchdowns in a season, the most points scored, and the most yards. Colleges were looking at him his senior year, but the war broke out. He signed up after graduation in June, 1942, which happened to be the day after the Battle of Midway was over. So much for a pro football career.

Cole handed back the rifle and examined Wickham's face for any stray whiskers.

"A pretty boy, are you?"

Wickham grit his teeth and continued to keep his mouth shut.

Cole smirked and started to turn away, but stopped long enough to lose the smirk and grumble to Adams, "Zero."

Next in formation was Staff Sergeant David M. Jones, known affectionately as Jonesy. He'd joined the squad in late June and had earned the slot as the sniper. His preferred weapon was a scoped M1903 Springfield, but today he carried the M1 like everyone else. Dunn had figured Cole would have gone nuts if he saw the non-standard issue Springfield. Jonesy was a slender six footer with dark brown hair and a widow's peak. He was from Chicago's Southside and a fervent White Sox fan. He'd attended the School of the Art Institute of Chicago for a couple of years before enlisting. He could draw anything, and often made the men laugh with his caricatures of them. Their favorite was the one of Colonel Cole, safely hidden away. Another was the one of Wickham where he wore a hat that was half Stetson and half British Commando beret to signify his peculiar Brit-Tex accent.

Cole inspected Jonesy's weapon and found nothing wrong. He handed it back and was about to turn away when a gust of wind swirled some of the dust at their feet. Cole looked down and grinned. A clump of dirt had fortuitously landed on Jonesy's right shoe.

"One demerit for dirt on the shoe."

Jonesy swallowed back his anger as the colonel moved on. Adams wrote down the gig point next to Jonesy's name. Adams looked at Jonesy and ever so slightly shook his head. Jonesy tipped his head a tiny bit.

Cole looked up at six-four Sergeant Bob Schneider II.

"You're a big one, aren't you?"

"Yes, sir."

"You're from Texas?"

"Born there, yes, sir."

Cole glanced to his left at Wickham. "The two biggest guys are both from Texas. Figures."

Dunn was surprised Cole knew that fact at all. He'd shown no interest in the men in any conversations with Dunn. That meant he either learned it from Adams or had actually taken the time to break into the men's files.

Schneider had indeed been born in Texas and, at twenty, was the youngest man on the squad. An excellent translator, he spoke

German and French fluently, a gift from his mother, who'd started him on the languages at four. His father was a career army officer and he'd lived all over the States. He was also the squad's radio operator. He remembered pretty much everything he heard or saw, much like Dunn. On their last mission into Germany about a week ago to blow up Hitler's Dam and power station, Dunn had been accidentally knocked into the dam's reservoir by the rolling bomb. Cross had jumped in and got his unconscious best friend out. Schneider, fighting panic, recalled something his dad had told him years ago, and did chest compressions on an apparently lifeless Dunn. Eventually, life shot through Dunn.

Dunn had invited Cross and Schneider to Sunday dinner with Pamela to thank them for saving his life. Pamela had expressed her gratitude with tears, hugs, and kisses on the cheeks.

Cole finished with Schneider and said, "Zero."

Black-haired and dark-eyed Staff Sergeant Alphonso (Al) Martelli slid his M1's bolt back and watched as Cole took the weapon. Martelli was the same age as Dunn, twenty-four. Born in the Bronx, his parents owned a grocery store with an apartment above. He was Dunn's Italian translator and had been borrowed from another squad for that skill because the squad was heading to Italy back in early August. He'd done a great job translating and in combat, so Dunn had requested that the loan become a permanent switch. He had an older brother flying a B-29 in the Pacific Theater. Martelli had fallen for an older Italian woman and planned to go back after the war.

Cole handed back the weapon and muttered, "Zero."

Next was Staff Sergeant Rob Goerdt. Cole took the M1. Goerdt's blue eyes followed his every move. Goerdt had joined the Iowa National Guard after high school and enjoyed the rigors of the military. He had a number of things in common with his squad leader: born and raised in Iowa, attended the University of Iowa, invaded North Africa, and fought his way up the boot of Italy. They'd never met until he'd been selected to join the squad following the mission to Italy. Goerdt had earned the Silver Star for using a bazooka to destroy seven Panzer Mark IV tanks, and for capturing three crews intact. A farm boy, he'd once saved city-boy Martelli from a viper in a foxhole in France by shooting it with his .45 and cutting off the head. From a German-American family, he spoke German fluently like Schneider.

A disappointed Cole handed back the weapon, and said, "Zero," and moved on.

Corporal Chuck Higgins was only five-eight, but had red hair which contributed to his feistiness and toughness. From Lincoln, Nebraska, he wanted to follow in his professor father's footsteps and become an archeologist. He'd proven he had some skill in that area on his first mission, which was to the Arctic, where the squad had discovered Himmler's Nazi SS trying to recover a treasure trove of jewels, ancient gold and silver coins, and a sword supposedly endowed with supernatural powers that transmitted to whomever held it as a leader.

Cole finished inspecting Higgins' rifle, but held on to it. He asked, "What's the serial number of your rifle, soldier?"

Higgins' face flushed. He hadn't checked and the squad interchanged weapons all the time.

"No excuse, sir. I don't know."

Cole smiled and handed back the rifle.

"Ten demerits for failure to know his rifle's serial number."

An embarrassed Higgins stared straight ahead as Cole moved on to the last man.

Cole took the rifle from Corporal Hugh Kelly, who was a particularly handsome man with black hair and blue eyes. An Irish lad from, of all places, Mississippi, Kelly's southern accent rivaled Wickham's. His great grandpappy, as he called him, had fought for the South and Kelly had gotten into plenty of fights with Northerners daring to criticize his heritage. He'd made it to Ranger School in spite of his troubles and stopped fighting his own men when he'd almost been sent back to his original unit. He'd set some records in shooting and problem solving and it had been enough for Colonel Kenton and Dunn to agree to take him on.

Cole handed back the rifle.

"From Mississippi."

"Yes, sir."

"Bet you have some confederate traitor's blood in you."

"Yes, sir. My grandpappy."

"You're proud of him, huh?"

"As you say, sir, he was a traitor. I'm not."

"Humpf."

Dunn, who had been staying to Adam's immediate left during the entire inspection, had been able to hear everything the colonel had said along the way. The exchange with Kelly was too much, but he forced himself to remain passive and not shake his head in disgust.

Cole said, "Zero" to Adams.

Dunn about faced and marched to his position in front of the squad.

Cole and Adams followed. Cole stopped directly in front of Dunn and eyed the Ranger.

"How many demerits, Captain Adams?"

Adams didn't have to look at his clipboard. "Eleven, sir."

Cole continued to regard Dunn for a moment before changing his focus to the formation behind Dunn. He scanned the line and said, "You're one man short, Sergeant."

Surprised by the comment, Dunn said, "Eugene Lindstrom is in the hospital recovering from a wound received in the Arctic. I expect him back next week. Sir."

"You should have arranged for someone to fill in for his absence."

"I did do that, sir, for our last mission. I released the man back to his original squad recently because Lindstrom is due to return soon."

Cole shook his head. "Not good enough. What if you'd been ordered on a mission with no time to prepare?"

"I would have requested a replacement again, sir."

"There might not have been time for that. Get yourself a replacement. Today. Understood?"

"Yes, sir."

"Ten demerits, Captain Adams, for failing to keep the squad at full strength."

When Adams hesitated in writing down the number, Cole snapped, "What are you waiting for, Captain?"

Adams felt he had no choice but to speak his mind. "I think that's an unusual demerit, sir."

"I will determine what is usual for a demerit, Captain," Cole replied coolly.

Adams' pencil scratched on the paper. "Yes, sir."

"That makes the total twenty-one, correct?"

"Yes, sir."

"Sergeant Dunn, you have amassed more than twenty demerits. Unacceptable. All weekend passes for your squad are hereby revoked."

"Yes, sir."

Dunn saluted. Cole returned it and about faced.

He and Adams got back in the jeep and drove away. Dunn watched the colonel's back until the jeep turned a corner and was out of sight. His lips compressed into a thin line and his dark eyes flashed black, a warning sign of anger. He forced himself to take a deep breath and push away the anger at the colonel's capriciousness.

Finally feeling calm enough, he about faced and eyed his troops. Their normally impassive formation expressions had given way to anger.

"Gentlemen, after I dismiss you, go immediately into the barracks. I will meet you there. Squad, dis . . . missed!"

The men raised their weapons to port arms and traipsed back into the barracks.

Cross hung back and waited for Dunn at the door.

"Asshole."

"Yep," was all Dunn replied.

The men gathered in a semicircle waiting for Dunn, still holding their rifles at port arms.

"To those of us receiving demerits today, I say only this: there is nothing we could have done. The inspection's outcome was ordained long before we even made formation. Is that understood?"

Jonesy and Higgins nodded.

"Weekend passes are not revoked, they are merely on hold. I will ensure you receive extra days down the road when Colonel Kenton returns to us. Is that understood as well?"

The men broke into smiles and all replied, "Yes, Sergeant!"

"Get the weapons secured, change into daily uniforms, and go get some breakfast."

"Yes, Sarge!"

Back in his private quarters, Dunn ripped off his tie and threw it on the bunk. Next came his jacket, although he slowed down and hung it up on a hanger. Couldn't risk getting dinged for a wrinkled uniform. He grudgingly picked up the tie and smoothed it out. He slipped it around the hook of the hanger and draped it over the jacket.

He picked up the phone and dialed the number for home. He looked out his window while waiting. When Pamela answered, he said, "Hi, Honey. I thought I should call you to tell you I won't be home this weekend. I can be there tonight only."

"Oh, no, really, Tom?" His wife sounded disappointed. "Why?"

"We had a surprise inspection by Colonel Kenton's temporary replacement and he revoked all weekend passes. I can't just up and leave the men in the barracks."

"Oh, I see. Of course. I understand. He's being awfully mean, isn't he?"

Dunn chuckled. "Not the word that comes to my mind, but it'll do."

"See you tonight."

"Yep."

They said their 'I love you's' and goodbyes and he hung up the phone.

He sighed and finished changing clothes. Time for breakfast and perhaps a visit to see how Colonel Kenton was doing. Maybe he'd come back sooner.

Chapter 3

Colonel Rupert Jenkins' office
Camp Barton Stacey
10 November, 1240 Hours

Sergeant Major Malcolm Saunders, a six-foot, wide-bodied Commando with red hair and a matching handlebar mustache, marched down the hallway toward his commander's office. Sergeant Steve Barltrop, a slim man just under six feet, viewed the world through bright blue eyes. He was on his squad leader's left.

At Jenkins' door, Saunders stopped and knocked. He waited for "Come," and opened the door. He stepped inside and came to a halt. Barltrop nearly ran into Saunders' backside because it was such a sudden stop.

Colonel Rupert Jenkins and his aide, Lieutenant Carleton Mallory, were seated, Jenkins behind his desk and his aide off to his right. What caused Saunders to stop so abruptly was the unexpected and completely out of place appearance of a man of the church, who sat to Jenkins' left. Saunders couldn't tell from behind which church the man represented, but he wore a black cassock.

Jenkins rose to his feet, as did Mallory and the man of the church. "Gentlemen, may I introduce The Archbishop of Westminster, Bernard Griffin?" Jenkins said.

Griffin turned around and smiled at the Commandos. He was in his mid-forties and a short man with disappearing hair trimmed short. He wore round wire-rimmed glasses. A heavy gold cross hung from a thick chain around his neck.

"Sir, may I present Sergeant Malcolm Saunders and his second in command, Sergeant Steve Barltrop?"

Griffin held out his hand and both Commandos shook it.

Even though Saunders was a member of the Church of England, he knew who the Archbishop was. "I'm honored to meet you, sir."

Griffin nodded, and said kindly, "The honor is all mine, gentlemen. So proud of what you are doing for our country and Europe."

He waved a hand at two chairs next to him. "Please, let's all be seated."

Everyone took a chair and stared at the Archbishop, including Jenkins.

"If you please, sir," Jenkins said.

Griffin nodded, bent over and lifted a small black satchel, which he opened deftly. He removed a stack of pictures. He handed one to each of the other men.

The color picture showed a man wearing a white cassock under a red robe that was carefully draped over the shoulders. A heavy, ornately designed cross hung from a short chain connected to a small button. A gold chain seemed to form the letter W with the middle peak on top of the cross and the wider peaks went up under the red robe. His hands were clasped in front of him. He also had round gold-rimmed wire framed glasses that seemed to make his dark brown eyes sharper. A small white crescent sat on the top, covering the back of his head, his zucchetto.

Saunders sucked a breath. Everyone knew who this man was.

The Archbishop rose to his feet and turned toward the door. "Gentlemen, may I present the Pope, Pius the Twelfth?"

Jenkins' door opened and the man in the picture walked into the office, his red robe flowing behind him. The Pope stopped and stood still.

Everyone rose.

All eyes in the room were on him. He returned the shocked gazes quietly, and gave a small smile. He raised his right hand with the first two fingers extended and touching the thumb, while the ring and little fingers were folded into the palm, and gave the sign of the cross while speaking in Italian.

When he was done, he pivoted away and walked out of the office, closing the door behind him.

Saunders exchanged a glance with Barltrop, who raised his eyebrows. What was that all about?

"Please take a seat, again, gentlemen," Jenkins said. He raised his voice and said, "You may come in again."

The door opened again and the Pope stepped through. Saunders and Barltrop jumped to their feet again, but Saunders noticed no one else had.

The Pope offered his hand to Saunders who shook it, although quite puzzled. Barltrop did the same. The Pope walked around to the right side of Jenkins' desk and sat in the last empty chair.

"Saunders, Barltrop, sorry for the subterfuge. This is actually Alfred Welford, a stage actor from London. Your photos are of the real Pope."

Saunders held up his photo and compared it to the man sitting not six feet away. He couldn't discern any differences. "You're a spitting image."

Welford nodded. "Amazing what can be done with stage makeup artfully done and props." He removed his glasses. Saunders immediately realized the eyes were different, this man's were slightly wider apart and the irises larger.

"Wow. Don't take off the glasses, sir."

Welford grinned.

Saunders turned to Jenkins. "I'm pretty sure this isn't some party game you want us to play."

Jenkins grinned at his top squad leader. He seemed pretty pleased they'd tricked the number one Commando in the company.

Saunders had joined the army in 1939 and first saw action in North Africa. That was where he'd met Barltrop. They'd both been selected to go to Commando School in Scotland, at Achnacarry House, which was where they'd come across Jenkins for the first time. Colonel Jenkins had been the no-nonsense training commander and the two men had survived. Shortly after, Jenkins took command of a special missions company. Saunders had been selected by Jenkins to be a squad leader.

Saunders was born in London's tough East End, and spoke like the true Cockney he was. He'd married Sadie Hughes toward the end of September. Barltrop had been the best man. Saunders planned to start his own construction business after the war. He had decided it would be based in or around London. He had three older sisters, all married to servicemen. So far, knock on wood, they were all okay.

Saunders had the reputation of getting the job done. Although because it was war after all, the cost could be terribly high. Just over a month ago, he'd lost half his men in a night fighter attack on their transport plane over Austria. It had been tough for Saunders and the rest of the men to recover.

Barltrop grew up in Cheshunt, a small town north of London. He'd met Sadie's cousin, Kathy, at the wedding and they were going steady. Where Saunders loved everything that had to do with buildings, Barltrop was the same toward cars. He could fix anything mechanical and dreamed of working on Grand Prix racing cars, preferably for the British team, if they ever got themselves back together after the war.

"Sorry for the trickery, gents. We needed to see if our intrepid Mr. Welford could pass muster with you. Archbishop Griffin, would you mind explaining what is going on?"

"Of course, Colonel." Griffin turned so he was facing the two Commandos. "We have it on good authority that Hitler is sending some of his elite and dreaded SS men to kidnap the Pope." He paused long enough for that terrible thought to bounce around Saunders' and Barltrop's heads.

"We need help in protecting the Pope, who, of course, is not interested in changing his scheduled events at all." He leaned closer to Saunders and Barltrop and said softly, "He can be . . .

stubborn, shall we say? Which makes keeping him safe a huge challenge for the Pontifical Swiss Guard. You've heard of them?"

Saunders nodded. "Yes, sir. They have quite a history."

The Pontifical Swiss Guard did have quite a history. They were established in 1506 by Pope Julius II, making it one of the oldest military units in the world with a continuous history of operations. When it had been disbanded at various times throughout history, the Guard was sometimes replaced by German mercenaries. It was always reestablished with Swiss members. The current version of the Guard was a result of changes made by Jules Repond, the commander during the years 1910 to 1921. The multi-color uniforms were one of the results of his tenure. He introduced modern weapons for the Guard in addition to the halberd, a long pike with an axe head on one side and a hook on the other. A week long mutiny against the changes took place in July 1913, but it was put down and thirteen ringleaders were dismissed from service. The Guard currently carried various rifles and had added the German MP40 submachine gun to their armory. Their primary role was to guard the Pope and Vatican City.

"They do indeed, Sergeant. Regrettably, their numbers are low, under a hundred men, and this threat to kidnap the Pope will require someone of your . . . particular skills to thwart. It is thought that the original order came directly from Hitler himself, although that hasn't been proven one way or the other.

"The Nazis haven't appreciated the Church's interference throughout the war. For example, we know that a monsignor in the Vatican is responsible for saving the lives of thousands of escaped prisoners of war and Italian Jews. I can't give you his name, although he seems to have been known by the SS in Rome prior to the liberation of the city back in June. They attempted to capture him numerous times. I'm happy to say they met with failure each and every time."

"How much about the German plan do you know, sir?" Saunders asked.

"Not any detail at all. Only that it is an imminent action. The Guard's commander, Gabriel Herriot, believes they might try it at the Villas of Castel Gandolfo, which is the papal vacation and holiday villa about twenty-five miles southeast of Rome. He personally asked for help from British Commandos. So here I am, asking in his stead for that help. Is it something you can do?"

Saunders replied immediately. "Absolutely, sir. You said the Guard is under a hundred men. How many exactly?"

"Sixty-two."

"Does your information happen to include the size of the SS unit?"

"It does not."

"Given the Nazis' predilection toward overwhelming force, they might deploy as much as a platoon to accomplish the mission."

"How many men would that be?" the Archbishop asked, his eyebrows raised.

"Somewhere between forty and fifty."

The Archbishop started to say something, but Saunders went on quickly, "We have to remember these are elite troops who have seen combat. I know the Guard would do their best, and I mean no disrespect, but it's unlikely they could hold off an SS platoon by themselves."

"And that's where you come in."

"Yes, sir." Saunders looked at Jenkins. "Gonna need help on this one, sir. Two squads to come with us. Who's available?"

Jenkins smiled. That was a bit rare, but had become more common lately. "I know you'd prefer to take Sergeant Dunn and his men along, but I'm afraid his new commander, Colonel Cole, takes a very dim view on . . . joint operations. Doesn't seem to like us Brits. Can you believe that?"

Saunders smiled. It was ironic because Jenkins himself used to be of the same view about the Americans. Only Dunn's incredible track record had changed his opinion.

"Seems hard to believe, yes, sir."

"We do have two squads ready to go. Sergeants Massie and Gilbert would be my choice. Do they meet with your approval?"

Saunders glanced at Barltrop, who nodded.

"They would be fine with us, sir. We know them pretty well," Saunders replied.

"Excellent." Jenkins said. He had selected the two men who were as close to being as good as Saunders as possible. "You'll be in command of the British platoon as of this moment. You'll liaise with the Swiss Guard commander. You'll need to work out a command structure that will work."

"Yes, sir."

"How soon can your platoon be ready?"

"I'll need a whole day, say, tomorrow, to get the men working together and responding correctly to situations. Also some work on the firing range would be appropriate. We should be ready to leave by Saturday night, barring any unforeseen issues."

Jenkins nodded. "Archbishop Griffin, would you be able to contact the Swiss Guard Commander secretly to tell him we're coming?"

"Yes, indeed, I can."

"Good. Lieutenant Mallory will make the travel arrangements and let you know when and where the men will arrive in Italy."

"I'm very grateful."

The archbishop stood and the others rose. He shook hands with everyone and left.

Jenkins looked at Mallory and tipped his head toward the still open door.

Mallory closed it and returned.

"Gentlemen. This is very important. Even though the world may never know about it if you succeed, if you don't, it will and the British Army and England will suffer immeasurable embarrassment. I expect you to succeed."

"Yes, sir. We understand perfectly."

Jenkins turned to the decoy Pope. "Mr. Welford, are you certain you are up to the challenge?"

Welford sat up straighter in his chair. "Absolutely, Colonel. Whatever needs to be done, I'll be ready."

"Good man, thank you. I'll hand you off to Sergeant Saunders."

"Yes, sir."

Saunders and Barltrop rose, saluted the colonel and left, Welford following.

After they got outside and looked around to make sure no one was in earshot, Barltrop said, "Blimey, Mac. Think there's enough pressure on this one?"

Saunders punched Barltrop in the shoulder. "This is why we get paid the big quid, mate!"

Welford smiled at the obvious friendship between the two soldiers. He remembered that feeling well.

Chapter 4

Colonel Jim Cole's office (formerly Colonel Mark
Kenton's)
Camp Barton Stacey
10 November, 1322 Hours

The empty office felt like more than that to Captain Samuel
Adams when he opened the door and stepped inside. He closed
the door quietly behind him and stood silently staring at the desk
from where Colonel Mark Kenton usually presided over mission
meetings.

Adams enjoyed working for Kenton, and was growing more
and more desperate for him to return to duty. He had recently had
the oddest conversation of his military career, maybe his entire
life. He was updating Brigadier General Hopkins, Cole's
commander, with some ongoing missions' details, at the
colonel's request. Bagley's squad was in eastern France, another
was in Denmark, and so on. The meeting had taken place at 1800
hours the night before.

"And so that's the complete update, sir."

Hopkins nodded. He regarded the young captain for a moment with a sour expression.

Adams had been around the block. He mentally prepared for what was coming.

"I had expected to hear this from Colonel Cole. Where is he?"

Adams knew perfectly well where Cole was. Lunch with a young redhead from Andover.

Adams hesitated, a rarity that Hopkins caught, but finally said, "I believe the colonel had another engagement, sir."

Hopkins raised his eyebrows in disbelief. "Colonel Cole told you he was otherwise engaged?"

Adams was in a tight spot. He was Cole's aide, even if it was temporary. And even if the man didn't instill loyalty.

Before he could reply, Hopkins held up his hand. "No. Don't answer that question."

Hopkins sat back in his chair. He eyed Adams as if taking the measure of the officer.

Adams waited.

"I know you feel you're in a box here, Captain."

Adams nodded carefully.

"Kenton trusts you explicitly. And from our own interactions, I do, too."

"Thank you, sir."

Hopkins shook his head. "No, don't thank me. I'm about to put you in a tighter box, if you're up to it."

"I don't understand, sir."

Hopkins leaned forward and rested his hands on the desk. "Colonel Cole is on his way out."

Adams nodded. "Yes, sir, I know, as soon as Colonel Kenton returns."

Hopkins shook his head again. "Not just out of here. Out of the European theater."

"I see, sir."

"I need your help. I was asked to bring him in here for one of two reasons: to prove he could straighten up and fly right or to prove himself unworthy. You tell me where you think he is at the moment between those two choices."

Adams swallowed nervously.

Hopkins noticed and said quickly, "You may speak freely here."

"He is not doing the first, sir."

"Give me an example."

"When he first met Sergeant Dunn during a post-mission briefing, afterwards, he told him never to include Sergeant Saunders and his squad on a mission again. That the assignments were to be American only."

"Dunn told you this?"

Adams flung up a hand to forestall that comment. "Oh, heavens no, sir. Dunn would never do that. No, sir, Colonel Cole told me himself later. He was bragging about it."

Hopkins' jaw muscles clenched and unclenched a few times. Finally, he said, "I see. Anything else."

"Sir, exactly how freely may I speak?"

"Completely."

"Yes, sir, thank you. This morning, Colonel Cole called a surprise inspection on Dunn's squad. He gigged them just enough to cancel their weekend passes. The demerits were bogus, made up on the spot. Old drill instructor tricks."

Hopkins rolled his eyes and shook his head. Petty.

"Anything else, Captain?"

"Only differences in office procedures. Nothing very important. Just unusual."

"I need your help, Captain."

"Yes, sir."

"This is an . . . unusual request by a commanding officer of a subordinate, and for that I apologize. This is all entirely between you and me only. Understood?"

"Yes, sir."

"Cole has quite a history. None of it very good. Here's what I need you to do for me."

Hopkins laid things out.

"Thank you, sir. Will there be anything else?"

"No. There is not." Hopkins stood and offered his hand, which Adams shook as he rose to his feet.

"The sooner the better, Captain. The sooner the better."

"Yes, sir."

Adams turned on the office lights. He waited in the hallway by the door for the colonel just the way Cole liked it. Like a church greeter.

Dunn and Cross arrived before the colonel.

"Morning, Captain," Dunn and Cross said together.

"Morning, gentlemen." Adams replied. He lowered his voice. "Sorry about the inspection."

Dunn shook his head. "It's okay, Captain. We knew what was up."

Adams nodded.

The two sergeants went on in the office and took their usual chairs.

About five minutes passed and they could hear voices coming from the hallway toward the front of the building. Soon after, Cole and another officer, a major, swept into the room. Cole sat down behind his desk and the major took Adams' usual seat. Adams closed the door letting it make some noise. He glanced at Cole who was looking down at his desk, and he quickly opened the door just a hair. He moved quietly to stand on Cole's right.

Dunn glanced at Adams, wondering why he hadn't just gone to the office next door to grab a chair. Adams' expression was stoic.

Dunn looked at Cole, and glanced at the major next to Cross. The man was round in most aspects, body shape and face, with the bulbous, red-veined nose of a heavy drinker. *Swell*, Dunn thought. He had short hair that was mostly brown with a touch of gray. He had piggy eyes that seemed to dart around almost furtively.

What the hell? Dunn thought.

He stuck his hand out, reaching in front of Cross. "Sergeant Tom Dunn, sir."

"Not now, Dunn," Cole chided.

The major, who had started to reach for Dunn's hand reflexively, pulled his own back and stared at Cole. Dunn suppressed a sigh, and purposely did not look at either Cross or Adams.

Cole unlocked his desk drawer and removed a red folder from it with a flourish. The red folders were for Cole's color-coded top secret missions. He laid it on the desk and flipped it open.

"We have a terrific opportunity here. We're going to stick it to the German High Command. Going to screw with their generals' communications."

Dunn nodded. Seemed like a good idea.

Cole rotated the folder and slid it toward Dunn and Cross. Dunn pulled it closer to begin reading. Dunn, who was the faster reader, got to the end of the first page and he glanced up at Cole. The man was practically beside himself with excitement.

Dunn looked back down, curious about something. He read the header information for the mission. This stated who requested the mission—General George S. Patton—who the authors were, the risk assessment and the sign offs by upper levels. Dunn stared at the header in disbelief. The authors were listed as company staff, two colonels whose names he recognized from previous missions, but Cole was also named for the tactical aspects. Risk assessment was marked as "low," an unheard of notation. He had never seen a Ranger mission marked as low.

Cross gulped out loud, and turned the page. The two Rangers finished the document a few minutes after that. Dunn flipped the folder closed and slid it back across the desk to Cole.

"What do you think, Dunn?" Cole asked, wide eyed and hopeful.

Dunn mentally shook his head. Cole was expecting him to ooh and ah over the mission's tactical plan. As written, it would fail. And men would get killed. His men. Dunn usually received missions that stated the goal of the operation, but not the how. He created the mission plan and shared it back to Kenton, who could approve or comment. In the end, Dunn's plans were always approved as is.

Dunn was hardly sure where to start. From what he knew of Cole, if he criticized the plan in any way, Cole would take exception and take it out on someone, either Dunn or his men. If he accepted the plan, he would be expected to run the operation that way. When he didn't, and there was no way in hell he was going to do that, he would get chewed to pieces by Cole during the post-mission debrief. Not typically diplomatic in his approach to idiots, Dunn opted to go for a smooth pre-mission meeting.

"It looks like a very challenging mission with great rewards, sir."

Cole beamed.

"I'll need maps of the area to determine the best routes in and out," Dunn said.

"Of course. Captain Adams will provide those for you."

Dunn nodded to Adams.

"I'd like you to meet my good friend and fine officer, Major Randy Miles, who coauthored the mission and who will be the communications officer going along with you."

Once again Dunn reached in front of Cross. The two men shook hands. Dunn's hand came away wet. He forced himself not to wipe it on his trousers. Cross shook hands next.

Dunn was thinking, *coauthored? Where was Miles' name?*

"So the mission plan looks good to you?" Cole asked.

Dunn realized Cole wanted some kind of validation of his work. *Good heavens.*

"Well, sir, as you know, missions tend to be fluid."

"Oh, yes, they sure do. But it looks like a good starting point?"

Dunn glanced at Cross, who refused to meet his eyes.

"Yes, sir. It's something we can work with."

Cole clapped his hands. "That's great. Why don't you take Major Miles with you and introduce him to the men when you give them the good news."

"Splendid, idea, sir."

Cole rose and the others joined him. He handed the folder to Dunn.

Dunn, Cross, and Miles saluted the colonel.

"Thank you, sir."

"Dismissed."

Everyone left the office except Cole and Adams, who closed the door behind the departing men.

In the hallway, Major Miles said, "Why don't you give me directions to your barracks? I'll meet you there later today. I have some important things to do first."

"Certainly, sir," Dunn replied. He gave the major simple directions to the barracks.

When the men stepped into the cloudy day outside the administration building, the major climbed into a jeep with a driver waiting and it trundled away.

Dunn and Cross jumped in their own jeep, but Dunn didn't start the engine. He sat motionless, staring through the windscreen.

"I think the major's meeting is down at the White Hart Pub," Dunn said.

Cross mimed drinking a shot while saying, *"Glug glug."*

"That is the worst mission plan I've ever had the misfortune to see," Cross said.

Dunn looked over at his friend. He shook his head. "The good news is, we're never going to use it."

Cross immediately looked relieved. "I was hoping you'd say that."

Dunn started the engine, but left the jeep in neutral.

"On the surface, it's actually not a bad idea. We'll have to completely rewrite the plan, though. Plus with Major Miles along, we may have to adjust our estimates on travel times. I suspect he won't be able to keep up with our normal pace."

"That's for sure."

Dunn started to put the jeep in gear, but motion to his right caught his attention. Adams was running down the steps carrying a rolled up map. Dunn pointed.

"Here comes the map."

Adams ran up to the jeep on Cross's side, the nearest point. "Here's the map you need." He handed it to Cross.

"Thanks, Captain," Cross said.

Adams' expression was worry-filled. "Please tell me you're going to come up with a different plan."

"Not to worry, sir. First thing we'll do back at the barracks."

Adams' face relaxed. "Whew. Okay. I read this last night and my knees wouldn't stop shaking."

"Yes, sir. My reaction exactly."

"Of course you realize what'll happen if you don't follow his plan."

Dunn grinned. "I would expect to lose at least another weekend pass, sir. Perhaps a stripe or two."

Adams and Cross laughed.

"It'll be worth it, though," Dunn said seriously. "At least we might all come home."

Adams nodded somberly.

"See you, guys."

"Yes, sir," the sergeants replied, and saluted.

Adams saluted in return, and stepped back. Dunn drove away. As Adams watched the men leave he had two thoughts: *thank goodness Dunn is so damn good,* and *that's good for at least another foot of rope for Cole.*

Chapter 5

White Hart Pub
Andover, England
3 miles southwest of Camp Barton Stacey
10 November, 1730 Hours

Two American Rangers and two British Commandos, good friends, sat around a table older than the United States. The White Hart Pub was established in 1692, during the reign of King William III. Located not far from Dunn's and Pamela's favorite Star & Garter Hotel and Restaurant, the White Hart was built of heavy dark wood with beams running over the doorways so low they had warning signs on them like "Go under, not through." People of the seventeenth century were far shorter. The men had selected the table nearest the roaring fireplace, with its welcome warmth against the British November cold.

Dunn and Cross sat across from each other, while Sergeant Major Malcolm Saunders faced Sergeant Steve Barltrop.

Each man had a glass of beer in front of him that was large enough to put out a major fire. Dunn wiped foam from his upper lip.

"How was your day, Mac?"

"Kind of quiet. Some routine hand-to-hand training for the lads," Saunders replied. He'd first met Dunn at Commando School. They had not hit it off at all. Saunders spent much of his time devising ways to make Dunn's life as miserable as possible. Over time and by working together, they'd become fast friends.

"Sounds like more fun than we had today," Dunn grumbled.

"Yeah, what happened?"

"Early morning surprise inspection by our new and intrepid leader."

"Oh, joy. Colonel Cole?"

Dunn and Cross both grimaced at the name.

"Yes," Dunn muttered. "Class B service uniforms with M1s. Dinged us for twenty-one demerits so we all lost weekend passes."

"Lovely."

"Not sure how much more of him we can stand. I'm gonna go see Kenton tomorrow. See when he's coming back."

"Can't blame you there, laddie."

"Dave and I had a mission meeting today with Cole and a friend of his, who we have to take along with us."

"Where you headed?" Barltrop wanted to know.

"Eastern France, behind the line."

"When do you leave?"

"Early Sunday morning before sunrise."

"We're leaving for Rome tomorrow, late. Looks like we might not see you guys again for a while," Saunders said.

"Yep." Dunn raised his glass. "Best of luck."

The other men raised their pints and took a long drink, finishing off the remainder of their beer.

"Good luck to you, too," Saunders said after he put down the glass.

"I need to get home to Pamela for tonight, since we lost our weekend passes. Although we're leaving early Sunday morning, so it's really just Saturday Cole took from us," Dunn said.

"Prick," Cross murmured.

The men laughed in agreement.

They stood and shook hands all around.

"See you guys around," Dunn said.

"Not if we see you first," Saunders said.

"Ha. Good one. Never heard that before."

Dunn dropped Cross off at the barracks and drove to the Hardwicke Farm five miles south of Andover. Parking the jeep in the barnyard, he shut off the engine and hopped out. He loved coming home to the farm. The main house where Pamela's parents lived was on the east side of the barnyard. Pamela's and his small house was left of the main house as you looked at it, and set back about twenty yards to give some space for each house. Both were made of light colored stone that reminded him of limestone. Maybe I should ask, he thought. At the north end of the barnyard was, well, the barn, which was painted red like they were in the States. A huge oak tree owned the land midway across the barnyard and on the western edge. To the west, a large pasture opened up and went quite a ways on a downslope. It had a marvelous view of sunsets and the valley at their feet. Pamela and he often went for hand-in-hand walks there.

Two happily barking dogs charged toward him from in front of his house. When they got there they licked his hands as he knelt to pet them. They were Pamela's dogs, raised from puppyhood. A black Labrador and a Collie. They were well trained, at least for Pamela. Whenever Dunn tried using her hand signals they just stared at him with their tongues lolling as if they were expecting a treat.

He rose. "Come on, dogs. Let's go see mommy."

The dogs took off and raced back to the house.

By the time he got there, they were sitting impatiently on the door stoop prancing their front paws in a happy dance. The door opened and they scampered inside.

Pamela stepped through the door and smiled. Dunn thought his heart was about to stop. She was so absolutely beautiful. Her blond hair was brushed and shiny and hung to her shoulders. Her oval face bore perfect, unblemished skin; the kind that never needed makeup. Her blue eyes danced at Dunn when she smiled. She wore a simple blue dress that went to her knees. She was three months pregnant and was just recently starting to show, although it was difficult to see when she was dressed.

"Hiya, Sweetheart," Dunn said, stepping close and enveloping her in a gentle hug.

"Hey, Tom. I'm glad to see you."

They kissed a couple of times. When Dunn pulled back he just stared into her eyes. She obligingly returned the gaze. He loved her eyes. It was on a recent mission to the Arctic, where he saw the blue ice inside a glacier's crevasse that he decided it was the exact color of her eyes. Except they exuded warmth, not cold like the Arctic.

Dunn met Pamela when he was in the Camp Barton Stacey hospital where she was a nurse. During a Ranger school training exercise with live fire, one of Dunn's trainees inexplicably stood up. Dunn had tackled the young man, but was rewarded with a bullet wound in the right shoulder for his efforts. Dunn had returned the man to his original unit, an automatic washout, while Dunn had been shipped to the Barton Stacey hospital.

Pamela had taken an interest in the quiet young man from Iowa. To the surprise of her coworkers, who unkindly called her the Ice Queen because she never dated a patient, or for that matter, a doctor, she had warmed to Dunn. She'd told the other nurses she would be taking care of him personally.

She sat with him, changed his bandage, washed his face, and all the other things a top notch nurse did to help her patient recuperate. He'd been apparently immune to her because she had, on multiple occasions, hinted that when he was released from the hospital, she would be interested in going on a date. He'd been such a knucklehead that she'd finally, exasperated, bluntly suggested it.

It was like having to hit a none-too-bright mule on the head with a two-by-four. Finally, it sank in. Even then he'd botched it by asking stupidly, "You wouldn't want to go out with me, would you?"

She'd replied calmly, "Yes, I'd love to," while inside she was screaming, 'Yes! Yes! You big lunk!'

And the first date was a complete fiasco, thanks to Dunn taking something she'd said the wrong way. He'd been rude to her all the way back to her flat in Andover. It was only while on a mission to Calais, France, he realized how dumb he'd been.

When he returned, he'd called her, begging forgiveness, and asking if they could start over.

Still angry over his behavior, she'd given him a hard time, but in the end, gave herself away with some unladylike laughter snorts. They went on a second date and everything went particularly well, with her telling him, "Take me home, Tom." This phrase became their secret code words for "take me home and make love to me."

They'd married seven weeks later. Whenever possible, he spent nights at their house. It gave him a sense of normalcy in an upside down world.

"Ready for supper?" she asked, turning toward the house.

"Yep, I'm starved. Lead the way."

She did.

During dinner, which was a marvelous roast chicken with a few red potatoes and green beans, Dunn related a more detailed story of Cole's surprise inspection, and the consequences. She commiserated with him and said she hoped Colonel Kenton got healthy real soon.

After dinner, they washed the dishes and retired to the small living room and its sofa. Pamela poured some tea for the both of them and added four sugars to his. They blew on the tea and took tiny sips of the lovely flavor.

She picked up an envelope from the end table next to her. "This came in the mail today. Your mom sent it for me." She handed it to him.

He pulled two pages out and read the top one, which had a Cedar Rapids, Iowa hospital's letterhead. Before he finished, he was grinning. "This is wonderful news. You only have to take a test to get a job as a nurse. Sure save the trouble of going back to school for a while."

Pamela smiled. "I was very relieved. It's kind of exciting, too. Of course, there's no way of knowing if nursing jobs will be available when we get to the States."

"I'm sure there will be. Don't you worry."

"I won't."

He put his hand softly on her tummy. "When will he start kicking?"

"Probably a month or two since this is our first."

"Well, I can't wait."

"Are you so convinced the baby's a boy that you don't want to check over my list of girl names?"

"It's a boy."

She grinned at him. He'd said it from about the first moment. "Not budging, huh?"

"No need, trust me." He was certain it would be Tom Percy Dunn, Junior. The middle name was for her late brother, who had been killed at Dunkirk four years ago when his unit fought a delaying action for the other 330,000 men who did escape from the Germans.

She laughed and nestled her head against his shoulder. He draped his arm around her and pulled her close. She laid her hand on his chest and could feel his heartbeat and breathing.

"I do love this, Tom."

"Yeah. I do, too."

"Don't tell me yet when you leave next. I need this moment."

"Whatever you want, dear. It can wait until morning," he said.

Dunn glanced over at her. For the first time, he was able to see her as the mother of his child. He realized she would constantly be in a state of flux and her behavior, needs, and wants would depend completely on whether she was Pamela Dunn, the wife, or Pamela Dunn, the mother. Truth be told, Dunn could hardly wait to see that in action. It made him grin and he got caught.

"What are you grinning about, Buster Boy?"

"Just imagining life with you and the baby."

"Hm. That's nice, dear," she said as she closed her eyes. Her voice was filled with sleepiness.

He bent to kiss the top of her head, and lay his head back onto the sofa back. He'd close his eyes. Just for a minute.

Two hours later, they woke up in pretty much the same position. Pamela's head had dipped off his shoulder and was tucked against his chest. She lifted her head and pecked him on the cheek.

"Time to wake up so we can go to bed."

Dunn yawned. "Okay. Sorry to drop off on you."

"I fell asleep, too. Did you read your mom's letter?"

"Ah, no. What'd she have to say?"

"They got a letter from Gertrude, who is still loving her work, but she misses Alan."

Alan was Alan Finch, who worked for Prime Minister Winston Churchill. They'd met almost by accident and fell in love in a short time period. He was off somewhere in North America.

"Hazel's husband got his own submarine."

"Danny a skipper? That's great."

Pamela frowned.

"What?"

"He got the boat because his skipper got killed in a car wreck. Danny couldn't say where it happened because the censors would have cut it out."

"Ah, man. That's awful."

"Yes."

"Anything else?"

"Not much. Your dad's fine. He snagged a deer when he and his friends went hunting."

"I miss going hunting with him. And Gertrude."

"Gertrude likes to hunt?"

"She does. She's an excellent shooter."

"I never would have thought. Your Mom said they really enjoyed their trip to Washington, D.C. to see you get the Medal of Honor."

Dunn smiled. It had been wonderful to see everyone. It had been three years, after boot camp when he got leave. He sighed. When was the damn war going to end? With Operation Market Garden's failure, it looked like any chance for the war to end by Christmas was out of the picture.

"Well, I'm awake now," Dunn muttered.

Pamela grinned. "Just how awake are you, buster?"

"Awake enough to take you home, Pamela."

"Excellent. Excellent idea. You're such a smart lad."

He got up and helped her to her feet. "Top of the class, I am."

She laughed.

He led the way to the bedroom.

RONN MUNSTERMAN

Chapter 6

Top Secret German Facility
75 kilometers southwest of Frankfurt, Germany
11 November, 0945 Hours, Berlin time, the next day

Dr. Volker Bauer and his partner, Dr. Rudolph Gerber, worked side by side at a long metal table. It was covered by papers filled with calculations, and maps of western Germany and eastern France. Both men wore white lab coats, mostly just out of a lifetime habit.

They were in an underground manufacturing facility southwest of Frankfurt that Speer had reopened for their use. Constructed in a soft limestone cave discovered in the early 1800s, it was about four hundred meters long, with branching offshoots that allowed for "rooms" to be built, like the one in which the two scientists were working. It was surprisingly dry, but the air was slightly musty, and seemed to maintain an even temperature hovering around ten degrees Celsius.

In the next "room" over, behind sealed doors, some of the workers who had been transported by Speer from a concentration camp in eastern Germany, were grinding the uranium into powder.

To test the efficiency of delivering the ground-up uranium, Bauer and Gerber had devised a method using an iron and steel composite that had been ground into a fine powder with the same weight characteristics of powdered uranium. They ran the powder through a dye process changing the color to a bright yellow. German workmen had filled a dozen 10.5 centimeter rounds with the powder and driven to a location fifty kilometers east of Frankfurt. There, each round was set for a different airburst height by an artillery unit. As each round was fired, Bauer and Gerber made notations on their notepads about the firing angle, the direction, and the distance. The rounds had been fired so they would explode a half-kilometer apart. This was to ensure there was no crossover between rounds and to make it easier to measure the spread of the yellow dust. Wind direction and speed had also been noted and its resulting effect on the dust.

Bauer pulled a piece of paper close. It was the test results.

"An airburst at thirty meters is optimal and will cause fallout covering a fifty meter circle with the density of powder we need for a fatal exposure," Bauer said.

"How close do you think we are to being ready?"

Bauer shrugged. "Maybe a couple of weeks."

"Any news from Speer."

"Oh, maybe."

He pulled an envelope he'd forgotten about from his coat pocket. It only had his name written on the front, which would have been done by the army radioman who'd received the coded message. He slid a folded piece of paper from the envelope and opened it. He read it carefully and groaned.

"What is it?"

Bauer sighed. "Message from Speer dated this morning. The generals demand we create enough weaponized uranium to cover a field three hundred kilometers in width." He did the math in his head. Three hundred kilometers divided by a fifty meter circle equaled six thousand cannon shells. "Six thousand shells! We have to make six thousand shells, Gerber! Can we do that in two weeks?"

Gerber looked at a sheet of paper on the table in front of him for the answer.

"Oh my god," Bauer said, his face white.

Gerber looked up in alarm.

Bauer had turned over the message for no other reason than just to make sure nothing was there. But there was. "They want the shells ready by this coming Wednesday. Three days. They're giving us only three days! Can we do that, Gerber?"

Gerber wrote some numbers down and did the math. When he finished he looked up at Bauer with a worried expression. "It will take one thousand eight hundred man hours to safely make and prepare the shells for transport. With only twenty-five workers that amounts to seventy-two hours per worker. That in turns equals three, twenty-four hour shifts for each worker. An impossibility. We need fifty workers, who will work twelve hour shifts only to reduce risk of accidents. Call Speer for an additional twenty-five."

Bauer nodded and reached for the black phone on the table. When the Minister of Armaments answered, he went into a lengthy explanation about why they absolutely must have another twenty-five workers.

Bauer listened to Speer's calm response and hung up the phone after saying goodbye.

"What did he say?" Gerber asked.

"We'll have them tonight. He recommends replacing the entire crew half at a time."

Gerber looked relieved. "Oh, that's good news. We might get through this mess after all."

Bauer nodded. "Yes, we just might."

Chapter 7

2 miles northwest of Sarrebourg, France
12 November, 0425 Hours, the next day

Dunn rolled up his parachute and ran toward the dark eastern edge of the clearing where the trees were waiting to hide his men and himself. He'd already done his head count and found all nine of his men plus the round Major Miles. Dunn had been surprised and relieved to learn that Miles had been on several jumps in the last few months, so he didn't need a rush course in jumping out of an airplane. Even still, Dunn had sandwiched the man between Cross and himself. Typically one would lead the stick and the other man would be last, but Dunn wanted to make sure Miles was in good shape.

Dunn had made a call on Saturday to Captain Adams requesting Sergeant Frank Barker again for the mission to complete the squad. He'd done it not because Colonel Cole told him to, but because he needed a tenth man for the mission. Barker had been borrowed for the attack on Hitler's Dam and had done a good job.

The weather forecast for France had been iffy before they left Hampstead Airbase. A storm system was predicted to arrive in France sometime the next morning. As Dunn look skyward, he noted some clouds farther to the west, but overhead it was clear and the fingernail moon and starlight made it possible to see well enough not to trip over anything or run headfirst into a tree. With the weather forecast set to bring heavy, cold rain with it, their fifteen mile march from the target city of Sarrebourg back to the American line would be a miserable one. Cross and he had estimated two miles per hour, partially because they'd have to be constantly on the look out for pockets of Germans, and partially because of Miles, who they thought would have trouble keeping up with a faster pace.

The Ranger squad gathered just inside the tree line and Dunn asked, "Anyone injured?"

No one said anything, which was good news. Even experienced jumpers such as themselves could have bad luck especially in night jumps. A large stone under a landing boot could twist a knee and that'd be it.

Dunn nodded. "We're two miles northwest of Sarrebourg. Remember, the target is a communications truck. It could be parked anywhere, but it's likely to be out in a relatively open space to improve their signals." He turned to Hugh Kelly. "Is the device okay?"

Kelly was carrying a mobile frequency finder. It was about the same size as the radio Schneider always carried. "Yes, Sarge. Want me to switch it on?"

Dunn glanced at Major Miles, who was standing a couple of feet away. "That okay with you, sir?"

Miles nodded and walked over to Kelly, who set the device on the ground and opened the lid. Inside were a variety of switches and dials, including a large dial for selecting a frequency, and some green and red lights that were off. He unhooked a ten-inch circle of wire that had a threaded bolt attached at the bottom from the underside of the lid. He gently screwed it into a receiving thread on the top edge of the open lid. Next, he flipped the switch for power. A light hum emanated from the machine. Miles edged around so he could see into the box from the same side as Kelly. Kelly picked up the device and held it at waist height. He rotated to the right so he was facing the target city. The red light bloomed to dim life.

Miles reached in and turned the frequency dial to a particular setting, one he knew the Germans often used for military radio traffic. The red light went out and the green one came on faintly blinking. Kelly rotated slightly to the right and the green light went out and the red came back on. He turned the other way and was rewarded with a solid green light and no red one.

Dunn checked Kelly's position with his compass and did a comparison with his mental map of the area. "A hundred and thirty-one degrees, just east of southeast. The signal is coming from the north side of the city, possibly just outside it."

Miles nodded. "Okay. Turn it off."

Kelly set about taking it down. When he was done, he lifted it and slid the carry straps over his shoulders as the box rested on his back.

Dunn slid over next to Martelli. "Al, take point. Be damn careful. Take your time. The heading is one thirty-one."

"Got it, Sarge. Confirming one thirty-one." Martelli faced Dunn and waited.

Dunn said to Cross, "Let's set our walkie-talkies to the same frequency."

Cross held his up and read Dunn's frequency dial. He twisted the knob on his radio and took a couple of steps away to prevent feedback whistles. He clicked the talk button twice.

Dunn heard the squelchy click on his own radio and nodded to Cross.

Dunn gave each man his position in the line. Dunn would be second, followed by Kelly and Miles. Cross would take up tail end Charlie. The men silently moved into their assigned positions, with two steps between them.

Dunn raised his hand and dropped it like a starter's flag.

Martelli turned around and took off, the squad trailing.

It took almost an hour to make it to the outskirts of the fairly large French city. North of the city, the forest covered the reasonably flat ground all the way to the rear of the northernmost houses and buildings. Some of the structures had backyards bordered by stone walls about three feet high, while others had fences, some wooden and some wire.

Martelli knelt behind a handy walnut tree that was at least three feet in diameter and ten yards from the nearest fence. Dunn and Kelly caught up. Kelly shucked off the radio beam tracker and set it on the ground. Once again he opened it and turned it on. The rest of the squad gathered around, kneeling, resting. Dunn assigned Wickham and Higgins to stand perimeter guard about ten yards from the squad, east and west, respectively parallel to the fences.

Major Miles edged closer to see over Kelly's shoulder as the younger man acquired a signal on the right frequency. Judging by the brightness of the green bulb, they were mighty close.

Speaking in a low voice, Kelly said, "It looks to be straight ahead about thirty yards away. I'd say on the road the other side of that house."

"I concur," Miles chipped in, perhaps to make his presence felt.

Dunn checked the compass heading. It was 180 degrees. This was because they'd curled around to the north and were coming in from that direction instead of from the west.

Miles turned to Dunn and whispered, "Are we ready to implement Colonel Cole's plan?"

Dunn grabbed Miles's upper left arm and steered him back from the tree, into the forest, leaving his men behind out of earshot.

"Major, our actual circumstances prevent us from implementing Colonel Cole's plan of attack."

Miles drew himself up. "What does 'actual circumstances' even mean?" He spoke a little too loudly.

Dunn held a finger to his lips. "Not so loud, sir. Sound really, really carries at night."

Miles seemed to be both embarrassed and angry at the same time. "I demand an explanation." He said, although he whispered, which took some of the heat out of the remark.

"Respectfully, sir, the colonel's plan to sneak into the mobile communications truck and neutralize the occupants by 'knocking them out' is unrealistic. I understand he wanted us to take the truck back to our front line. But we have to allow you to use their equipment to send false orders under General Runstedt's name. I know the plan is to get the Germans to reallocate their men, to change positions on the line facing Patton's Third Army. I appreciate that.

"The thing is, driving any German vehicle through German occupied territory is problematic. Add to that the distance involved and it's simply not possible. I will not risk my men for a ludicrous plan. We can't risk leaving survivors or evidence of our presence. The men in that truck have to be killed at the onset and when you're done, we're setting off incendiary devices that will burn the truck, the equipment, and any evidence that we were even there."

"You're just going to kill those men?"

Dunn's eyes narrowed. "Sir, Ranger missions are not the time or place for a philosophical discussion. The plan is changed. I changed it."

Miles shook his head. "You can't just override the colonel's plan."

Dunn simply stared at the major. "As the mission commander, I have complete authority over it and the power to change it as I deem necessary. Check the book, sir. You will do as I ask, by completing your critical task, and leave the rest to us."

"I will have no choice but to report this insubordination to the colonel."

"Major, you do what you think you have to, but I really suggest you read the book on Ranger missions. On page two under command structure and authority you'll find a section on 'adapting the mission.' "

Miles still didn't believe Dunn.

"Sir, are you going to follow my mission orders or not?"

Miles grit his teeth. He knew his friend Cole would be furious, but what could he actually do? This man in front of him was simply going to ignore the well-thought out plan and proceed the way he wanted to. Best to go along to get along.

"Yes, Sergeant Dunn, I will acquiesce to your orders, even though I strongly object."

"Objection noted, which will appear in the after-action report. Sir."

"Fine."

Without another word, Dunn led the way back to the squad.

In one minute, Dunn reviewed the plan. Cole's plan had never been mentioned to the men. This way, when the shit hit the fan, only Dunn would take the heat.

"Any questions, men?" Dunn asked, eyeing each man in turn, something he often did on missions. His way of checking their readiness. Everyone shook their heads.

"Martelli, go take a look and report back," Dunn said.

"Will do, Sarge."

Martelli advanced toward the street and disappeared between two houses.

A few minutes later he was back.

"All clear, Sarge. No one on guard and no one walking around."

It was no surprise that there were no guards stationed outside the truck. Why would there be fifteen miles from the front line?

Chapter 8

British Airfield
10 miles southeast of central Rome, Italy
12 November, 0515 Hours

Saunders woke up when the C-54's tires hit the ground. The plane bounced once and settled into a more or less smooth roll across the field. At the end of the run off, the pilot guided the plane left to clear the runway, coming to a stop not far from a gaggle of various-sized tents that made up the airfield's command buildings.

Saunders was sitting near the cockpit, where he typically liked to be. He glanced down the long tube of the aircraft's interior toward the rear. He had twenty-nine men with him this time. In any other unit, he would have been expected to have an officer with him, a platoon leader. But why bother to send an officer when you had a perfectly capable sergeant major? He chuckled lightly at this thought and grinned. It hadn't even been mentioned. He liked that. It showed Colonel Jenkins truly did trust him.

A crewman opened the door at the rear of the plane. The men rose and stretched. Soon, everyone was moving toward the exit and stepping out into the bright sunshine. When Saunders climbed down the stairs, he noted how cool the morning air was. He exhaled a large cloud of human steam, which told him it was probably fifty degrees or less outside. According to Lieutenant Mallory, who'd done some research for Saunders, the average highs in Rome this time of year would be in the low sixties and the nights could reach the mid-forties. November was the highest month of precipitation at almost two inches, which Mallory said was twenty percent of the annual total. The forecast was for sunny days and no rain for the next several days, but a storm front would move in on day four if they were still there.

He stood still for a moment, looking northwest toward the heart of Rome. He thought he could make out a few tops of the famous Seven Hills of Rome, at least the ones on the south and east sides of the city. He couldn't remember the names of the hills, but did know their history. Around 750 B.C., separate settlements formed on the top of each of the hills, which might be thought of as more of a ridge. These groups began to mingle and often played games together. Eventually, they decided to drain the swampy area in the center of the ring of the hills and place open air markets on the new dry land. Three hundred years later, in an effort to protect the area, they built the Servian Wall which surrounded all seven hills. As Rome grew and prospered, some of the famous monuments were built on the hills.

A half-dozen Italian-made panel trucks rumbled up close to the men and stopped. A man dressed in a brown suit walked toward the British Commandos. He stopped to speak to a Commando and that man turned and pointed at Saunders. The man nodded his thanks and strode toward Saunders.

Saunders headed toward the new arrival. When they met, they eyed each other carefully. The man was shorter than Saunders' six feet, and much slimmer. He had blond hair combed straight back with no part. His intelligent cobalt blue eyes examined Saunders, settling on the Commando's monstrous red handlebar mustache. The man's lip twitched as if he was almost ready to grin. But he didn't. He stuck out his hand and said in good English tinged with a French accent, "Hello, my name is Gabriel

Herriot. I am the commander of the Pontifical Swiss Guard. You are Sergeant Major Saunders."

Saunders took the man's hand and was unsurprised by the strength of his grip. "Aye, I'm Saunders. I'm very glad to meet you, sir."

"Thank you for wearing civilian clothing. We have to consider the possibility of spies noting that the Swiss Guard is talking with British Commandos."

When Lieutenant Mallory had told Saunders of the request coming from the Swiss Guard, he'd almost argued against it because of the international law of war stipulation that combatants not wearing uniforms could be considered to be spies and treated accordingly. Which invariably led to execution. But he realized they were going to be behind their own lines the whole time and were unlikely to get captured by the Germans.

"You're welcome. Seemed important to me. We did bring our uniforms and weapons in case we have to cross the front line at some point."

"Good. I thought we might begin at the Villas of Castel Gandolfo, the Pope's vacation home. It is just twenty-four kilometers away. Perhaps twenty-five minutes. I'd like to give you a tour of the grounds and the palace. Are you ready?"

"Yes, sir. We'll load up. Where do you want me?"

"I would appreciate it if you joined me in the cab of the first truck. That way we can get to know one another."

"Certainly, sir. I'll just see to getting the men aboard."

"When we first arrive at the Villa, we should take some time for breakfast. No doubt your men are starving after a long night's flight?"

"That would be correct, sir." Saunders smiled a thanks at the man's thoughtfulness.

"We can discuss the mission while we eat. We'll want the leaders of your squads to join us."

"Yes, sir."

"I understand you have brought with you a doppelganger for the Pope."

"Yes, sir. We did. Would you like to meet him? He's with the men."

"No, I'll meet him later. See you at the truck." He turned and walked away.

Saunders marched toward his men who were standing in a large clump. He caught the eye of Barltrop, and the other two squad leaders and tipped his head to the right. Each man nodded and headed his way as he moved to the right.

The two squad leaders who were along on the mission with their men, Sergeants Cecil Massie and Lionel Gilbert, caught up to Barltrop and the trio stood close to Saunders.

Cecil Massie was a wide shouldered man, nearly as bulky as Saunders. He was born in Leeds, but moved to London with his family at the age of ten. He wore his black hair short, nearly a crew cut, and he had an angular face dominated by brooding dark brown eyes. He'd been a Commando for a year.

Lionel Gilbert was built the opposite of Massie with a tall, lean form that carried strong, sinewy muscles. His sandy hair was long, almost touching the collar in the back and he sported a mustache that rivaled Saunders'. The combination of the long hair, the drooping mustache, and the first name had earned him the nickname Lion. He was from Liverpool, the son of a dock worker.

"All right lads, the gent I was talking to is the Swiss Guard commander, Gabriel Herriot. We're going to the Villa first. He wants to give us breakfast when we get there."

"Good. I'm bloody starving." Barltrop looked at the Swiss Guard commander from a distance and asked, "What'd you think of him?"

"Too soon to tell much. I do know you don't get to be commander without some pretty outstanding credentials and skills. I'll introduce you three to him when we get there."

Barltrop nodded.

"Let's get the lads loaded. I'm going to be in the first truck in the cab with him."

"Right, Sarge," the men replied in chorus. They ran back to the men and set about getting each squad into the trucks.

Saunders made his way over to the front truck and waited, facing the trucks behind him. When the Commandos were aboard, Barltrop and the other two squad leaders raised a hand. Saunders acknowledged them with a wave. He climbed in and nodded to Commander Herriot, who said something in French to the driver.

Soon the convoy was away from the airfield and on a narrow two lane road, heading southeast.

"I understand you and your men are all Swiss."

Commander Herriot smiled. "Yes, we are. An old tradition we're happy and honored to continue."

"Where in Switzerland are you from?"

"Lucerne."

"I've heard it's beautiful."

Herriot sighed. "It is indeed. Right on Lake Lucerne. Marvelous scenery. You should come see it someday. You know, after."

"I would love to bring my wife, Sadie."

"You are married?"

"Yes, a couple of months. You?"

"No. We are all single men. Marriage is for after serving."

"How long do you serve?"

"Usually two years." Herriot shrugged. "But with the war, we all feel we are in for the duration." He glanced at the big Commando. "Much like I imagine you and your men are."

Saunders nodded solemnly. "Aye. For the duration. Until we beat the bastards." Saunders realized what he'd said and immediately said, "Oh, I beg your pardon, Commander."

Herriot laughed. "Not to worry, Sergeant. We have the advantage of swearing in up to four languages. Makes things interesting."

Saunders laughed. "I see. Anyone ever combine languages in the middle of a rant?"

"As a matter of fact, I'm rather famous for it. Away from the Vatican, of course."

"Of course."

Herriot pointed at a grove of something or other on the right side of the road, Saunders couldn't tell exactly what.

"Olives. We're in the middle of harvest season all over Italy."

Saunders peered through the windshield. The olive grove seemed to go back to the horizon. Not too far from the road, workers were surrounding some trees with some kind of netting.

"They shake the trees and the olives fall into the netting."

"That's really something to see."

The grove disappeared and they fell into a comfortable silence.

They passed a crossroad and Herriot said, "Five more minutes. Keep your eyes just to the right of the road ahead. It'll be quite a sight."

Saunders stared in that direction and was soon rewarded. It certainly *was* quite a sight, he thought.

Chapter 9

Sarrebourg, France
12 November, 0540 Hours

Dunn peered at the dark street from beside a quiet French home. He had Miles with him as well as half the squad. Cross had taken the remaining half to a point between houses two to the north from Dunn's position.

Dunn spotted the truck parked right on the street, which ran east-west. It was facing away from him, toward Cross. The top of the large van was covered with antennae, including one that was similar to the one in Kelly's box. It would be connected to their own radio beam finder. It wasn't rotating, a good sign; they weren't searching. The truck engine was not running, which meant they were using battery power. Dunn examined the houses and their dark windows on the opposite side of the street. Curtains or shades covered the windows, which were closed due to the cold temperature of the mid-November night. Dunn assumed the general and his staff were staying in one or more of the houses nearby.

Except for Major Miles who had a 1911 Colt .45, Dunn's men were carrying the 9mm Sten submachine gun, which had the stealth advantage of an integrated suppressor, a must on this mission. The Sten derived its name from the two designers, Major Reginald V. Shepherd and Harold Turpin, and for Enfield, its first manufacturing facility. It had a 32-round magazine and could fire at a rate of 500 to 600 rounds per minute. The suppressed version fired at a lower muzzle velocity to help reduce sound, at 1,001 feet per second, which was lower by 197 feet per second. Its effective range was about 100 yards, about twice that of the American Thompson .45. Dunn's men were deadly with either, and for that matter with any weapon in their hands. The men also carried the Colt .45, a seven-round semiautomatic pistol, and combat knives.

Cross's face appeared two houses down and a hand was stuck out at about knee height. That indicated the street was clear and that no one was in the cab of the truck. Dunn returned the signal. The street seemed all clear on his end. While Cross's team edged out and took up prone positions, Dunn's men dashed toward the rear of the truck. Right behind Dunn, Jonesy ran and raised his Sten. He was by far the most accurate shooter in a squad of outstanding shooters. Dunn put his left hand on the handle for the rear entrance, which was made up of two doors. Martelli, Kelly, and Higgins formed a shooters' semi-circle aiming away from the truck, toward the empty street. Miles stood to Dunn's left, holding his .45 in his left hand aimed at the ground.

Jonesy took a position that would put him to the extreme right of the entrance once Dunn opened the doors.

Dunn looked at Jonesy, who nodded once crisply. Dunn slowly turned the handle. When it was at its farthest point, he pulled gently on it. The door swung open all the way. Dunn pushed open the other door and ducked back.

Jonesy had a split second to take in everything inside. A faint lightbulb burned in the center of the space, shedding plenty of light for Jonesy. Three radio operators sat along the right side, their faces intent on what was in front of them. All three wore headsets, which would make it unlikely they could hear the ratcheting sound of the suppressed Sten's bolt when it fired. No one else was present. Jonesy lined up his sights on the closest man's temple and fired. The enemy soldier toppled off his chair and hit the truck's floor. The second man noticed movement out of the corner of his eye and turned to see what had happened to his colleague. It earned him a 9mm hole in the forehead, between the eyes. He also collapsed to the floor. The third and last operator turned his face toward the dark form in the doorway. His mouth dropped open and Jonesy shot him in the bridge of the nose. Another body slammed to the floor. Three seconds had passed.

Dunn grabbed Miles by the arm and pulled him toward the door. A metal staircase attached to the truck's rear reached almost to the ground. "Up you go, sir," Dunn whispered.

Miles clambered aboard and navigated around the dead Germans lying on the floor. He examined the three radio sets carefully and, choosing one, sat down in front of it.

Jonesy jumped into the truck.

To the other three men, Dunn whispered, "Go."

They ran up the stairs and Dunn followed, closing both doors behind him.

Cross and his men remained in position. Some were aimed east along the street and others west. Cross shifted his attention between the area in front of him and the point directly across the street from the truck. He was watching for lights coming on. Everyone was listening for vehicles. Nothing yet.

Dunn stood behind Miles as the communications officer worked the radio dial. He had opened his bag and laid out a notepad filled with rows of letters. Dunn knew the messages that were going out were in German because he'd asked the man before leaving Barton Stacey. Miles had said he was fluent in German. He also knew the specific manner in which German radio operators sent their messages. While he couldn't know the particular fist each man used on the telegraph key, the way he tapped the key, like an individual's signature, he knew enough to be able to mimic someone sending in German. If anyone asked who he was, he had an identity ready to send saying he was a new arrival from the eastern front.

Miles had told Dunn that it would take only three minutes to send the entire page of messages. It would take another minute or two to receive acknowledgments from the recipients. They would be done after receiving those replies.

Dunn checked his watch, noting when five minutes would be up. The only sounds Dunn could hear were the breathing of his men and the *clickity-clack* of the telegraph key.

While Miles was working, Higgins was setting up several incendiary devices around the interior of the truck, including three attached to each of the radios. Another was placed beside the left rear wheel well, which would place it just above the fuel tank. The devices were courtesy of the SOE and were specially designed to obscure their presence after the fire burned out. He cut lengths of fuses that would also in essence disappear. No German soldier would find anything. Higgins would light all the fuses when Dunn gave him the go ahead. They would burn for two minutes.

The messages had a life-span of about ninety minutes. They would be decoded, sent to the appropriate generals, who would issue the order to move certain units to the wrong locations. Locations beneficial to Patton. Dunn didn't believe the Germans would figure out what had happened in an hour and a half. If the bodies didn't completely incinerate, they might discover the bullet wounds in the charred skulls, but that would take some time. If they did finally determine the cause wasn't an accident, the messages would have already done their strategic damage to the German Army.

Miles appeared to be reaching the bottom of his hand written page. He used one finger to keep track of his position and used his other hand to key. He suddenly reached the end and stopped.

Dunn checked his watch. Three minutes exactly. He was impressed. He loved it when someone did what they said they could do.

The next two minutes seemed to drag on as they waited for confirmation of receipt. Suddenly the replies started coming in. Miles wrote furiously, drawing a short line under each separate incoming message. When the last one arrived, he drew a double line under it and whispered, "No one suspected anything. We're done here."

Dunn reacted by telling Higgins to light the fuses. He stepped to the rear door and opened the one with the handle enough so he could see the street. It was clear. He took off his helmet and peeked around the edge of the other door. Also clear. He swung the doors open.

"Time to go, gents."

They left in reverse order and each man returned to the space between houses. Dunn had Miles precede him, and when he got to the ground, he turned around and closed and latched the doors. He ran to catch up to his men, who were waiting just out of view between the two houses. He waved at Cross as he ran. Cross raised a hand and his men rose and melted away in the darkness.

Dunn joined his group and got down on one knee. He checked his watch.

Miles knelt beside him and whispered, "How much longer?"

"Less than a minute."

Dunn looked over his shoulder at Jonesy and pointed toward the forest behind the house. Jonesy nodded and he grabbed the others. They took off into the darkness to go meet Cross and the rest of the squad in the trees.

"Nothing's happening," Miles complained.

"Patience, sir."

"Something must have gone wrong."

Dunn put a hand on Miles's left arm. "Sir. Either keep quiet or go join the rest of the men."

Miles stared at the sergeant who dared speak to him like he was a recruit.

"But—"

"No 'buts', sir. Are you staying quietly or going?"

"Staying."

Smoke began to sift into the truck cab.

"Here we go, sir."

Miles watched as the cab filled up with smoke. There was a low *whump* sound from inside the back of the truck and flames burst into the cab. Soon the fire was roaring in the cab and the driver's window cracked and shattered, the glass peppering the ground below.

Dunn could hear the roar of the fire.

The rear of the truck exploded, sending one of the back doors clanging into the street. The rear hopped up and crashed back down on the ground, the rear tires ablaze.

"Wow," murmured Miles.

Up and down the street lights came on behind the window curtains, and soon people's faces appeared to see what had happened.

"Time to go, sir."

"Okay."

Dunn led the way between the houses and they made it back into the forest where they found the rest of the Ranger squad.

"Everyone here?" Dunn asked Cross, who had been tasked with taking the head count.

"Ayup, we're all here," Cross replied in his Nor'easter accent.

"Good. You've got point. I'll take the rear. Men, we better go ahead and get our ponchos on. It's gonna rain on us sometime."

The men spent a minute getting their raingear on.

When they were done and ready, Cross gave the order and the men assembled into a column.

Cross took off and the men followed.

Chapter 10

Villas of Castel Gandolfo
25 miles southeast of Rome
12 November, 0603 Hours

Saunders' convoy drove up the curving road toward the Villas of Castel Gandolfo. As they neared the front gate, his eyes almost bugged out in excitement at the sight of the buildings.

Commander Herriot glanced over at Saunders and smiled at the Englishman's reaction. "Beautiful, no?"

"Very. I've been fascinated by architecture since I was a kid. I plan to start a construction company after the war."

Herriot nodded. "You'll enjoy your time here. We'll stop first at our headquarters where we can stretch and relax while we discuss plans to safeguard the Pontiff over that breakfast."

"Sounds good."

"Later, I'll take you and some of your men on a tour of the grounds, the areas where the Pope is usually present at various times."

"Right."

The truck stopped in front of a two-story stucco building and the driver shut off the engine. The building was painted a pale yellow with white trim. High above the front door the square Swiss Guard flag flapped gently in the breeze. Saunders was able to make out that it was divided into quarters by a white cross with a colorful circle in the center. The upper right and lower left quadrants were identical with five horizontal stripes: red, yellow, blue, yellow, and red. The upper left and lower right quadrants, which had a red background, were also similar, but not identical, to each other and appeared to be coats of arms.

Saunders stepped out of the truck and stretched. His men were doing the same thing in the early morning sunshine. He looked up and down the street. A few people were about, walking purposely toward their place of work.

As each squad formed itself into a column, he admired the way his men moved quickly and efficiently, and was proud of them. Going from squad leader to platoon leader was something he just took in stride. He wanted to make sure he helped everyone do the best possible job for a successful mission.

Herriot had been watching the commandos, too. He nodded to himself, also impressed by their speed. He had high hopes for them.

To Saunders, he said, "Shall we go in?"

"Aye. Lead the way, sir."

Herriot strode away and Saunders gave a signal to the platoon, which immediately started his way. They entered the Guard's Headquarters and went up a flight of stairs. Once they reached the top, they were met by a long wide hallway. Herriot led them half way down, opened a door on the right, and waved them inside. It was a large cafeteria. The food line was to the left. Round tables with chairs were spread about the rest of the room. Morning sunshine filtered through windows opposite the door. Smells of eggs and toast, and some kind of sausage filled the men's noses and made their stomachs growl. There were several older men working the food line. They wore crisp white clothing and white hats styled like a fedora.

The men lined up and quickly made their choices and found seats at the tables. Saunders, the other two squad leaders, Gilbert and Massie, and Barltrop stayed back, as did Herriot. Only after all the Commandos had been served and seated did the leaders get their food and coffee. Herriot led the group to a table by the window. Large overhead fans spun lazily, but moved a surprising amount of cool air. A man a few years younger than Herriot entered the cafeteria. He practically ran through the food line and took the last chair at the table sitting next to Herriot, who introduced him as his second in command, vice commander David Surbeck. The men all nodded "hello" with their mouths full.

Saunders, like his men, was starving and made quick work of his scrambled eggs, sausage, and toast. He wiped his mouth with a linen napkin. That surprised him to find those on the table.

Herriot said, "It's no secret that the Nazis distrust the church, and naturally vice versa." He sighed deeply, as if offended by what he was about to say. "We thought that after the liberation of Rome last June, we would be finished with the Nazis' desire to hurt the church. Alas, that is not the case. They intend to kidnap the Pope in an effort to terrify church members around the world. We don't know what they will ask for, whether a monetary ransom or some speech of support by the Holy Father. But we do know they are about to make the attempt."

"How soon?"

"Within the next few days, I'm afraid."

"How'd you even find out about what must certainly be a top secret mission?" Barltrop asked, leaning forward.

Herriot's cheeks flamed pink. "We employed the oldest trick in the book. A honey trap set on a high ranking SS officer in Bologna, Italy. It was really blind luck, although we had targeted more than one officer. Our woman agent was able to get the information from him without raising suspicions. She's still active with him, but we have no new information as of yesterday."

The Commandos seemed surprised the church had used such a distasteful technique, but it was war, after all.

Herriot continued, "I think they intend to kidnap the Pope from the grounds of this villa because it's easier to access than the Vatican. The Pope's schedule is publicized ahead of time, so it's known where he will be. We've asked him to cancel public appearances." He shrugged.

"He said no," Saunders said.

Herriot smiled. "Or something to that effect, yes."

"Winston Churchill is much the same. It drives his security team mad."

Herriot nodded enthusiastically. "That's where we are. So tell me of your proposal to use the doppelganger."

"I know you'll have to get the approval of the Pope, but here's what we have in mind. First, we'll need to outfit my men as members of the Swiss Guard. Is that something you can live with?"

Herriot looked at Saunders for a long time before speaking. Long enough for Saunders to wonder whether the question was so wrong the man couldn't form an answer.

"You understand that the heritage of the Guard is so intertwined with the papacy it's impossible to separate them?"

Saunders compressed his lips and nodded. "I believe I do understand, sir."

"Members of the Guard are always, and I mean always, Swiss nationals and Catholic. We take enormous pride in becoming a member. My family, for instance, has had members going back to the sixteen hundreds. I'm not even sure how many greats in great grandfathers that is."

He looked away, out the window, where tree branches swayed in the wind. Still staring at the outside world he said, "However. Exceptional times such as these require us to take exceptional steps. Yes, it is something I, and the Pope, will be able to live with."

He finally returned his gaze to Saunders. He seemed to be sizing up the big Commando in more than one way. He grinned. "We might have to make a custom fit uniform for you."

Saunders laughed. "Indeed."

"Please continue with your plan."

Saunders laid it out, step by step, taking his time to be sure to deliver a clear and concise explanation of the events. He concluded with, "I know a lot depends on the actual layout of the grounds here, as well as the Vatican. What do you think?"

"Do you have this written down?"

He shook his head. "No. We never take any paper with us, except for unmarked maps." He tapped his noggin. "We keep everything up here."

Herriot smiled. "We do the same. At first hearing, I think everything you laid out will work. We'll meet with some of my sub commanders and finalize the details with, as you mentioned, the layouts of the Villas of Castel Gandolfo and the Vatican.

"But first, if you're ready, a small tour of the grounds. We'll focus on the areas the Pope tends to use the most which, unfortunately, includes the gardens. You'll see what I mean."

"Very good, sir. We brought a few cameras to share amongst the men. Help us blend in as tourists."

"Good idea," Herriot said, pleased the Commando sergeant seemed to be thinking of everything. He stood and everyone at the table did, too. After the platoon had cleared away their plates, they lined up at the door.

Saunders was at the head of the line. He spoke to his men, "Remember lads, we're tourists. Those with cameras take lots of pictures, even if you run out of film, keep at it for appearances sake. I want you to group yourselves into threes and fours, no formations! Walk out of step. Don't line up in any way. We have to look like civilians, so play the part. Laugh and joke and point wildly at things. Squad leaders will be with me and Barltrop and Commander Herriot." He touched the commander on the shoulder to make sure the men knew exactly who he meant.

Dickinson raised his hand.

Saunders frowned. Dickinson would undoubtedly be up to no good. "What is it, Dickinson?"

Dickinson frowned and shook his head. "Sarge, I don't think the lads can remember how to joke and laugh. It's been a while."

The room erupted in laughter and Dickinson beamed. He'd done his job.

Saunders just shook his head and glanced at Herriot, who seemed more or less amused by it all. *Probably thinking: those idiot Englishmen*, he thought.

Soon the men were in the hall and striding toward the rear of the building trying for the first time in years to not look like the tough, lethal Commandos they were.

The tour had started.

Chapter 11

7 1/2 miles west of Sarrebourg, France and
7 1/2 miles east of the American Line
12 November, 0810 Hours

Cross held up a hand to stop the column. They were moving through yet another wooded area and Cross checked his watch. Time for a break.

He gave a hand signal for the men to take a seat on the ground and rest. No one hesitated, including Miles. Dunn made his way quietly up next to Cross. They walked a few yards away from the men so they could talk privately and sat down side by side, legs crossed.

Cross unfurled a map. He marked a point on it and said, "We've been on the move for two and a half hours. We've covered a surprising seven and a half miles. That's two more miles than we expected."

He looked over his shoulder to make sure Miles was still sitting down yards away.

"Major Miles has kept pace without complaint."

"I noticed. That's a pleasant surprise. We've been lucky so far. We've only had to stop once and wait a couple of minutes for that small column of German vehicles to pass by."

"Ayup."

"Things'll get harder the closer we get to the front line."

"I'm wondering if we should hunker down, rest and go the rest of the way after nightfall."

Dunn didn't reply right away. He'd been thinking the same thing the last twenty minutes. The biggest problem with trying to move through the line at night was just having bad luck and stumbling right into the enemy. That was the deciding factor.

"We'll continue on. Worried we might trip over some Germans in the dark."

Cross nodded. "Okay. How long a rest do you want to give the men?"

"Another five minutes. Then five minutes per hour."

"Got it."

"Let's get back," Dunn said, getting to his feet.

Cross got up and the two men walked back to the squad.

Dunn knelt and eyed his troops. They were in good shape. Eyes still clear.

"We're half way home, men. We need to really stay alert. We'll stay in a column except for Martelli and Goerdt. I want you guys paralleling Wickham, who will have point. Stay about five yards out and pace him."

"Right, Sarge," Goerdt said.

"Okay, Sarge," Martelli said.

"Schneider, take the rear."

"Okay, Sarge," said the big man.

"We'll take five minute breaks about every hour. Our goal is to stay within the woods whenever possible. Let's go."

The men rose to their feet and everyone took up their positions.

Dunn, who was behind Wickham, gave the Texan a nod. Wickham nodded in return, spun around and walked off toward the front line.

Five minutes later, the rain came. It sprinkled first, with few drops actually making it to the ground through the tree limbs. Then the skies emptied. The ground became soaking wet in a few minutes and the fallen leaves, which had been a problem for making light crunchy noises, grew quiet and slippery. A plus and a minus for the hikers.

An hour later, Wickham caught motion to his right. Goerdt was headed his way. He stopped walking and Goerdt stepped close. Martelli noticed Wickham had stopped and spotted Goerdt standing next to him. He maneuvered himself over to join the two. Behind the trio, Dunn held up his hand to stop the column and he waited in place.

"There's a farm house. Maybe a hundred yards ahead and twenty-five north of our line of march," Goerdt said. "There's a small cleared area on the south side, but the house faces north. Smoke is coming out of the chimney, so someone's there."

Wickham looked in that direction, but just being five yards farther away was enough to block his view of it.

"Okay, good catch. I'll check with Sarge." Wickham looked to the southwest. "We'll probably just go around."

Wickham walked back to Dunn and explained the situation, got his instructions, and headed back.

"Going around."

Goerdt and Martelli nodded and moved away to resume their relative position to Wickham, who waited until they were in place. He glanced over his shoulder at Dunn, who nodded.

Wickham started walking and the column followed.

A half hour later, he stopped, holding up his fist. He motioned for everyone to kneel. The column halted as did Goerdt and Martelli, and everyone tensed up and took a knee. He'd heard something ahead. He advanced a couple of steps and leaned his left shoulder against a white birch tree. He peered around the right side of the tree and was greeted by a view of a large five-point buck only twenty yards away. A flurry of good memories flooded in of hunting deer with his dad and three brothers back in East Texas. God he missed it. Missed them. He blinked his eyes rapidly to rid them of the unexpected moisture that came not from the rain, but from him. When that didn't work he had to use a finger to wipe it away. He took a deep breath to gather himself, and he turned around facing the rest of the men. He raised his left hand with the fingers and thumb outstretched. He placed his wrist against his wet helmet in a sign for antlers. Everyone grinned and relaxed.

He turned around and marched off to the west, the squad following.

Dunn was concerned about breaking through the German front line from the *wrong side*. He and his squad had done it before back in early July. They'd been on a nighttime mission to break into German Headquarters in La Haye, France, which was about six miles south of the front line stretching across the Cotentin Peninsula. They'd stolen important documents and found top secret papers that allowed them to later destroy the Nazis' electromagnetic pulse weapon. Along the way to the front line, they'd created some havoc by destroying a supply depot, rescuing a priceless painting stolen from a museum in Cherbourg, and blowing up four German 88s. They'd weakened a point on the German line by attacking it from the rear giving the American forces on the opposite side an advantage.

Dunn wasn't so sure they'd be as lucky this time. The Germans were compressed into a smaller area not too far ahead, which meant stealth was going to be the only way through the line. Back then, he'd opted for a daylight crossing and he still believed it was their best chance here.

He estimated they had another hour to go, or about three miles. He'd been pleased and impressed with the major's ability to keep pace. Dunn had positioned the communications officer right behind himself so he could keep an eye on him just by looking over his shoulder. Every time he'd done that, the major had smiled and given him a thumbs-up.

Wickham suddenly stopped again with a fist aloft.

Dunn kept on moving and joined his point man. He immediately saw why the Ranger had stopped. Just ahead about fifty yards another road running north-south lay in their path. Dunn thought about it for a few seconds and made his decision.

He leaned close to Wickham and whispered, "We're going to form a tight skirmish line. Get Martelli and Goerdt over here while I go get the rest of the men."

Wickham simply nodded.

Dunn walked carefully back to his men. He waved a hand for them to come close in a semi-circle. When they formed up around him, their alert eyes peered out from underneath their dripping helmets.

Keeping his voice low, he said, "Need to cross another road. We're about three miles from the line, so we're going into a tight skirmish line, two yard interval. I'll be in the center. Major Miles, you'll be on my right."

Miles nodded. If he was upset at Dunn wanting to keep an eye on him, he kept it to himself.

The men moved forward to join Wickham, Martelli, and Goerdt, spreading out as instructed. Their line was about twenty yards wide with Dunn in the middle. He checked the men on each side and pointed with his left hand.

The line rushed forward. When Dunn reached a point five yards from the road, which was mud and gravel, he signaled to stop. The men reacted immediately. Dunn moved forward until he was behind the last tree near the road. To his right, the road curved away from him at a point about seventy-five yards distant, heading off to the northwest. To his left it ran straight until it crested a hill at about two hundred yards. The road was empty, but something made Dunn continue to stand still.

What was it?

He closed his eyes and listened. It was hard to hear over the sound of the rain beating on his helmet, so he took it off. He stood stock still for nearly a minute.

He was rewarded for his patience.

A light repeating pattern of crunching sounds came from the north.

Men marching toward his position.

Lots of them.

Chapter 12

SS Headquarters
Bologna, Italy
307 kilometers north-northwest of Rome
12 November, 0830 Hours

SS *Hauptsturmführer*, Captain, Werner Möller sat at the head of a beautiful seventeenth century dining table in the Bologna SS Headquarters, a mansion which had, at one time, belonged to a wealthy Italian banker.

The Nazi SS, the *Schutzstaffel*, protection squadron, predated the war, and Heinrich Himmler was named its leader in 1929. Over time it grew in size and became one of the most feared military units in the world.

Möller was in his mid-thirties with a round, almost cherubic, face that belied his darker violent nature. He'd first seen combat in Russia as a fledgling member of the sadistic murderous SS *Einsatzgruppen*. His performance there, going from one village to another, leaving a trail of burned out homes and dead bodies everywhere, earned him the reputation as a man who got results whatever it took, whether torture or murder, or both. He'd quickly been promoted and eventually transferred to Italy, where he commanded an SS company, a *Sturm*.

When he'd been awarded, for that's how he thought of it, the mission to capture the Pope, he realized he was destined for greatness and a place in the annals of history forever. It had made him smile, although fortunately no one had seen it. His smile was a baring of the teeth with the lips compressed, much like a wolf might do when snarling. Men on the receiving end of Möller's smile always looked away as soon as it was politically possible.

He looked at the five men around him and gave them that smile. All were able to maintain eye contact, which made him proud of them. He opened a black leather notebook which had a silver SS death's head attached to the front. His rank and name were engraved in the leather below the death's head. Everything he'd done of any importance started its life in that notebook.

Hauptscharführer, Master Sergeant, Horst Sauer had the seat to the captain's right. Across from the sergeant were four squad leaders, all ranked *Oberscharführer*, Staff Sergeant. Everyone looked at Möller expectantly.

He removed six maps the size of letter writing paper. Passing them out, he kept one for himself, which he set aside.

"The purpose of today's meeting is to conduct a final analysis of our plan to capture the Roman Catholic known as Pope Pius the Twelfth. The code name of our operation is Devil's Advocate." He looked up and smiled again. This time the men returned it. He had dreamed up the code name himself and was quite proud of it.

"This mission was ordered by the *Führer* himself, therefore we will do everything possible to make it a success.

"To remind you of why you are here: although I command a company, I decided an oversized platoon will provide sufficient man and firepower. You four lead the best squads in my company, and you, *Hauptscharführer* Sauer, are the best platoon sergeant, not only in my company, but the battalion."

The five men chorused, "Thank you, *Hauptsturmführer*!"

Möller nodded. "Take a look at the map of Villas of Castel Gandolfo. I've indicated where we'll make entry, where I expect the capture to take place, as well as from where the Swiss Guard commander will attempt to strike back after the capture. Take your time and ensure you know the locations by memory.

"Each squad leader, and I, will carry one of our Feldfunk-Sprecher two-way radios in case we need to adapt our attack."

The men nodded. The radio was of high quality and having good communications would increase the likelihood of success.

Möller waited patiently as the men examined the maps. When one by one they looked up to indicate they were done, he reopened his notebook. He removed six more maps and distributed them.

"If you look about fifteen kilometers southeast of Villas of Castel Gandolfo, you'll find the city of Lariano. I have contacts there who will provide us with farmer-style trucks. We will air drop a few kilometers south of Lariano. A night drop of course, and low level, which will carry some risk. We will be dressed like Italians and carry our MP40s, and other weapons in civilian satchels.

"Our escape route will be difficult. Each truck will take a different path to the west coast two kilometers north of Anzio, which is clear of Americans. A submarine will pick us up and transport us all the way to the sub pens at Wilhelmshaven. From there, we'll transport by air to Berlin, where the *Führer* will greet our prisoner."

He glanced at Sauer, who was still examining the map closely. "Questions coming to mind, *Hauptscharführer* Sauer?"

Sauer looked up. "Are we still confident in the numbers for the Swiss Guard? Was it sixty-two in total?"

The captain nodded. "*Ja*, that's the number we've received several times from our contact in Rome. The number who travel with the Pope when he goes to the villa is about half that. The others remain at the Vatican. We'll have about a one and a half to one superiority. Comparing the experience of our men to that of the Swiss Guard, it'll be a straightforward and short battle, should they even attempt to fight back. That's why we've selected the ambush spot so carefully. The part of the garden they'll be passing through has two-meter high stone walls along both sides of the walkway, which, at that point is only three meters wide. It would be practically a duck shoot. Two squads will be positioned one behind each wall. The other two will be in position to close the walkway at each end of the ambush site. Any resistance will be met with immediate firepower. That's why we selected two of our men to carry sniper rifles. They will pick off the guards nearest the Pope, if necessary. If they don't immediately surrender.

"Our contact will be in St. Peter's Square this afternoon. The Pope is scheduled to make one of his public appearances on the ellipse. We'll get good photos of the Pope and his guards from him."

He looked around the table, meeting each soldier's eyes. "Are there any other questions?"

"Nein, Hauptsturmführer."

"Hauptscharführer Sauer, have you located a suitable rehearsal spot?"

"I have, Captain. It's not far from here. North a few miles along the main road going out of the city. Matches up in size quite well. I've arranged for the rehearsals this afternoon. I selected other squads to act as the Swiss Guard and someone to be the target. Blank ammunition will be distributed and double checked to prevent accidents.

"For the squads who are guarding the target I've told them they are practicing moving an SS target of value and protecting him from the Italian resistance. I may have led them to believe they are guarding *Reichsführer* Himmler."

Möller chuckled. "I'm picturing their expressions when they lose the battle."

"Yes, sir. It's going to be led by *Hauptscharführer* Becker, third platoon's master sergeant."

"I believe you've outdone yourself, Sergeant Sauer."

Sergeant Becker was an ultra-competitive man with no sense of humor, which proved to be a bad combination.

"Yes, sir. I'm looking forward to this."

"I'd like you to show me where this will take place and help me find a good spot to watch from."

"Yes, sir. Would you like to do that now?"

Möller looked at the ceiling, thinking about the rest of his morning. He lowered his gaze to Sauer. "Yes. That would be perfect. Meet me outside my office in five minutes."

"Yes, sir."

Möller rose indicating the meeting was over. The others stood and saluted him. He returned it and left.

Sauer said to his men, "Have your men ready at thirteen hundred hours at the departure point. Remember, blank ammunition only."

"*Jawohl, Hauptscharführer.*"

RONN MUNSTERMAN

Chapter 13

12 miles west of Sarrebourg, France and
3 miles east of the American line
12 November, 0950 Hours

Moving quickly, Dunn slapped his helmet back on and wound his way farther back into the thick woods. He stopped and turned around, taking a knee behind an oak tree. He could still see the roadway through the trees, and eyed the curve to the north. The leading edge of what might be at least a German platoon came into view. Their boots' crunching sounds grew louder with each step.

Dunn wondered whether this movement was the result of the messages Major Miles had sent hours ago.

As the formation came closer, Dunn was able to discern that the makeup of the platoon was of men in their late twenties and early thirties. This meant these were veterans, and probably had transferred from the Eastern Front some time ago. As soon as the platoon cleared the curve, another came into view. Dunn waited until the first platoon was almost right in front of him before he did a quick count. Three columns of ten for a total of thirty. The majority of the men were carrying Mausers, the Germans' standard field weapon. The rifle was a bolt-action weapon whose internal magazine had room for a five-round clip of 7.92 mm ammunition, which was 1/100 of an inch bigger than the .30 caliber American Garand M1. With a muzzle velocity of almost 2,500 feet per second, it had an effective range of 550 yards. However, it wasn't nearly the weapon the M1 had proven to be because of its semi-automatic fire and an eight-round capacity, but it was still deadly.

As the second platoon passed by, Dunn counted again, after noting the men were of the same age range as the first. There were twenty-seven for a total of fifty-seven. One more platoon rounded the curve. Dunn immediately noticed a difference in their uniforms, which were completely clean. Replacements. As the last platoon went by, Dunn counted forty-five, a full complement. He listened carefully, but heard no other footsteps coming from the north.

He waited until the rear of the last platoon disappeared over the hill to the south. He rose to his feet and made his way back to his men.

"One rifle company, a hundred and two men, heading south," Dunn said. He looked at Major Miles. "It could be a result of your messages, sir."

Miles gave Dunn a grateful smile. "Well, I sure hope so."

Dunn nodded.

"We'd best get across the road quickly. Everyone up to the tree line."

Dunn took off without waiting for the men, who he knew would be right behind him. When he reached the tree line, he looked up and down the road. The men were lined up on either side of him, ready and waiting for his signal. He checked the road once more and then gave the signal. The squad ran across the road and into the forest on the opposite side. They stayed in formation and began moving through the forest. Dunn kept the pace up, but not so fast that the Rangers couldn't slide quietly along. After thirty minutes, he called a halt. He waved for the men to come close.

After they crowded in around him in a semicircle, he said, "We're really close. Maybe a mile and a half. Everybody stay alert. Anyone who sees a German stops the line. Remember, our goal is to make it back, not wipe out the enemy. That's for another time."

Dunn made eye contact with each man as he talked to make sure everyone heard what he was saying.

"Any questions?"

They all shook their heads.

"Okay. Back in formation."

The men quickly resumed their positions and watched Dunn, waiting for the go-ahead signal.

Dunn checked the line on both sides and raised his right arm. He dropped his arm level and pointed straight ahead. The line of Americans moved forward.

Dunn checked the time: almost 1030 hours. The rain had lessened in the last half mile and visibility was better, up to several hundred yards. He knew his men were tired from the long night and day of marching. Major Miles was still holding his own.

Wickham, who was on the right end of the line spotted a shape just off to the right and halted the line. He pointed at Higgins, who was next to him, to come with him. They advanced slowly toward what turned out to be a cabin, possibly a hunter's one-room hideaway. No smoke came from the chimney. A small cleared area surrounded the cabin, although the grass appeared to be about knee high.

Wickham maneuvered to within fifty yards, staying behind trees whenever possible. There was a narrow trail leading to the front of the cabin from the west, coming out of the woods. There was no track for vehicles. There seemed to be only one window in view and it was on the south side with the front door.

Wickham moved farther to the right to get out of the window's sightline. He stopped at the next tree. There was a gap between his tree and the next one of about ten yards. He could move in such a way as to still remain hidden from the window, by following a straight line that started a little farther to his right. The space he was about to cross was covered with short grasses and a shrub or two.

He turned and gave signals to Higgins indicating he wanted the other man to follow him exactly. Higgins nodded.

Keeping his eyes on the cabin, he made his move. Higgins slid in quickly a few steps behind.

About half way across the gap, he was in mid step, with his right foot just lifting off the ground to begin its journey forward. Something grabbed him and yanked backwards. He fell back against Higgins, who struggled to keep the much larger man on his feet. Wickham got his balance and turned to face Higgins with a questioning look. He wasn't angry at the man because he knew there had to be a reason, but he sure wanted to know what it was.

Higgins knelt and pointed a finger toward the ground in front of them.

Wickham also knelt and peered at the ground. Something shiny was stretched along the ground about six inches above the dirt. Wickham's gaze followed the wire to the right. Five feet away, a German potato masher grenade dangled head down from a stick stuck in the ground. The wire was tied to the stick. If Wickham had hit the wire, it would have knocked the grenade loose. As it fell from the stick, the already unscrewed end cap would stay in place and the fuse inside the handle would be lit as the striker slid along it.

He gulped, and followed the wire the other way. Another ambush grenade was set up there, too.

Wickham motioned for Higgins to put his head right next to his own.

"Thanks. I owe you," he whispered. His Brit-Tex accent was gone and he reverted to his native Texan accent instead, something he invariably did under stress.

"No you don't, Sarge," Higgins whispered back.

Wickham frowned at Higgins. "You saved my life. I owe you. Period. End of story."

Higgins nodded. "Okay. You're welcome."

Wickham nodded. "Let's go tell Sarge what we found."

Another nod from Higgins.

The two men moved quickly making sure they still were out of sight of the cabin window. When they made it back to the squad, they found the men resting on any relatively dry spots they could find.

To Dunn and Cross, who were sitting side by side, Wickham explained what they'd seen and how Higgins had saved his life by seeing the tripwire.

Dunn looked at Higgins and gave him a somber nod. "Good job, Higgins."

"Thank you, Sarge."

"What do you want to do, Tom?" Cross asked.

"Avoid, avoid, avoid. That's our mantra for the day."

"But why would they set up booby traps around a hunter's cabin?" Cross persisted. "Might be something worth looking at inside there."

Dunn nodded. "Yep, there might be. But I don't give a damn. We're leaving it alone."

Cross nodded. His curiosity was trying to get the better of him, but he would never go against Dunn's orders.

"Get the men up and ready. We're going southwest for a quarter mile and back northwest to return to our travel line."

In short order the men were up and rearranged facing southwest. Dunn checked the line and pointed again.

He slowed the line's forward motion a little bit, from the three miles an hour they been traveling to about two, which seemed like a crawl. It allowed them to take their time observing things in front of them and would keep them from running up on a problem before they could react and prepare.

After a little over an hour and a half, Dunn called another halt. By his reckoning, they were almost on top of the German front line. The American line would be about two hundred yards farther. They'd seen absolutely no activity, which had been a blessing. Dunn wondered whether their luck would hold up.

The terrain had been primarily flat with a few rises and valleys along the way. The same was true in front of the men. Dunn advanced a few yards and suddenly dropped to a knee. The line stopped moving. Dunn got down on his belly, his Sten gun cradled in his arms and he combat crawled forward several more yards until he was on top of a small rise. He stopped and raised his head. Not fifty yards away, tucked into a small swale sat a German machine gun two-man crew. From his position behind, Dunn couldn't tell if it was the feared MG42, "Hitler's buzzsaw," or the less powerful, but still deadly, MG34. He scanned the area to the north of the machine gun. Twenty yards along, he found a pair of German soldiers poking their heads up from their foxhole. Their rifles were on the berm around it, aiming west. He continued his scan and he spotted the next foxhole about another twenty yards from the first one. Turning his attention to the south he was only able to locate one foxhole the same distance from the machine gun emplacement. He thought about the situation. If the Germans had a ten-man squad here, it would have just the one machine gun and everyone else would have rifles. If each foxhole contained two men and they were twenty yards apart, the squad's front covered eighty yards. What he needed to know was whether there was another squad on the left, or if there would be a gap, like you sometimes found on the line between platoons.

Scooting backwards until he was underneath the top of the rise, he rotated his body and crawled back to his men. He waved at Cross. When Cross crawled over to join him, he whispered, "Squad dead ahead. Light machine gun and to its left twenty yards, a foxhole with two in it. We need to find out if this is a platoon's flank. Maybe we can squeeze through."

"I'll go check."

"Okay."

Cross moved away, still on his stomach.

Ten agonizing minutes passed before Cross returned safely to Dunn.

Dunn looked at his friend expectantly.

"Our luck's holding. That is the platoon's left flank. The next one is on the other side of a very thick copse of pine trees. They're set up about two hundred yards away."

Dunn made his decision instantly. "We'll go through the pines on our stomachs. Column formation."

Soon after, the squad was inching along and entered the pine tree area. The air smelled so fresh, it was a welcome change. By the time the squad made it to the western side of the pines, the men were nearly exhausted, not to mention wet and cold and covered in mud, and also brown pine needles that stuck to the mud on their uniforms.

Dunn raised his head and examined the terrain ahead. More trees, but they were maples and white birch. He figured they were about fifty yards from the American line and a hundred fifty from the German line. Often called no man's land. He eyed a small crest in the terrain which was where he thought the Americans would be. He carefully scanned the area. It took two visual passes, but he finally spotted a pair of green American helmets just above the ground. He continued looking, but didn't see any other foxholes.

To Cross he whispered, "I'm going to go way off to the left, see if I can get past those two guys and come back from behind them where they'd expect someone to be. I'll give you a signal when it's safe to come across."

"Be damn careful, Tom. I don't want to have to explain to Pamela why you got shot by another American."

Dunn grunted in reply and took off to the south, still crawling along. Every ten yards or so, he raised his head slightly to check for foxholes. Nothing so far. He was able to still see the foxhole he'd found, which helped him know where he needed to get to.

When he was about ten yards from the American line, he heard footsteps somewhere ahead. Two men walking toward the north. Replacements for the foxhole, perhaps? He waited until the sounds faded. He sped up his crawling efforts. He wanted to be behind the line before the men being replaced left their foxhole.

Just as he reached the line, and was passing a maple tree, which was on the left, he felt something hard and cold press against his neck.

Chapter 14

Vatican City
Swiss Guard Barracks
12 November, 1000 Hours

Saunders was still on cloud nine because on the drive from the Villas of Castel Gandolfo through the center of Rome, they had driven right past the enormous Colosseum. He'd dreamed of seeing it one day and when Commander Herriot mentioned in passing on the drive that they would go right past the ancient structure, Saunders had become as excited as he'd been in a long, long time.

Herriot must have noticed his excitement because he'd asked the driver to slow down as they approached the Colosseum. Saunders had rolled down his window and stared at the almost sixteen story tall building. He was impressed by the design with its many, many archways and the intricate scroll work at the top of the outer wall. He regretted not having a camera in hand. Herriot must have read his mind for he said he would arrange for them to get postcards of the Colosseum and any other buildings they wanted. Saunders was beside himself and grateful.

The trucks had driven across one of the many bridges crossing the River Tiber and past the outside of Saint Peter's Square on the north side. They parked near the Swiss Guard barracks and armory.

Herriot led the men into a long narrow room and stood to the side as they entered with eyes wide. The room was filled with shiny silver armor, including helmets. Long pike-like weapons, the halberds, and silver swords were carefully stored along the wall opposite the armor. At the far end on the left, past the weapons, tricolored uniforms hung on long racks. A Guard stood at the front of the uniforms, facing the men.

"Gentlemen, please do not touch the armor or the weapons. They have been carefully polished. Please see the man ahead of you for help in finding a uniform that will fit you," Herriot said in his commander's voice.

Herriot turned to Alfred Welford, the Pope's stand in. "Sir, would you care to sit down? I can have a chair brought in."

Welford, the actor, said in Italian, "Thank you, no, Commander. I'll just stand here with you, if that's all right."

Herriot's expression changed to one of wonder. "You . . . sound just like him. How . . . ?"

Welford grinned. "One of my many talents, Commander."

Saunders watched the exchange and asked, "What was that about?"

Herriot replied in English, "I'd asked Mr. Welford if he'd like to sit. He replied in perfect Italian and even sounds like the Pope himself."

Saunders eyed Welford with a new perspective. "An added bonus, then."

Welford grinned again. "Indeed." He set his suitcase down. It contained his papal clothing. He also carried a satchel which he placed next to the suitcase. It held all the makeup and other items, like the glasses, he'd need to transform himself into Pope Pius XII.

Saunders took up a position next to the commander and Welford, and watched as his men began the slow process of selecting a uniform. Each one was made up of three colors: blue, red, and yellow. After about fifteen minutes, everyone except Saunders was almost fully dressed as a Swiss Guard. The man helping led them to a table where stacks of black berets were stored. Soon, the men had their heads properly covered.

Saunders was proud of the men. Not one had involuntarily giggled at the sight of a mate in the unusual uniform. They all seemed to sense the history behind the clothing and the mood stayed rather somber, which Saunders thought was fitting.

"How long have you been a Commando, Sergeant Saunders?" Herriot asked quietly.

"Well, let's see. It was sometime last year. I think we graduated in April of forty-three. I guess that makes it what, a year and seven months."

"That's a long time."

"Aye. And you? How long have you been a Guard?"

"Twenty years next May. We're always sworn in on May the sixth in honor of the Sack of Rome, which occurred on that date in fifteen twenty-seven. The Papal States fought Charles the Fifth. One hundred eighty-nine Swiss Guards fought the Imperial troops on the steps of St. Peter's Basilica. All but forty-two were killed, but Pope Clement the Seventh was escorted to safety. The years following were difficult for Romans, but eventually the city recovered as did the papacy."

"Twenty years! I thought you said it was typically a two year stint, except for the war."

"It is for the average Guard. For command level members, they can stay on as they are promoted. It's the best way to provide continuity of command and to have veteran Guards."

"Sounds like the British Army and its professional soldiers."

"Yes, same principles."

"I'm only familiar with the Guard's overview history. Looks like I need to read up sometime."

"It will certainly be worth your time."

"Do you have family?"

"Mother, father, sister and brother. You?"

"Mum, Dad, three sisters. Got married in September."

"Recent. Congratulations. Her name was Sadie?"

"Aye."

"Lovely name."

"Thanks."

"I imagine you've been to a few places during the war."

Saunders sighed. "I have. Egypt. Twice. Germany, France, Italy, Belgium. Poland. Austria. Those are the ones I can think of at the moment."

"Do you always fly in?"

"Most of the time we parachute in. We took a sub once and that was once too often. We got depth charged on our way back. A horrible, terrifying experience."

Herriot looked at Saunders. "I'm having trouble seeing you terrified."

Saunders snorted a chuckle. "I'm an enigma. Calm as can be on the outside. Churning like crazy inside. Had to learn pretty bloody fast how to function effectively in spite of the churning."

Herriot nodded. "Yes. Overcoming fear. A difficult task." He gently put a hand on Saunders' shoulder.

Saunders glanced his way.

"I am deeply grateful you are here to help us."

The Commando nodded solemnly.

"Okay. How about we get you dressed?"

"Should be interesting, sir."

The wardrobe man searched for five minutes before coming back to Saunders with a uniform. He held it up against the Commando's large frame and smiled. Nodding, he held out the uniform for Saunders, who took it. Saunders stripped off his suit and laid it on a table nearby. He put on the tricolor shirt followed by the matching pants. He pulled the shoe cover pieces over the tops of his black shoes.

The man handed him a beret and he slipped it on with the flat part facing his right, positioned so it covered his right ear. He walked over to one of the many mirrors situated around the room and stood in front of it.

Barltrop sidled up beside him. "Want me to take a picture for Sadie? I think she'd like the colors on you. Go real well with your mad red hair."

"We should get pictures of everyone together. Be a great keepsake."

"Okay. Let's do that soon."

Commander Herriot joined Saunders and Barltrop and examined them both closely. When he was done, he said, "You'd pass inspection. Very good job. I think we should get you armed."

"What do you have for us?"

"We have Sig MKMOs available."

Saunders frowned. That was an older weapon made by the famous Swiss company, Schweizerische Industrie Gesellschaft. It would not be his first choice. He cleared his throat politely.

Herriot was bright enough to get the hint. "We also have some captured German MP40s. Perhaps those would be more to your liking."

"Aye, they would, sir. Thank you. I assume you must have a firing range somewhere?"

"We do. It's outside Vatican City, of course. Not far, though."

"Good. We'll need a little time to reacquaint ourselves with the 'forty.'"

"I'll arrange it. We should go out in the courtyard and do a little close order drill. We do some things differently starting with the hand salute. We use the American style with the palm face down rather than facing front. Also will want to pass along commands in French, which is what we're using most of the time. I'll have my second in command handle all that. Oh, and two other things before we go outside. When marching we do not exaggerate our arm motions like you do. When we are making turns in place, we do not lift one leg high and stamp the ground."

"You've studied our methods."

"We study all methods to see if anything of value can be borrowed to improve."

"Interesting."

Herriot raised his voice, using his command tone. "Gentlemen."

The Commandos immediately stopped what they were doing and looked his way.

"We're heading out into the private courtyard for some close order drill. My second in command, David Surbeck, will conduct a short class in commands in French as well as point out some of the differences between our styles. Sergeant Barltrop, would you please lead the men to the courtyard. It's back through the door we came in, down the hall to the right and out the first door on the left."

Barltrop nodded. "Yes, sir."

He quickly got the men into formation, a single file, and marched them out of the room.

Herriot looked at Saunders and Welford, the actor. "We'll go to a meeting room and while Sergeant Saunders and I examine maps, Mr. Welford, I'll show you where you can . . . transform yourself."

"Wonderful. Can't wait." Welford's eyes seem to sparkle.

"I will be the only person to see you dressed as the Pope, well, except for Sergeant Saunders, so, please refrain from just walking out of your room by yourself. It could cause quite some confusion if you're spotted by someone who just saw the Pope."

"Understood, Commander." Welford's expression turned professional. "Whatever you need me to do."

"This way, please."

Chapter 15

On the front line and 15 miles west of Sarrebourg, France

12 November, 1012 Hours

"What'cha doing down there, buddy?" someone growled at Dunn.

He was shocked that he hadn't heard a thing, but he was relieved to hear an American voice above him. He moved his arms so they were stretched out in front of him, the equivalent of raising his hands if he'd been standing.

"My name's Tom Dunn. I'm a Ranger returning from a mission with my squad. I'd really rather you didn't shoot."

"Uh huh. Right."

With his M1 still aimed more or less in Dunn's direction, the man asked, "So who won the last World Series?"

"The Cardinals."

"How many games?"

"Six."

"Good. Doing good so far. So how long has Teddy been in the White House?"

"That would be a good trick, since Teddy Roosevelt has been dead for twenty-five years. Franklin is president and has been since 1933."

"Okay, here's what you're gonna do: keep your hands where they are and roll over onto your back. Don't make any sudden moves."

"Whatever you say."

Dunn rolled over slowly and got his first look at his captor.

The man was about Schneider's size. He had several days' worth of stubble and wore three stripes. He had dark eyes under a heavy brow. Dunn didn't think he'd stand a chance with the guy one-on-one, even if he wasn't lying on his back.

The man grinned and chuckled. He eyed Dunn's filthy uniform, but was able to see the five stripes on each sleeve, and the Ranger patch on the shoulder. "Aren't you a sight, Sergeant Dunn?"

He safed and slung his M1 over his shoulder, and stuck out a hand. He pulled Dunn to his feet as easily as if the Ranger had been a little boy, but kept them positioned safely behind the maple tree. Standing next to the man, Dunn realized he'd been wrong. The guy was three inches taller than Schneider's six-four. He was enormous.

"So what's this mission?"

"Top secret."

"Of course. I take it all went well?"

"Yes. Can you let your men know I need to get the rest of my squad through here?"

"Will do. By the way, the name's Warren Humphrey."

"Nice to meet ya."

"Yeah." Humphrey lifted a radio off his shoulder and raised the antenna. He spoke into it for a moment. He evidently got the responses he wanted and put it away. "You can give your men the all clear from our side, but they still need to keep their faces in the dirt. Our guys will light things up if the krauts get cute."

"Great, thanks."

Dunn pulled out his walkie-talkie and pressed the talk button three times: dit-dit-dit, "S" for safe. He waited a couple of seconds and sent another series: dah-dit-dah-dit, "C" for crawl.

He received the same two signals in return to prove Cross had read them correctly, followed by a "U" for understood.

While Dunn and Humphrey waited for the Ranger squad, they faced the enemy line, but chatted quietly. Humphrey was from South Carolina, not far from Myrtle Beach. He'd been in the army since late 1942 and was assigned to Patton's Third Army. He was a squad leader, too.

Dunn watched the area he'd used to arrive and after ten long minutes, he finally spotted an American helmet seemingly sliding along the ground. Then the bulk of Cross came into view. Soon, the remaining ten men were safely behind the American line, kneeling, catching their breath. Dunn introduced the major and Cross to Sergeant Humphrey.

"Can you get us to Twelfth Corps' Second Battalion HQ? Their intelligence officer is expecting us and we need to arrange for a flight back to England with the logistics officer."

"Can do. Follow me."

When they arrived at the 2nd Battalion's HQ, Dunn thanked the big sergeant, who went back toward the front line.

Dunn asked around and was pointed toward a major, the intelligence officer. The major was glad to see Dunn and took his verbal report. He was grinning by the end of it.

"Sounds like you did everything we needed. We're already getting reports of troop movements, and the ones you saw are very helpful. Thank you."

"Our pleasure, sir."

The two men shook hands and Dunn asked where the logistics officer might be. The major tipped his head toward a group of officers, who were staring down at a large map spread out on a portable table. He wondered whether an attack was in the offing. Should be one, he thought, based on the messages Major Miles had sent. There should be an opening on the line to the north, if all of the German commanders fell for the trap.

He introduced himself to the officer, a captain, and made his request for transportation back to Hampstead. The captain motioned for Dunn to follow him and he led him to a dark green field desk on which a large radio sat. The operator glanced up when the captain tapped him on the shoulder. The radioman slid one of the headset ear muffs off. The captain explained what he wanted. The radioman nodded and turned back to his machine. He made a quick call and signed off.

"All done, sir," the radioman said. He turned back to the radio, immediately forgetting the interruption.

"You're all set, Sergeant Dunn. I'll get you and your squad a truck. The airfield is about ten miles west. Or would you rather grab some chow first?"

"Yesterday's dinner was a long time ago, sir. Chow would be swell."

The man nodded. "Follow me."

"Thank you, sir."

After the men gobbled down breakfast and lunch combined, they boarded a deuce and a half, which trundled away toward the airfield, where a C-47 would be waiting for them.

Chapter 16

The Vatican
12 November, 1530 Hours

While Saunders and Herriot were seated at a large table, Welford was busy in the room next door. There was a connecting door between the rooms and when he was made up and dressed, he knocked on the door gently.

Saunders, still wearing his tricolor Swiss Guard uniform, rose and strode over to the door, opening it. He eyed the ersatz Pope carefully, looking for anything out of place. Satisfied, he stepped back. The Pope stepped through the door.

Commander Herriot, who got his first full look at the Pope's doppelganger, dropped his mouth open and his eyes seemed to bug out. Welford walked slowly toward Herriot and stopped directly in front of him. As a test, the commander immediately dropped to his right knee and bowed his head.

Welford held out his hand, palm downward and Herriot looked at it, surprised. Welford was wearing an ornate ring with a ruby set in the center. It looked exactly like the one Pius XII wore every day. Herriot kissed the ring.

"Rise, my son," Welford said in Italian.

As Herriot rose, Welford gently placed his left hand on the commander's right arm.

"How nice to see you, Commander Herriot."

"Thank you, Holy Father."

Herriot looked at Saunders, shaking his head. "I don't know how you did this, but he's incredible. Perfect in every way."

Saunders smiled. "I can't take credit for it. Some folks back in England arranged it all."

"Marvelous. Simply marvelous. I can't wait to introduce him to my men later." He turned to Welford. "We'll be going outside with you as the Pope for the first time at sixteen hundred. The Holy Father sometimes walks the circumference of the ellipse on Sunday afternoons."

"Of course, sir. That will be my premier performance, won't it?"

"Yes, it will be. I must say you've captured the Holy Father's mannerisms and movements wonderfully. How did you do that?"

"I watched hours of film over and over again, and practiced in front of a full-length mirror."

"Impressive."

Welford nodded his thanks.

"In a minute, we'll go over how the Holy Father interacts with the Guards and the public. My men won't believe it when they see you. I didn't believe it. If I hadn't known the Holy Father was about to start Mass, I would have sworn you were him."

Welford smiled gratefully at Herriot.

"One thing I need to alert you both about. The Holy Father has a habit of changing his mind about public appearances, and can be . . . strong willed about ensuring his wishes are followed."

"Well, that figures. Hope we can just work around that," Saunders said.

"Me, too," Herriot said ruefully. "Let me explain how the Guard works security for an event like this afternoon. We have specific plans for repetitive events to simplify things for the men."

He talked for ten minutes, pointing occasionally at the map of Vatican City. After he finished explaining the Pope's interaction with the Guards and the public to Welford, he checked his watch. "We should bring the men together, yours and mine, and go over the details for this afternoon. We have a much larger room, an auditorium actually, where we conduct these type of meetings with the men who will be on duty."

He stood and walked over to a dark walnut table by the door to the hallway. He picked up the white phone's handset and dialed a two-digit number. He waited a moment for someone to answer, and said something in French, and hung up.

"The men will be on their way." He lifted a hand toward the door. "Shall we?"

RONN MUNSTERMAN

Chapter 17

Outside the administration building
Camp Barton Stacey
12 November, 1455 Hours, London time

Dunn took one last puff from his Lucky Strike cigarette and dropped the butt to the ground, where he smashed it with his boot toe. The squad had arrived at the camp a half hour ago. Dunn had sent everyone to bed to get a few hours of shuteye, even though most slept some on the plane trip from France. He had slept himself and was glad he did. When he'd called Colonel Cole from Hampstead Airbase to tell him they were back, the man had been his usual brusque self and ordered him to be in his office at 1500 hours. Dunn had debated whether to bring Cross, but in the end decided to go ahead and do it.

Cross finished his cigarette and dropped and crushed it, too. He looked at his best friend. They had changed out of their mud-covered uniforms and replaced the helmets with flat garrison caps.

"You look like something the cat would drag in," Cross said with a grin.

"I feel like I've been dragged in."

"Maybe you'll get some rest tonight."

"Probably depend on what happens in the next five minutes or so. I can't imagine him being very happy with me."

Cross shrugged. "We completed the mission, what's not to like?"

"Oh, I don't know, something about 'following orders' is bound to come up." Dunn put his hand on Cross's shoulder. "You ready to take over the squad if I get demoted to buck private?"

"That won't happen," Cross replied immediately. When he saw Dunn's expression change to grim, he asked in a low voice, "Will it?"

"Don't know with this guy."

A jeep roared up to the front of the building, avoided the two Rangers, and parked nose in toward the building. Major Miles climbed out, looking about the same as Dunn and Cross, with puffy, tired eyes.

"Maybe the major will come to your defense."

"They're friends, remember?"

Cross nodded. "I remember."

"He did do a good job, though."

"True."

Miles made his way around the jeep and approached the two men, who saluted when he got closer. After returning the courtesy, Miles's face broke into a wide grin. "Hello, gentlemen." He came to a stop nearby and continued, "I have to say, I was so very impressed by you and your men. It was my distinct honor to have worked with you."

Dunn and Cross were momentarily speechless with surprise.

Dunn recovered first. "Thank you, sir. We thought you did a great job yourself."

Miles beamed at the compliment. "Thank you. That means a lot to me coming from you, Sergeant Dunn. By the way, Sergeant, I wanted to apologize for how I spoke to you about the mission plan. I was wrong."

He offered his hand and Dunn shook it.

"Thank you, sir. No hard feelings on my part."

"Mine either." Miles looked toward the door. "Shall we?"

"After you, sir," Dunn said, sweeping an arm toward the stairs.

Miles bounded up the steps. It was as if Dunn's kind words had rejuvenated the major. Dunn and Cross glanced at each other and let small grins slip. They followed.

When the three men arrived outside Cole's office, they found it occupied only by Captain Adams, who was sitting to what would be the colonel's right, his usual spot. He stood when he saw the men and smiled. He saluted the major, and Dunn and Cross saluted him. A sort of round robin salute party.

"Welcome back, gentlemen. I heard it was a success."

"Well, the major sent the messages anyway," Dunn replied.

Adams nodded. "Colonel Cole will be here soon. Please, have a seat. Here, Major, take this one." Adams offered him his own chair, where he'd been seated in the first mission meeting.

Everyone settled into a wooden chair. Dunn glanced around the office. Something was different. It took a couple of eyeball sweeps around the room to realize the new colonel had hung an eight by ten picture on the wall to the right of the desk. Dunn's eyes narrowed as he took in the details of the photo. It showed a slightly younger Cole shaking hands and looking toward the camera. The other man was FDR's opponent in the 1940 election, Republican Wendell Willkie. Both were wearing dark suits. Dunn inferred it was from a time during the election campaign. Wilkie's signature was across the bottom. Dunn recalled listening to the results in Iowa City with his college buddies on the radio. FDR had won with over 400 Electoral College votes to Willkie's eighty something. It had been considered a real trouncing. Why in the hell would a guy keep a picture of the opponent of his Commander in Chief? He nudged Cross and tipped his head toward the photo.

Cross stared for a moment. "Who's that with him?"

Dunn whispered the information. Cross shook his head and rolled his eyes. Cross was mostly apolitical, but he listened when Dunn liked to talk about American politics. Dunn was a history major after all, even if he had quit school one semester short of his degree. That had been in response to Pearl Harbor. Dunn and several of his friends had been in line at the army recruiter's office at eight o'clock the next morning.

Adams checked his watch and stood. He walked over to the door and waited. A minute later Cole came storming through the door and walked to his place behind the desk, which was cluttered with folders of various colors and stacks of papers. A complete opposite of Kenton's neatness. Adams once again closed the door loud enough for everyone to hear, opened it a hair, and took a position on Cole's right. He eyed the door. Would this be the time that Cole hanged himself? He sure hoped so. The first time, General Hopkins had listened to the entire meeting out in the hallway, but Cole hadn't crossed the line far enough.

Cole looked at each of the men and leaned forward with his hands folded on the desk in the one clear spot available. He turned to Dunn.

"Mission report."

Dunn started at the beginning and Cole listened attentively. When Dunn described the blitz attack on the radio command truck, he frowned and held up a hand. Dunn stopped talking.

"You've already departed from my mission plan, Sergeant. Why is that?" Cole gave Dunn a stern look.

"The situation called for a different plan, sir. Had to adapt to conditions."

"I told you to follow my plan without deviation."

Adams watched Dunn react to Cole's outrageous statement. He was amazed by Dunn's calm. He took a quick peek at Miles, whose expression seemed to be one of being embarrassed for a friend. He wondered whether this had happened a lot during their friendship.

"Yes, sir. I remember."

"I wanted that truck captured and brought back to the front line."

"As the commander on the ground and in charge of the mission, I deemed that an impossibility given the distances involved, over fifteen miles, and the compactness of the enemy forces on the front line." Dunn had carefully rehearsed this particular comment in his head on the way over from the barracks. He'd crafted it in such a way that Cole would respond in the only way he knew how.

"What the hell is wrong with you, Dunn? Are you unable to follow simple instructions? I gave you explicit instructions on how I wanted this mission to be run and you immediately start by ignoring my carefully constructed plan." Cole fumed for a moment. "Well?"

As Dunn repeated his comment word for word, Cole's face grew redder and redder. Dunn thought he might explode.

"You've ruined everything, you idiot!" Cole turned to Adams. "Start the paperwork for demoting Dunn down to private for blatant insubordination."

"Now hold on, Jim," Major Miles said. He appeared to be surprised to hear his own voice, but he continued. "I was there. Everything Sergeant Dunn did worked perfectly and I, for one, completely support his decisions."

Cole completely lost it. He shouted at his, presumably, former friend, "Shut your trap, Miles. In fact, get out. You're dismissed. Return to your unit."

Miles started to say something, but Cole pointed a finger at him. "Get . . . out!"

Miles's jaw muscles tightened. He glanced at Adams then at Dunn next to him. He stood and placed a hand gently on Dunn's shoulder. "I'm sorry, Sergeant."

"Get out!" Cole shouted again.

"Thank you, Major," Dunn said.

Miles headed toward the door, but stopped to hear the rest.

Cole glared at Dunn. "I knew I should have gone on the mission with you to make sure it was done right."

Cross, unable to allow such a rank amateur treat his best friend this way, said, "Colonel Cole, Sergeant Dunn did everything right and we completed—"

Cole turned his fury on Cross and jabbed the same finger at him. "You shut your mouth, Cross, or you can join your buddy as a private."

Cross's eyes narrowed and flashed his own fury. "Why you arrogant little—"

Dunn quickly slapped a hand over his friend's mouth.

Cole smiled smugly. Again he spoke to Adams. "Start the paperwork for our out of control Sergeant Cross to be demoted to private. Both men will be transferred out of the Ranger unit and will join the replacement pool. We'll see how they like being on the front line."

"Sir, I must protest—"

"Do you want to join them on the front line?"

With no hesitation at all, Adams said, "Yes—"

He was interrupted when the door flew open so hard it bounced off the wall.

Chapter 18

St. Peter's Square
Vatican City
12 November, 1600 Hours, Rome time

Saunders and his men were intermingled with Herriot's Guards. They formed a double line, each side facing the other. They were standing at attention at the bottom of the stairs which the Pope, Welford, would walk down. Herriot had told Saunders earlier that the real Pope had retired to his private residence to reflect and read the bible.

The day was sunshine filled, with few clouds above. The temperature was in the upper sixties and there was a pleasant southerly breeze. The square was filled with people who stared with rapt fervor toward the large double doors that would soon open and give them their Pope.

Earlier, when Herriot had gathered his men with Saunders' in the auditorium, there was an audible gasp from the Guard members when Welford stepped into their view from offstage. They rose to their feet and broke into polite applause, which was the custom in small gatherings such as this, and beamed at their Pope.

Herriot walked over beside the Pope and said, "Members of the Guard, I apologize for some deception on my part. While the man standing next to me for all intents and purposes 'looks' like the Holy Father, I assure you he is not. He is here to help us protect the Holy Father, who, as we've previously discussed, has been threatened by the deadly Nazi SS, who intend to kidnap him.

"This afternoon, this man will meet the public in St. Peter's Square. This is the real test of his abilities to portray our Holy Father. We, all of us, must be certain that our demeanor towards him is exactly the same as if he actually *is* the Holy Father. We must remain vigilant at all times. There could be Nazi spies in the crowd, even today, as they look for weaknesses in our protection umbrella.

"*Acriter et Fideliter!*" he said sharply, quoting the Guard's motto. Fiercely and Faithfully!

"*Acriter et Fideliter!*" the men responded.

"Attention!"

The men snapped into the position.

"To your posts! Dismissed."

With practiced movements, the Guards departed the auditorium in less than a minute.

Saunders stood next to Commander Herriot on the line facing south. Directly across from Saunders was Barltrop. The men were at the end of the line, the farthest from the stairs of St. Peter's Basilica so they would be first as the Pope began his walking ministry around the outside of the elliptical portion of St. Peter's Square. They would be moving clockwise, starting from the nine o'clock position.

The crowd suddenly cheered wildly as the Pope exited through the double doors, greeting them with a gentle wave and a loving smile. Saunders thought the crowd seemed to be well behaved even though some appeared to be beside themselves with excitement.

The Pope was dressed in his white cassock and wore his zucchetto. His cross and his glasses sparkled in the afternoon sunlight. Two cardinals trailed the Pope. They wore black cassocks with red trim and red buttons. Their zucchettos were red. The trio walked through the manmade corridor of Swiss Guards keeping their eyes on the people in the crowd at the end of the line.

Saunders knew from studying a map that a complete trek around the ellipse was about a quarter of a mile. Herriot had told him that it could take the Holy Father an hour to make the full revolution due to his penchant for stopping and talking with the people.

When Welford and his cardinals reached the end of the line of Guards, Herriot, Saunders, Barltrop, and Herriot's second in command, the vice-commander David Surbek, took positions in front of the trio in single file, with an interval of two steps. They would precede the Pope and cardinals. Ten Guards, which included five of Saunders' men, fell in behind the Pope in two columns closing the box of protection. All of the accompanying Guards' eyes were on the crowd at all times.

The box moved slowly as the Pope walked within a few feet of the crowd. Every mother with a child held the child out as the Pope neared. He sometimes would stop and put his left hand on the child's head and make the sign of the cross. The mother would invariably turn and raise her child to the crowd, which cheered.

Saunders watched the people closest to the Pope's line of travel, the ones at the front of the crowd, which amazingly didn't press forward. After checking the people in the front row, he scanned the faces and, when possible, the hands of the people farther back.

They were on the last quarter of the trip, heading toward the starting point. Saunders thought his head might explode from all the smiling faces he had studied. He suddenly spotted a man in his twenties who wasn't smiling. Instead, he had a camera to his right eye and was clicking away, advancing frame after frame. Saunders kept his eye on the man. When the man lowered the camera he turned his attention to the Guards behind the Pope. Saunders had to turn his head to keep the man in sight.

Herriot had been clear in his instructions to Saunders and the men. Rely on your instincts. If something looks wrong with a person, it was always better to take steps to find out what that person was doing, than to risk putting the Holy Father in danger. Saunders sped up and tapped Herriot on the shoulder. The commander stopped and faced Saunders, his expression worry filled.

Saunders leaned close so he could speak directly into Herriot's right ear. "Got a bloke I don't like. Camera. No smile. Brown hair, white shirt, dark jacket, black hat, cigarette."

Herriot nodded. "Lead the way."

Saunders broke through the crowd which parted like the Red Sea for Moses. Saunders kept his eyes on, not the target, but a man to the target's right. Herriot moved to a position to Saunders' right. He spotted the man, who had raised the camera again, aiming at the rear guard. Herriot picked a woman to the target's left and headed for her.

As soon as Herriot and Saunders left their position, the two Guards leading the rear group double-timed forward to take the vacated slots. The remaining members of the rear guard focused intently on Herriot and Saunders, trying to discern what had attracted their attention.

The target lowered his camera and swung his gaze back toward the Pope. He spotted the two men wearing tricolors headed more or less toward him. He immediately ducked and ran bent over toward the east. He plucked his hat off his head and jammed it into his back pocket. He wiggled out of his jacket and carried it. Turning to his left, he straightened and walked normally to the north. In his peripheral vision he spotted the larger of the two Guards running through the crowd like a bull in Pamplona. The Guard was headed the wrong way, still going east. The target smiled and kept walking.

Saunders stopped running and stood with his hands on his hips. His head swiveled like a radar unit. As soon as the target had dropped out of sight, he'd run straight toward him. But it was no use. The mass of the crowd was too much and it was impossible to pick up the target again. He glanced over his right shoulder. Not far away, Herriot was standing still also and looking into the crowd, who seemed unperturbed by the Guards' actions. Herriot faced Saunders with a raised eyebrow. Saunders shook his head. Herriot frowned and tipped his head toward the Pope. The two made their way through the crowd and returned to their original positions. Herriot motioned for the two replacements to return to their posts.

Welford discovered he'd had to invoke all of his willpower to ignore the sight of two of the Guards running into the crowd. A hollowness he'd experienced many times before hit his stomach, but like before, he did what he needed to do. He continued waving and smiling.

When the Pope concluded his tour around the ellipse, he stopped and faced the crowd. He raised both hands and smiled. The crowd roared. He turned and walked toward St. Peter's Basilica.

Saunders, Herriot, and Welford, wearing his suit and not wearing the glasses, were seated around a small, but ornate table in Herriot's personal office. Saunders guessed the table was at least two hundred years old. Its top was polished to a sparkling shine.

"I'm bloody sorry I couldn't catch the guy, Commander," he said.

"I lost him, too, Sergeant. He must have taken off the hat and jacket and just walked away. Smart. Unfortunately. We've learned that if we don't catch him within a few steps, it's impossible with the crowd. Did you get a good look at him before he disappeared?"

"I did. I'll recognize him if I see his face again."

Herriot nodded, obviously pleased. "It appears that Mr. Welford has passed muster with the people. Well done, sir. I'm impressed."

"Thank you," Welford replied.

"Please tell your men they have the afternoon off, but they should remain in the barracks. After supper, we'll gather to plan our trip tomorrow back to the villa."

"Yes, sir," Saunders said, rising to his feet.

Welford stood, and the two men left the office, heading toward the barracks.

Chapter 19

Colonel Cole's office
Camp Barton Stacey
12 November, 1505 Hours, London time

General Hopkins stomped into the office, nearly knocking over Miles, whose mouth had dropped open.

Cole's face drained of color.

Hopkins' face looked like there was a hurricane brewing behind it. He pointed a large finger at Cole. "You! In my office this instant!" He glanced at Adams and tipped his head toward the hallway. He spun on his heels, narrowly missing poor Major Miles again, and thundered out of the office, leaving the door wide open.

Adams caught Dunn's and Cross's eyes and winked. Dunn and Cross, still unaware of what was happening with the general's arrival, didn't react.

Adams stood. "We should—"

"Shut up," Cole snapped, as he jumped to his feet and left the room, his shoulders slumped.

Adams leaned over and whispered to Dunn, "Follow us in one minute and wait outside the general's door."

He left.

Dunn and Cross stared at each other.

"What the hell just happened?" Cross asked.

Dunn shook his head. "Whatever it is, I'd say we might be done with Colonel Cole."

The men waited the minute and got up. Miles, still frozen in the same place, looked at them.

"Sir, do you want to join us?"

Miles thought about it briefly. A wide grin broke out on his face. "I believe I would."

The three men moved quietly down the hallway and stopped outside Hopkins' door, which was cracked open an inch.

They exchanged glances. Adams wanted them to hear what was happening. It wasn't difficult.

"Your arrogance and incompetence has caught up with you, Colonel Cole. How dare you come in here and treat my best Rangers the way you have."

"But, sir, if I might—"

"I don't want to hear your excuses. There is no excuse. You crossed the line. You made poor, dangerous decisions and it's going to cost you. At long last. You will be stripped of your theater rank of colonel and demoted to captain. You'll be shipped home where a desk job at a supply depot is waiting for you in Arkansas. I have it all lined up. Or you can go home, resign your commission, and crawl back under whatever the hell rock you came out from under."

"Sir, that's awfully unfair. I was just trying to make the unit stronger."

Silence came from the office and the three men outside glanced at each other.

The general began to guffaw, which went on for a time. When he stopped, he said, "Cole, you are hereby relieved of command. Get yourself out of my office. Captain Adams will arrange for your transportation back to the States and be in touch. You may retrieve your personal belongings from the office. Captain Adams will accompany you. In particular, take that disgusting picture of you and Willkie. God Almighty, what an embarrassment you've been."

"But, sir—"

"Get . . . out."

The scraping sound of a chair moving across the floor came.

The three men outside the door looked wildly around the hallway. Dunn pointed at the empty office across the hall. They dashed inside just as the general's door swung open. Dunn peeked out through the partially open door.

A red-faced Cole exited and was followed immediately by Adams.

Cole and Adams disappeared into Kenton's office down the hall. Dunn opened the door and stepped into the hallway. Miles and Cross were right behind him.

"Wow," Cross said.

Suddenly, General Hopkins was standing in his doorway. He eyed the three men, who stared back with deer-in-the-headlights expressions. A tiny smile crossed the general's lips.

"Come in, gentlemen, won't you?" He turned away and disappeared inside the office.

The three men shared a glance, and Dunn shrugged. They went in the office and saluted the general. He saluted back and waved at the empty chairs. The men sat down, Miles to the left, then Dunn and Cross. They looked at Hopkins expectantly.

"We'll wait for Captain Adams to return." He busied himself with a monstrous stack of reports.

About five minutes later, Adams joined them. He took a seat to the left of Miles.

Hopkins looked up at Dunn. "Sorry that you were treated so unprofessionally. It was very unfortunate. I owed someone a favor. Captain Adams answered my questions honestly about how Colonel Cole was behaving, so I took steps to see for myself, or hear for myself, I guess. The good news is, I heard from Colonel Kenton. He thinks the docs will release him next week. As for your demotions, that never happened. I don't think Captain Adams even made a written notation of it." He looked at Adams.

"Never crossed my mind, sir."

"Sergeant Dunn, I'd like to hear your mission report. Start at the beginning. I missed a few parts of it from the hallway." He grinned.

"Yes, sir." Dunn gave a succinct report, leaving out nothing, including getting an M1 barrel in the neck. Hopkins chuckled at that, but said nothing.

At the end, Hopkins smiled. "Well, sounds like a great job. I do have reports that the Germans did react to the messages. In total, three infantry battalions were rerouted away from the main line of attack, which is currently underway. Excellent work. Major Miles, I want to thank you for your assistance on the mission. Very crucial as you just heard."

"You're welcome. It was a great learning experience for me, sir."

"Good." Looking at Dunn, the general continued, "Sergeant Dunn, until Colonel Kenton returns, I'll be handling the next mission for your squad. I'm in the process of finding the right one. You'll hear from me soon."

"Very good, sir."

"Captain Adams, you've done an excellent job. I think it's time to reward you by shipping you out to your training command. You're free to leave as soon as Colonel Kenton returns."

"Why, thank you, sir."

"Gentlemen, thank you. That'll be all."

The four men rose and saluted the general, and left the office. Adams closed it behind them and walked beside Dunn down the hallway. At the front door, he stopped, and the others did, too.

Eyeing Dunn for a moment, Adams was suddenly overcome by feelings of deep friendship and comradery for Dunn and Cross. He swallowed the lump in his throat and offered his hand, which Dunn and Cross shook.

"We'll miss you, sir. But best of luck. I know you'll be great."

"Thanks, Tom."

"And thank you, sir, for getting us out of a mess with Cole."

Adams grinned. "It was truly my pleasure."

Dunn and Cross laughed.

"By the way, sir, if you're still around on the afternoon of the twentieth, we're having a party for Pamela's birthday. It'll be out at her family farm."

"Thank you. I'll plan to be there."

He shook hands with Miles and walked back toward his own office, where he had some packing to do.

Once outside, the three men stood around at the base of the steps.

"It was an honor working with you both," Miles said.

"You, too, sir. Glad to have you along. Sorry about your friend."

Miles chuckled. "Don't be. Our friendship was solely one way. When he wanted something, I heard from him. Never liked him much at all."

The men laughed.

"You know, I learned a lot from you two. Thank you."

"You're welcome," Dunn replied, smiling.

"By the way, gentlemen, I'd like you to know that my red nose is genetic, not because I'm a drinker. I have my father to thank for it."

"No kidding, sir," Dunn said, careful not to look at Cross. "We hadn't thought anything about it."

Miles gave Dunn a knowing smile. "Well, thank you for your kindness. Hope to see you again."

They exchanged salutes. Miles jumped in his jeep and roared away.

"Well, now I feel like a real heel," Dunn said, "for thinking he was a drunk."

"Me, too. That's what we get for making assumptions."

Dunn sighed in embarrassment. "Yeah." He shook his head. "Okay if I drop you off?"

"Ayup. A bed awaits me. You headed home?"

"Yep."

"Let's go."

The two Rangers hopped into their jeep and drove off.

"I am so grateful we no longer have to deal with Colonel Cole," Cross said.

"Captain Cole, you mean."

Both men laughed a long time on that.

RONN MUNSTERMAN

Chapter 20

General Hopkins' office
Camp Barton Stacey
13 November, 0800 Hours, the next day

General John Hopkins held his dark thoughts right on the surface. While Dunn and Cross hadn't had many meetings with him, when they did, he always seemed perfectly under control, as you'd expect a general to be. Not today. He was worried. If Dunn didn't know better, it seemed the general had just been scared to death. What kind of news could provoke that kind of reaction? In addition to Captain Adams, another officer was present, a full colonel. Dunn eyed the man's brass lapel insignia and was quite surprised to see the Medical Corps' caduceus, two entwined serpents climbing a winged rod. Dunn nudged Cross and tipped his head toward the doctor.

Cross's eyebrows lifted when he, too, saw the caduceus, and he shrugged.

Hopkins sighed. He probably didn't mean to, but there it was.

"Gentlemen, I really didn't expect to see you so soon. I received intelligence last night from Churchill's office. This mission is on a tight deadline, so here we are."

Looking directly at Dunn, he said, "I re-read your Operation Devil's Fire mission report last night. You stated that Dr. Herbert, the German project leader, mentioned they'd had a radiation poisoning death at the atomic bomb lab."

Dunn nodded. The little German scientist who had requested that Dunn take him back to England had indeed told Dunn about the death of a worker who had been accidentally and fatally exposed to uranium.

"Yes, sir. He also said it had been an agonizing death, but he didn't go into any detail." Dunn thought about all the horrible attempts the Nazis had made to create weapons of mass destruction, to kill as many people as possible. It made him angry. Furious. His face turned red.

"Are you all right, Sergeant," Hopkins asked.

Dunn shook his head. "No, sir. Not really. Tell me, what are the bastards up to now?"

Hopkins tapped a folder on his desk. "What's in here is so horrible it defies humanity. We've learned from Bletchley Park that the Germans have a stockpile of uranium-235, what they were going to use for their bombs if you hadn't destroyed their facility. They've decided to grind up their leftover uranium. They're going to spread the deadly powder and create a lethal ground that our troops, as well as the British and Canadians, will have to cross to get into Germany."

"I knew it," Dunn grumbled just loud enough so the others could hear.

Dunn and Cross exchanged a look. To each of them the other looked sick. Dunn understood the general's expression.

"Exactly how bad would it be, sir?" Dunn asked.

"Gentlemen. This is Colonel Elmer Mason from the Medical Corps. He'll enlighten us. Colonel, if you please."

Mason turned his chair slightly so he was facing the two sergeants. His face was craggy and he appeared to be in his early to mid-forties. He had brown, kind eyes. Dunn thought he'd be a good doctor for someone who was ill, especially terminally ill.

"Pleased to meet yaz, *Sahgeant* Dunn, *Sahgeant* Cross," Colonel Mason began. His voice was smooth, like a jazz singer's, but it carried clear indicators of a Boston upbringing. "Radiation poisoning is something I've have been studying closely. I'm not allowed to say where, of *couahse*. We measure exposure by something called a gray. If you've ever had an X-Ray, you received well below one tenth of a gray. So let me give you a little explanation of different exposures and what they do to the human body. Okay?"

Dunn and Cross nodded.

"A mild exposure would be one or two grays. It would make the patient vomit within six hours. Within four weeks, he would feel weak and suffer from fatigue, but could recover. On the other hand, exposure to ten or more grays cause these things." He held up a hand and ticked off each item by raising a finger. "Vomit in ten minutes, diarrhea within one hour, headache and fever within one hour, dizziness and weakness. In twenty-four hours, hair loss, and infections. Ten or more grays is always fatal. Always. Death usually occurs within two days to two weeks. As Dr. Herbert said, it is a horrible way to die.

"What the Germans are planning is to grind up the uranium and spread it on the ground. They're going to use artillery shells with air bursts to maximize the spread of the radioactive dust. If our men walk, or worse, crawl over ground and plants dusted this way, I estimate their exposure to be anywhere from six to greater than ten grays. What this means medically, is that those exposed to six grays will show the exact same symptoms as those exposed to ten or more, however it will take a little longer for them to appear. The good news would be that they could survive. Those at ten or more, as I said, are dead men in two days to two weeks.

"Entire armies would be wiped out. Those who don't die, will be completely useless *foh* months."

Mason stopped talking and silence blanketed the office.

After a short time, Hopkins cleared his throat. "The Germans, knowing the poison is on the ground, wouldn't dare attack across it. However, they would gain an enormous amount of time, which would allow them to reinforce the German border with large numbers of divisions. Our healthy troops would be frozen in place, while the ill would have to be shipped back to England.

Without a danger on his west, Hitler might then be able to stop the Russians in the east. We would be at a stalemate. Much of Europe would still be under his thumb. Who knows, if they have enough uranium, he might threaten to bomb Paris with the same poison. My God, imagine if that happened."

"There's something else to know about radioactive material," Mason said. "It would be dangerous, in essence, forever. Uranium-235 has what we call a half life of over seven hundred million years. That's the point at which one half of its radioactivity would decay. It could kill people thousands of years from now.

"The only hope for long term protection would be to cover the entire affected area with ten-foot-thick concrete. Picture that. A wall a couple of hundred miles long."

Dunn felt shell shocked. He couldn't seem to form a rational thought, the fear had risen so high. What if the Germans were able to bomb England, too? Or the States? He swallowed hard and rubbed his eyes hard enough to see flashes of light.

He calmed down a bit and his brain started working again. "Damn bastards," he muttered to no one in particular. "What kind of human thinks up this kind of shit?"

No one in the room had an answer.

He took a deep breath, much like the general's sigh earlier. "General Hopkins, what else do you have in that folder? Do we know where those bastards are preparing this attack? And do we know when it will be?"

"Yes, we do know those things," Hopkins said. "We know exactly where they are doing the grinding and filling the artillery shells. It's in a former bomber factory built under a hill about fifty miles southwest of Frankfurt. According to Bletchley Park, the German High Command wants the shells ready to be shipped by this coming Wednesday. Two damn days from today! We've got to get a plan today, who's going, and what you're going to do when you get there so you can fly out tonight."

"Got a map, sir?" Dunn asked.

"I have it," Captain Adams said. "I marked the location of the facility."

He handed it across to Dunn, who unfolded it.

Dunn laid it on top of the general's desk without bothering to ask permission. He and Cross leaned over looking at Germany. Dunn poked the map.

"Frankfurt." He found the map's scale markers and used a thumb and forefinger to get the length of fifty miles. He put his finger and thumb on the map, creating a line to the southwest of Frankfurt. He found Adams' mark right away. It was situated on a hill halfway between the towns of Dannenfels and Steinbach am Donnserberg.

"Getting there should be no problem. There's plenty of farmland around there and wooded areas for concealed travel to the facility. General, do we know what kind of defense they have there?"

Hopkins frowned. "I'm afraid not. That seems to be the one thing we don't know."

"Well, we can't go in there short of men. I want Newman's squad. Is he available, Captain Adams?"

Adams grabbed a clipboard he'd set on the floor leaning up against his chair. He flipped a couple of pages and ran a finger down a list. "Yes, they got back yesterday from Belgium."

"Okay, good. Who else is available?"

Adams checked the list again. "Porter, Rollins, Turner. And, uh, Bagley." Adams knew Dunn couldn't stand Bagley. He thought he ran a sloppy outfit and wanted no part of him.

"Give me Porter, sir. I know him pretty well and he and his men are quick thinkers, excellent shots, and tough hand-to-hand fighters."

"You mean they're exactly like your men," Hopkins said.

Dunn smiled for the first time in the meeting. "That's right, sir." He turned to Colonel Mason. "It would be very helpful to us if you could come along, sir. Have you ever jumped?"

Mason's face paled. "You mean out of an airplane?"

Dunn grinned at the colonel's discomfort. "Yes, sir. That's exactly what I mean."

Mason closed his eyes briefly, and opened them. "I took jump training last year. It was not my favorite, uh, thing."

"But you passed?"

"*Moah* like I almost passed out in the door. But, yes, I passed." He seemed to admit this reluctantly. Dunn didn't blame him. Jumping wasn't for everyone. But he needed the man.

"Will you go with us, sir?"

"Of *couahse*. I'll bring a standard first aid bag with me, but also some items that have proven helpful in the treatment of radiation exposure. I will bring some little film badges *foh* the men to *weaah*. They'll show us if anyone has gotten exposed, and if so, how much.

"There's one more thing we need to discuss." Mason's expression darkened. "It's about preventing radiation exposure." As he explained, Dunn's expression grew darker, too. At one point he muttered, "Dear God."

When Mason was finished, the mood of the room was somber. It was silent for some time as the men reflected on just how dangerous this mission would be. In addition to fighting the Germans and their weapons, Dunn and his men might have to fight a metal and its invisible, yet deadly, properties.

Dunn seemed to shake it off first and said, "General, I'd like to get Newman and Porter over here in Colonel Kenton's office so we can use his map table and make our plans. Is that okay with you?"

"Yes. Whatever you need. This knowledge goes to the very top and Eisenhower is extremely concerned," Hopkins said.

"Understood, sir. Would you like to attend the meeting?"

"No. You gentlemen work out the details and go over them with Captain Adams. He'll update me later. I trust your mission planning skills."

This surprised Dunn, but he was grateful for the general's faith in him. "Thank you very much, sir. Is there anything else, sir?"

Hopkins shook his head. "No. Just go save the world, son. This is a bad one."

Dunn stood, as did the other guests. "Yes, sir."

The men all exchanged salutes with Hopkins and left the office.

Out in the hallway, Adams said, "I'll call Newman and Porter to get them over here ASAP."

"Thank you, sir. We'll head on over to Colonel Kenton's office. By the way. Have you talked to him recently?"

"I did last night. He was quite pleased with Cole's, uh, outcome."

Dunn and Cross laughed.

"I just bet he was," Dunn said. "Couldn't happen to a nicer guy."

"No, it could not," Adams agreed.

Mason looked from Adams to Dunn, an eyebrow raised.

"I'll explain it to you, sir, in a minute," Dunn said.

Mason nodded.

RONN MUNSTERMAN

Chapter 21

Villas of Castel Gandolfo
13 November, 1648 Hours, Rome time

The convoy to the villa was so large that Saunders suggested to Herriot that he send each truck by a different route from the Vatican. They would rendezvous a few miles outside of the city and roll together the rest of the way. Saunders was concerned about the spy who had gotten away and he didn't want the man to be able to report on such a sizable troop movement. Herriot had agreed. Some of the trucks were borrowed American deuce-and-a-halfs, while a couple had been captured from the Germans and they had the German crosses painted over with black paint. Saunders rode with Herriot, and Barltrop with Herriot's vice-commander. Alfred Welford was with Saunders. He was dressed as himself and would change later at the villa. Saunders' men were in three of the six trucks.

Saunders' own squad was in the same truck as he. He peeked into the back of the truck. The men were dressed in their Guard uniforms and seemed to be getting used to the much looser fit of the clothing. They were chatting about nothing of importance.

Saunders had lost one man, Geoffrey Kopp, on their last mission. They'd gone to western Germany with Dunn and another American squad to blow up Hitler's Dam. While Dunn and his men focused on the dam itself, Saunders' squad had the responsibility of destroying the power station underground. That was where Kopp had been killed during a firefight. Of the nine men remaining, only four had been in the squad from the beginning: Saunders, Barltrop, Chadwick, and Dickinson. The rest joined the group in early October, just over a month ago.

Lance Corporal Tim Chadwick was a fisherman's son from the fishing village of Amble which was almost on the Scottish border. He had blond hair that he combed straight back and blue eyes. He could pilot any watercraft he touched and had once stolen a German patrol boat to help the squad escape from the submarine pens they'd just blown up at Wilhelmshaven, Germany.

Sitting next to Chadwick, as usual, was Lance Corporal Christopher Dickinson, who was Chadwick's best friend. As a young teen, a misjudged header shot allowed a soccer ball to break his nose, which he wore with pride. He was a rugged man, a tough fighter, but for some reason delighted in performing magic tricks for anyone, especially for kids. The night before, after dinner, he'd amazed some of the Guards with coin and card tricks, what he always called the "C & C of magic."

Corporal Albert Holmes had red hair which was, incredibly, brighter than Saunders'. His father served in the Diplomatic Corps and he spent much of his childhood in Cairo, which helped him become Saunders' Arabic translator. It had proved to be useful on a recent mission to Egypt to help protect the Suez Canal by locating and destroying a rebel group intent on preventing the British from using the canal.

Lance Corporal Ira Meyers, Saunders' sniper, was a big man, almost Saunders' size, but with narrow hips. He seemed to be a natural athlete. From near Sheffield, he'd grown up on a farm and was an excellent shooter, which had earned him the sniper's spot. He'd left his sniper rifle in England for this mission at Saunders' request.

Lance Corporal Martin Alders was one of the older men at twenty-four, which made him third in age order behind Saunders and Barltrop. A thin man of five-nine, he had surprising strength and stamina. His face was narrow, his hazel eyes set close together. He, like Saunders, was from London, but where Saunders was from the East End, Alders came from the more affluent West End.

Corporal Billy Forster was one of the three twenty-one year olds in the squad. His angular face had a strong jaw line and he had no trouble lining up dates on the weekends. Born in Southampton, he'd almost joined the Royal Navy because he'd fallen in love with the huge cargo ships coming in to the port. He chose the army instead because his father had served as a soldier in the Great War.

Corporal Cyril Talbot was also twenty-one and from Birmingham. He was adept at mimicking others' voices, and he tentatively took over that humorous role from the late Geoffrey Kopp, who could do a perfect Saunders. Talbot hadn't tried that out yet in front of the big sergeant. He had, however, done King George VI several times. He used the same slow controlled speech pattern as the King, but out of respect, never tried to mimic the King's stutter, which the King had fought his entire life.

The new man, Corporal Teddy Bentley, was from Bristol on the west coast of England. Saunders had selected him from a pool of replacements because he'd scored very high at Commando School in shooting and problem solving. A slender six-footer, he could run anyone into the ground.

The lead truck with Saunders and Herriot on board made the first turn onto the curving road to the top of the villa property. Soon all the trucks pulled in behind the Swiss Guard's building. The men climbed down and stretched. It hadn't been that long of a journey, about forty-five minutes, but the hard wooden bench seats on the trucks took their toll.

Saunders and Herriot instructed the men to get inside quickly and prepare for details on the planned roving guards around the gardens area, where the Pope's replacement would begin taking walks the next morning. The intent was to provoke the German assault team into showing their hand and wiping them out.

As the Guards and Commandos headed indoors, carrying their equipment and weapons, Saunders and Herriot stepped off to the side of the building. Saunders looked around, entranced by the beauty of the area. Trees still had their leaves, which were green. Shrubs were trimmed neatly, much like in an English manor's garden. Flowers were still blooming.

He took one more look around, and walked through the door, ready to finalize their defensive measures.

Chapter 22

Dunn's Landing Zone
3 miles south-southwest of Nazi Uranium Facility
14 November, 0620 Hours

The engine sounds of the two C-47s necessary to carry Dunn and his platoon of Rangers slowly disappeared to the west as the aircraft turned for home.

Dunn had wanted to arrive at the landing zone much earlier in the morning, but the moon phase was against them as it was coming into new, which meant no moon at all. With the risk of overcast also high according to the weather planners, he'd had to opt for arriving right at first light. This meant they'd be able to see the horizon, especially from jump altitude, and maybe would be lucky enough to see the ground rushing up under their boots. It turned out that the sky was only partly cloudy, so the jump went well. Dunn had organized the platoon so that his squad was in the lead plane along with Colonel Mason, the doctor. Newman's and Porter's squads jumped from the trailing plane. As Dunn's squad had jumped, they dropped into a cloud and when they popped through, their light-colored parachutes ended up blending in with the clouds, an unexpected but welcome bonus.

Gathering the platoon had gone well. The landing zone he'd selected was between two large wooded areas, each of which was only a hundred yards from the touchdown points. In the growing light, which might have been a misnomer, it had been relatively easy for the Rangers to see each other and form up in their squads. In the pre-mission meeting with all three squads, Dunn had instructed everyone to create a skirmish line facing the woods on their north.

Dunn checked the line to his right and left and, satisfied everyone was ready, gave the advance arm signal. The three squads, thirty men, plus Colonel Mason, who was next to Dunn, pounded toward the tree line. Even with full gear, weapons, and fifty pounds of explosives each, the men reached the safe, dark woods in less than thirty seconds.

It was harder to see, so Dunn had to pass the word to the other two squad leaders to come join him. Sergeant Randy Newman and Staff Sergeant Don Porter ran over to Dunn and the three of them took a knee.

Dave Cross sent two men from each squad farther into the woods to set up a picket line, just in case.

Newman had recently accompanied Dunn and Saunders on a raid that destroyed a dam in western Germany. He and his squad had acquitted themselves well and Dunn was glad to have them along again. Newman was twenty-three, a year younger than Dunn and about the same size as Dunn's six-two. He had blond hair and hooded blue eyes that gave him a hawkish appearance. He was from Baltimore.

Don Porter was a stocky man with powerful arms and legs, which had served him well for two years at linebacker for Notre Dame. A native of Indianapolis, he'd dreamed of racing at the Indy 500 someday. If football didn't work out. The fact that he might have trouble getting into the race car's cockpit didn't sway him a bit.

"Everyone okay?" Dunn asked. He assumed they were since they'd made the run, but wanted to be certain.

"Yeah," Newman replied.

"Yes, Sarge," Porter said. His voice was deep and if he could ever carry a tune he would sing bass.

"Good. We're right where we're supposed to be, which is a minor miracle. How about the men's equipment?"

"All good," Newman said.

"Same with us."

"We're three miles straight line from the uranium facility. I wish we'd had time for recon photos, but it was too late in the day already. We don't know what the place looks like. We don't know what's between us and it. We might run across a farmhouse or two. We do know it's out in the country, but there's bound to be some heavy roads to it since they used to make bombers there.

"We're maybe a hundred miles in front of the American lines, specifically, Patton's Third Army, which is spread out from Nancy. I have to remind you that we must complete this mission one way or the other. I'm hoping our plan hangs together, but if it doesn't, I'm relying on you to be able to make snap judgements in the field."

The two squad leaders seemed to be bolstered by Dunn's confidence in them and they smiled gratefully. It was no small thing to have a man such as Dunn say those things to you. He had been a legend in Colonel Kenton's company since forever due to a top secret mission back in June for which he'd earned the Medal of Honor. Getting to work for Dunn was like making it to the Major Leagues.

"Before we set off toward the target, we need to check every man's gear especially the stuff the doc had us bring along. Also make sure everyone's detonators are packed and will stay nice and dry. The weather guy said rain was in the forecast starting around noon and it might last a day or so, off and on."

"Will do, Sarge," Porter said.

"Right, Sarge," Newman replied.

Dunn stood and so did the other two men. "That's all. Let me know when you've finished your checks, and then we'll get going."

The two squad leaders returned to their men and gathered them around for the gear inspection.

Dunn returned to his squad, still at the platoon's lead. He quickly told the men what he needed to do and they stood patiently while he checked everything. When he was satisfied the doc's special gear was where it was supposed to be, and the detonators were safe and dry inside the packs, he asked Cross to check his.

"So, little boy, did you pack everything like I taught you?" Cross asked.

The squad managed to keep from bursting out laughing, but some had to cover their mouths to stifle a chuckle.

"Yes, daddy," Dunn replied, grinning, as Cross poked and rummaged around in his gear. Since Dunn was attached to the gear, it was like he was being shaken first one way then another.

Cross patted Dunn on the arm. "Good boy. You did a very good job."

Dunn considered raising his hands like a dog's paws and panting with his tongue out, but decided that might be a touch too close to silly to do in front of the men. Instead he just nodded.

"Okay, men. Hang tight."

He turned to face the squads behind him, waiting for the word from Newman and Porter. Cross stood beside him. After a moment, Cross cleared his throat lightly.

Dunn looked at his old friend.

Cross tipped his head toward a spot a few yards away.

"Lead the way, Dave." Dunn wondered what his friend wanted to say that he couldn't say in front of the men.

When they reached a place between two white birch trees, which were losing their leaves, they stopped.

Cross nervously cleared his throat again.

"Okay, Dave, what's going on?"

"I just wanted to tell you I wrote to my mom about that girl."

"Girl? You want to tell me about the girl now?"

Cross shrugged. "Just in case something happens to me, Tom. In case she writes to me, but it's . . . too late."

Dunn stared at his friend. Comments like this were not uncommon among men headed into battle. Cross was clearly worried about it. "I understand. This is the one you admired from afar all through high school?"

Cross nodded sheepishly. "Ayup, that's the one."

Dunn grinned. "Well, I'm proud of you, Dave. Wow. You surprise me."

Cross gave a little aw-shucks head toss and kicked the ground with the toe of his boot. "Betty Warner. That's her name. Betty."

Dunn patted Cross on the arm. "I hope something good comes from it for you."

"Thanks. Me, too."

"I take it you'll let me know if it does."

"You'll be first."

"I better be." Dunn smiled. He was deeply happy for his friend and hoped that maybe this Betty girl would actually write a letter to him. Who knew, maybe she'd been admiring *him* from afar.

Dunn spotted Newman and Porter making their way toward him.

"We're all set, Sarge," Newman said.

"Us, too," Porter said.

"We'll get underway. Remember, keep everyone in line and no closer to any clearings than five yards."

Both squad leaders nodded, and headed back to their men.

The three squads formed into one long column, Newman's behind Dunn, and Porter's last. Dunn wanted an interval of two steps between men, so the line extended about sixty yards. A long, lethal snake sneaking through the woods.

Dunn took point and glanced over his shoulder once more. The men looked ready. They wore camouflage grease on their faces and hands. Since it wasn't raining yet, they kept their ponchos in their packs. Each man carried the Rangers' favorite weapon, the Thompson .45 as well as the 1911 Colt .45 handgun. Jonesy would have normally brought his 1903 Springfield sniper rifle, but Dunn had said he didn't see a need for it this trip.

Dunn took the first step and the line surged forward.

.

Ronn Munsterman

Chapter 23

Landing Zone of Möller's SS platoon
18 kilometers southeast of Villas of Castel Gandolfo
14 November, 0622 Hours

SS *Hauptsturmführer* Werner Möller was in roughly the same position as Dunn: checking to make sure his platoon had parachuted safely to earth. They were eighteen kilometers southeast of their target, the Pope's holiday property. They'd also required two aircraft to carry all of the men and equipment. In their case, they were the tri-motor Junkers-52s. The planes had been painted black to blend in with the night and the markings had been changed from the white and black German crosses to the Italian roundels of the insignia of Regia Aeronautica. This was three fasces, black vertical shafts with what looked like axe blades set at the midpoint, facing right. The fasces represented the three powers of the Italian State: the King, Parliament, and of course Mussolini's Fascist Party.

Möller hoped the aircraft would make it back safely, although with American airpower being what it was, he'd didn't think they would. The markings might fool them temporarily in the daylight, but when the planes refused to land, they would be shot down. If so, he'd make sure the crews would all receive medals.

As for his men blending in, they wore Italian-made clothing plus various hats and coats. Each man carried a large satchel in which his MP40 submachine gun and ammunition was hidden from sight. Under their coats, in holsters on the belt, they carried the Italian Beretta Modella 1934, an eight-round .380 semiautomatic. In sheaths strapped to their calves, they also carried the eight-inch-bladed Italian knife, the M91.

They'd landed in an open field that was bordered by heavy woods on three sides and a vineyard's grape stand, which was to the north. As each man gathered his parachute, he ran to the woods to the south, where they would hide them.

Möller took off at a run, carrying his chute. When he reached the woods, the majority of the platoon had gathered together and ordered themselves into their respective squads.

There was a lot riding on this particular mission. It had come down with the notation that the *Führer* himself had ordered it and had high expectations. The reason for the order was not given, but Möller wasn't stupid. Hitler hated the Pope, who it was known was doing things in secret that countered the Nazis' worldview including interrupting plans to rid Europe of Jews.

Möller was happy, and honored to have been selected for this mission. He hated the Pope as well and looked forward to seeing the man's terrified expression when he realized he would be sent to Germany to come face to face with Hitler. What his eventual fate would be, he didn't know. He doubted Hitler would execute the Pope, but he would certainly keep him prisoner as long as possible. He might even threaten the Pope, not with his own safety, but the safety of others, to force him to make radio speeches supporting Hitler. Yes, that would be quite wonderful. He smiled to himself in the growing morning light. Yes, what a mission to lead.

While his men checked their gear and hid their chutes, he waved at *Hauptscharführer* Horst Sauer, his platoon master sergeant. Sauer waved in return and jogged over to join his commander.

"Sir, it looks like everyone made it safely, no injuries."

"Yes, that's good. I was concerned about the low-level jump. You almost always have one or two men who get hurt, or worse."

He spread out a map he'd pulled from his coat pocket. "Just between us, Sauer, it feels quite weird to be in civilian clothing."

Sauer smiled. "*Ja*, very weird, sir, after so many years."

Möller tapped a spot on the map. "Here's our rendezvous point. It's only a kilometer to the north."

Sauer leaned in to look, although he already knew from pre-mission planning where it was.

"I hope our friends have all four of the trucks we need," Sauer said.

"I was told they would be there without fail. Not all Italians welcomed the arrival of the Americans and British."

"Very good, sir."

"Get the men ready for the short hike," Möller said.

"Yes, sir."

A few minutes later, the platoon formed into four columns and marched into the woods.

RONN MUNSTERMAN

Chapter 24

1/2 mile south-southwest of the Nazi Uranium
Facility
14 November, 0724 Hours

The trek through the woods was going well, except the
weatherman had been wrong. It had already started raining
instead of waiting until noon. It was a steady drizzle, and you
could hear it striking the leaves still on the trees. Dunn wondered
how much longer before it really started coming down. They
were very close to the facility and so far had seen no one. The
terrain had been challenging at times, with low valleys followed
by hills. With the leaf-covered ground becoming wetter by the
moment, footing was turning into an issue. He decided he would
tell the men to dig out their ponchos before they got soaked to the
skin.

Dunn periodically stopped the column and edged closer to the
tree line where he would check the open areas. He halted the men
and carefully picked his way toward the opening on the east. He
stopped behind a large oak and knelt so he could see the clearing.

He was immediately glad he'd called for a stop. Not a hundred yards ahead, to the northeast, he spotted a farmhouse.

The white two-story house faced north and a barn sat across from it at the other end of the barnyard. An old car that resembled an early 1920s Ford Model T was parked near the house. A similarly-aged truck with wooden slats around the bed sat forlornly next to the car, closer to Dunn.

He listened carefully, praying he wouldn't hear a dog bark. He didn't, but it didn't mean there wasn't one or more around the house. Smoke curled out of the chimney, so he knew someone was home. No one left a wood burning stove or fireplace alive while gone. The risk of fire was too great. The question was: who was home? He watched the house for a little longer. Nothing changed.

He rose and backed straight away from the tree, keeping it between himself and the house. When he was several steps away, he turned and walked around another tree and rejoined the men.

Cross looked at him expectantly. He'd been gone longer than the previous times.

Dunn told him what he'd seen. "We need to get a little deeper in the woods and keep our eyes open in case the farmer is out here in the woods checking his property or hunting. Also, have the men get on their ponchos. Pass the word down the line."

Cross nodded and turned to Schneider behind him. He passed on the message to the big man, who turned and did the same thing. In no time, it reached the last man in Porter's squad and the men were in various stages of working their ponchos on.

Dunn patted Colonel Mason on the shoulder. "How are you doing, sir?"

Mason was just finishing pulling on his poncho.

"I'm fine."

Mason had been spared the fifty pounds of explosives, but he carried a pack with the special equipment he'd told Dunn about in the mission meeting. He carried a Colt .45, but not a Thompson. He'd never fired one and there had been no time for training.

"Good. We're heading off again."

"Okay."

Dunn checked the column of men out of habit. He turned and walked off, headed to the northwest to get farther from the tree line. After a few more yards he turned back to the north. They were ten yards inside the woods.

A few minutes later, the terrain changed. It was all uphill. He changed direction to the northeast and when they were again five yards inside the tree line, he called a halt. He waved at Cross to go with him this time. The two Rangers worked their way to the edge of the trees and stopped behind one. They knelt and looked out.

About two hundred yards to the east, a raised road ran from their right to left. Dunn thought it was a paved road. He lifted his binoculars and verified it. "We're close. There's the highway."

He lowered the field glasses and looked north. The hill they'd been climbing continued to the northwest, but some sort of outcropping seemed to grow out of the foot of the hill about a quarter of a mile away. He raised the glasses and studied the oddity.

"Huh."

"What is it?"

"There's something at the foot of the hill extending toward the east. It's strange because it's far too straight for nature. I think it's manmade. But there's grass and shrubs growing on it."

Dunn took off the glasses and handed them to Cross.

"I see what you mean. What the hell is it?"

"Only thing I can think of is a well camouflaged entrance tunnel to the underground facility. From the air it'd be impossible to spot for the bombers."

"I think you're right. Do you think it'll make it harder to gain entrance?"

"Not sure. We need a place where we can see straight into it."

Dunn looked at the huge open space in front of him. He figured that toward the northeast, he could see about a mile, before trees got in the way. Closer to him, he found a small grove of trees. It was maybe two hundred yards away. From inside the grove, he'd be able to see the front of the entrance. There were no buildings in sight and the grove was the only cover anywhere near the entrance to the facility. The problem was, there was exactly zero cover between his men and the grove.

"Well, shit, Dave."

"What?"

"I'm going to have to crawl to that grove of trees out there. See it?"

"Ayup. That's going to take a while."

"Yep. You want to go along?"

"Wouldn't miss it for the world."

"Go have Newman leapfrog our men and set up at the tree line. Have our men and Porter's set up, too. Let everyone know what we're gonna do."

"Will do. Be right back."

"Okay."

Cross headed back.

Dunn studied the entrance. Nothing was happening. He checked his watch: 7:40.

A few minutes passed and Cross returned.

"You ready?" Dunn asked.

"Ayup."

Dunn slung his Thompson over his right shoulder and got down on his stomach. The ground was soaking wet and he was grateful for the poncho as he started his combat crawl. Behind him, he heard his friend plop down and start moving.

Chapter 25

Villas of Castel Gandolfo, the Gardens
14 November, 0745 Hours

Saunders walked next to the Pope stand in, Alfred Welford, while Barltrop was on the Pope's other side. A few yards ahead, Commander Herriot and three of his men formed the front box. Behind the Pope, Barltrop, and Saunders, his squad, plus one from Massie's squad, formed another, longer box. The full effect was that the Pope was inside a protective cordon of fourteen Guards. Everyone was armed with their German MP40, a substitute for their usual Stens. All wore the tricolor Swiss Guard uniforms.

"How are you doing, Mr. Welford?" Saunders asked, his voice low.

"I should have had another cup of coffee. This is my prime sleeping time. You know actors. Up all hours of the night. Sleep 'til afternoon."

Saunders chuckled.

The garden was beautiful. Various types of roses adorned one side for about twenty yards, while on the other side, multicolored flowers Saunders didn't recognize seemed to hang from the wall bordering the garden.

As they walked, the sounds of nature awakening filled the morning: bird song and the chittering of squirrels angry at having been disturbed in their perpetual search for food. The air was cool, crisp, and smelled heavenly to him.

They passed a three-tiered fountain, which was on their right up about eight steps. It was surrounded on three sides by a half dozen white statues on pedestals. Trimmed hedges bordered the fountain's space at the rear. Turning right they entered a garden of low hedges trimmed square. It was like a short maze. Saunders hated mazes and was glad he could see where everything was.

"It's just up ahead, sir," he said.

Welford, wearing his white cassock and zucchetto, replied, "*Grazie.*"

They reached a small white stone bench. Herriot and his men walked past and halted. Welford sat down, careful to smooth his cassock behind him as he lowered himself to the stone. He closed his eyes and folded his hands in his lap. The real Pope always stopped at this particular bench and prayed, sometimes as long as ten minutes. Saunders sneaked a glance at his watch so he'd know when ten minutes had passed.

One mile away
Roof of four-story apartment building

Scharführer, Sergeant, Heinz Huber watched the Pope. He was one of *Hauptsturmführer* Möller's men. Huber had carried a telescope with him up all four flights of stairs to the roof. It was an astronomer's telescope. A standard sniper scope wouldn't have the magnifying power he needed. The lens was fifteen centimeters, nearly twice the diameter of the famous German 8.8 centimeter artillery shell.

He studied the Pope carefully for several minutes taking in the glasses the man wore. His eyes were closed, evidently praying to his ridiculous idea of a God. Huber snorted reflexively at the silliness of the church. Here was a man who obviously truly believed a spirit of some kind watched over humans and would even deign to intervene when asked, or maybe you had to beg. Huber had no idea and didn't care. He knew the mission was to capture the man, but if it were up to him, he'd just kill the old man. Who cared? The Catholics? They'd get over it and just appoint, or was it elect, another one. He idly wondered whether, if he had a weapon capable of making the shot, he would shoot the Pope. He sighed. Probably not. Be against orders.

He changed his view to the man standing protectively beside the Pope. He wore the horrible uniform of the Swiss Guard. Huber couldn't imagine having to wear such trappings. The guard seemed to be looking everywhere at once, the sign of a good bodyguard. He had a wild mustache. A bright red one at that. It almost seemed to have a life of its own. Huber couldn't imagine wearing that either. He shook his head.

There were a dozen other guards arranged in dual boxes around the Pope, one of the standard defensive measures the Swiss Guard was known to employ.

He aimed the scope back at the Pope. The man suddenly opened his eyes and looked around, blinking in the bright morning sunlight. He looked like he'd been napping, not praying. Huber laughed to himself. Maybe that's what he was doing all those times he was seen in public with his eyes closed.

The Pope rose to his feet and his bodyguards resumed their respective positions. The procession moved toward Huber. It gave him the opportunity to study the faces of the guards. All were alert and their eyes were constantly on the move.

He realigned the telescope, using the smaller aiming scope on top. He found what he was looking for. A place in the garden where the pathway became enclosed on two sides by high stone walls for a distance of about twenty-five meters. There were various statues along the path inside this area. He assumed there would be a name for it, but he didn't know what it was. This would be the ambush point. It was ideal because it was in essence a ready-made funnel that could be closed at both ends.

As the procession approached the far end of the funnel, he pulled out a stopwatch. When the first pair of guards entered, he started the watch. He waited impatiently for the Pope to reach the middle of the ambush zone. He stopped the watch and checked the time. Just under sixteen seconds.

He put away the watch. Turning to his right, he powered up his radio, and made a call.

"Georgio's," a voice said in Italian, one of the two other men in the platoon besides Huber who spoke fluent Italian.

"I'd like to reserve a lunch for two at noon today," Huber said, speaking in Italian. The code word for the Pope being in the garden was "lunch."

"Your name, sir?"

"Lucio Ricci."

"I have you down for lunch for two at noon, Mr. Ricci."

"Thank you."

Huber switched off the radio and resumed watching the Pope walk through the gardens.

Chapter 26

200 yards southeast of the Nazi Uranium Facility
entrance
14 November, 0802 Hours

The rain had started coming down harder when Dunn and Cross were about half way to the grove of trees. Dunn was glad of the poncho, but he still felt the water seeping in through his trousers where they weren't covered by the poncho or his boots.

The two Rangers were still flat on their bellies, but they'd made it into the grove safely. Making their way to the front side they found a good lookout spot between a tree and another one that had fallen over, forming a perfect viewing spot. Dunn rose to a kneeling position, peeking over the top of the fallen tree. Cross joined him.

"I hate the damn mud."

"Yep," Dunn replied.

Dunn lifted the front of his poncho so he could get at his binoculars. They were still dry. He raised them to his eyes.

"I can see large doors, recessed about ten feet maybe, at the entrance, probably metal. They look like hangar doors. They'd be big enough to tow an airplane through and the roadway there is very wide."

Cross tapped Dunn on the shoulder. "Someone's coming from the east."

Dunn lowered the binoculars as he followed Cross's point.

A convoy was headed toward the facility. In the lead was a black Mercedes staff car. It was a four-door vehicle with a solid top, rather than the more common convertible. A good choice in the rain. A second car, not a Mercedes, followed the staff car. Three troop trucks completed the convoy. All had their canvas tops in place, so Dunn couldn't see inside.

He focused the field glasses on the lead car. He could clearly see the driver from the side as the car passed by less than a hundred yards away. He thought there was a passenger in front. In the second car, the driver and front seat passenger both wore white coats.

A rumbling sound came from the entrance and he lowered the glasses to look. The hangar doors were swinging open, obviously on rollers. When there was a gap of about ten feet, the doors stopped moving. To Dunn's surprise, the convoy stopped outside, rather than driving inside. The staff car's driver jumped out and ran around to the other side, where he opened the door.

The second car turned left, pulled up a short distance, and backed up. The driver maneuvered it to face east.

Dunn raised the glasses. The staff car's passenger climbed out, stretched his back, and walked toward the front of the car, where he stopped and turned to face Dunn, evidently waiting for the men in the second car to join him. He wore a brown officer's hat and a long brown leather coat. A red armband with the black Nazi swastika inside a white circle adorned his left bicep. Dunn stared at the man, who seemed oblivious to the rain.

"Holy shit, Dave. That's Albert Speer."

"Speer? You're kidding. The Minister of Armaments?"

"Yep."

Dunn handed over the glasses and while Cross studied Speer, he watched a squad's worth of soldiers jump down from the first truck. They appeared to be armed with the MP40 submachine gun. As he watched, half ran to the second truck's rear and the other half to the last truck. He was too far away to hear anything, but soon a gaggle of men appeared. They wore striped prisoner uniforms. They were guided toward the entrance by being jabbed with the barrels of the weapons or by being kicked in the behind. The men looked exhausted and starved. Dunn tried to imagine the prisoners who the Nazis *didn't* bring with them and how bad *their* condition must be.

Speer and the two white-coated men watched the workers, for that's what Dunn knew they were, shuffle by. From their bored expressions, they may have just as well have been watching a herd of cattle going into a building for slaughter. Dunn's jaw muscles worked. It looked like about twenty-five prisoners were being driven inside the facility.

Cross handed back the glasses. Dunn lifted them and studied the three men, who stood talking.

"Sure love to hear what they're jabbering about," he muttered.

The line of prisoners reached the hanger door opening and slowly disappeared from sight. Speer and the other two men turned and walked inside. They, too, soon disappeared. The hangar doors began closing.

"Well, now what, Tom?"

"I'm surprised they didn't leave sentries outside. I wish I knew whether it was because there really are some men hidden out here, or if they just don't see the need for it, here in Germany."

"Yeah, I see what you mean. I think it's the latter. Why would they bother? They're still over a hundred miles from the front line. I mean that's why they picked this place isn't it? So they wouldn't have to transport the uranium-filled artillery shells very far?"

"Yeah, that's what Bletchley Park seems to think. Okay, so no sentries outside. They probably think they're impregnable under the hill there," Dunn said.

"Yeah, but how do we get inside?"

"That's what I'm wondering, too. I'm interested in Speer and the other two guys. Maybe when they leave we can gain entrance."

"Except we don't know when that'll be."

"Right."

The two men grew silent for a time, thinking about the problem.

"Okay, what if, when Speer or the other two leave, we follow them?" Dunn asked.

"Uh, we don't have a vehicle, Tom."

"Sure we do. Back at that farm."

"What, go back and steal one of them?"

"Yep."

"Why not use one of those trucks sitting there?" Cross pointed. His expression was saying, how'd you miss those?

"Or, yes, we could use one of those trucks. We chase down one of them and they get the doors open for us."

"Give me those."

Dunn gave Cross the glasses.

Cross examined the entrance for a time. "There's a personnel door built in the right hand door, near the center."

"So?"

"Let's just enter through that. If it's locked, we'll blow it."

"Not exactly stealthy."

"No, but I think your idea of chasing down some guy to open the door for us is not one of your best ideas."

"It's not?"

"Oh, hell, no."

Dunn sighed. "Okay, sometimes I might, possibly, could be . . . uh, wrong."

"Good heavens, that must have hurt considerably."

"You've no idea."

Cross laughed gently. "Never fear. It's just between us."

"Good to know. So we sneak around from the south of the entrance, go to the personnel door and go in there?"

"Ayup. Simple."

"If only."

"Well, there is that, of course. How many soldiers do you think there are inside?"

"The little convoy felt like they were the main group. There might be a few folks who were already there, but maybe not many soldiers. Only one way to find out. Is there a window in that personnel door?" Dunn said.

"Yeah, there was. Like on a house front door."

"If it's lit up at all inside, we might be able to take a peek before trying anything."

"Yeah, could do that."

"Let's head back to the men."

"Lovely. I'll go first."

"Great. Thanks for giving me the crappy view."

"Any time, buddy." Cross chuckled. He gave Dunn back the glasses and hit the deck.

Dunn soon joined him on the watery ground.

Half way back to the platoon, Dunn glanced over at the entrance. He could no longer see the doors, being at a more side on angle, but he saw Speer exit and head toward the staff car. Dunn stopped moving to keep an eye on things. Speer appeared to be alone. The driver jumped out and opened the door for his boss, who climbed in. A minute later, the car turned around, passed the three trucks, and went back the way it had come.

Dunn laughed to himself. Cross had been right. It was a dumb idea to think they could have followed and captured one of the Germans.

He resumed his seemingly interminable crawl.

Chapter 27

The Vatican
14 November, 0903 Hours

Pope Pius XII closed his personal bible, the one he'd owned since childhood. He was in his private study, where he preferred to do his reading. He rose and stepped away from the ornate desk, which was where he penned his letters, and other items necessary to the running of the Church and the Vatican.

His assistant had departed to bring some coffee.

He glanced at the glass doors that led to the small balcony from where he gave his speeches to the crowds in St. Peter's Square. The bright sunshine shone through the glass in the doors, brightening the room and his spirits. He walked to the doors and stood there briefly. He enjoyed the view from the balcony, but understood the importance of not going outside while the Nazis were up to no good. His stand in, he knew, was walking through his favorite gardens. He felt a pang of loss. He missed the gardens. He leaned closer to the door so he could see the square better. Being a Tuesday, there were few people about. Possibly less than there were pigeons.

The Pope's assistant opened the hallway door and entered the study carrying a coffee tray in both hands. When he saw the Pope standing right in front of the door, and not sitting at the more secure desk, he nearly dropped the tray. He rushed across the Pope's study, practically slamming the tray down on the desk on the way by.

"Holy Father! Away from the door! Hurry!"

The assistant picked up the phone on the Pope's desk.

Scharführer Hans Richter, another of *Hauptsturmführer* Möller's men stared through his own astronomer's telescope. He frowned. From his vantage point directly across the square from the Pope's balcony, he thought he saw some movement behind the glass doors. He was situated in an apartment facing the square and was in complete darkness. He was set up a couple of meters from the window. No one could see him.

The shape behind the Pope's door moved again, coming closer. It took form in the scope. Richter blinked, looked away from the eyepiece, and back again. No doubt about it. The Pope stepped away from the door and out of sight.

He turned on his radio and made a call.

"Giorgio's," came the reply.

"I'm calling to confirm a reservation for Ricci."

"Yes, I have one for lunch today."

Richter was confused. Lunch? Had Huber already called in a sighting? The Pope was still at Castel Gandolfo? Who had he just seen?

"Please contact Mr. Ricci for me and confirm that it's for lunch."

"I will do that, sir. I'll call you back in a few minutes."

"Thank you."

Richter sat back in his chair. What the hell? He'd asked the man to contact Huber and confirm the Pope was still in his sight. He waited for what seemed like an hour, and his radio chirped to life.

"Hello?"

"I'm calling to re-confirm lunch for Mr. Ricci at noon."

"Lunch?"

"Yes, sir."

"I'm sorry. Something's not right. I'm positive it should be for dinner." *The Pope is here!*

"I will speak to the manager, sir, and we'll call you soon."

"Thank you. Please hurry."

Hauptsturmführer Möller stared at the radio from his position on an old wooden chair. *Hauptscharführer* Sauer stood by his side. He and his men were a couple of kilometers south of Castel Gandolfo. The barn they were using as a kind of command post was owned by a longtime German sympathizer, who'd been smart enough to change his name and appearance, and get out of Rome just before the Allies invaded the city. Reprisals that were expected did come and were terrifying examples of what an occupied nation could do to its own citizens who were only trying to survive.

The SS men were sprawled out, resting, preparing for the upcoming attack.

Möller had been pleased when he first heard from Huber, confirming that the Pope was right in front of him in the Castel Gandolfo Gardens. But the message from Richter suddenly made the waters murky and uncertain. How could the Pope be confirmed in the Gardens *and* the Vatican? He shook his head as he thought about it.

He glanced up at Sauer. "It doesn't make any sense."

"No, sir."

"Well, let's say that both Huber and Richter are correct. That can only mean one thing: the Vatican knows what we're planning and have found a look-alike. A decoy. It's the only explanation."

Sauer's eyes widened at Möller's conclusion. "If that's the case, sir, what do we do?"

Möller gave his sergeant a grim smile. "We have to deduce which one is the decoy."

Sauer, who couldn't think of a way to do that, just nodded.

Möller looked toward the rafters in the barn, thinking. "If you had the responsibility of protecting the Pope and you had a perfect decoy, what would you do?"

He didn't wait for an answer from Sauer, who still didn't have one.

"The safest location is obviously the Vatican itself with its many hiding places. He could be protected by the Swiss Guard, possibly indefinitely. However, if you had a decoy, you could parade him around the open and less secure gardens and entice the enemy to attack there. If you lose the battle, you don't really lose the Pope and our plan would be exposed. Therefore, the real Pope is in the Vatican." He lowered his gaze to meet Sauer's eyes.

"Recall Huber. Inform Richter. Prepare for our backup plan: the Vatican."

"Yes, sir." Sauer spoke to the radio operator who passed on the message.

Chapter 28

200 yards southwest of the Nazi Uranium Facility
entrance
14 November, 0915 Hours

Dunn had his squad leaders, Major Mason, and Cross in a small group at the edge of the tree line. All were kneeling, eyeing the protruding foliage-covered entrance. It was pouring and the sound of the rain beating against the leaves still clinging to the trees plus those on the ground made a considerable racket, almost like rain on a tin roof. The wind had shifted to the northeast and it was blowing the rain sideways making it difficult to see clearly.

"Damn, this is cold," Cross complained.

"Didn't you wear your sweater?" Dunn asked.

"Of course I wore my sweater. It's not helping."

"Wait until it's actually real winter here."

"Yeah, thanks for that. Don't worry about me," Cross said in a careful monotone.

Dunn and the other men laughed at Cross's Eeyore impression.

Dunn explained the plan, such as it was, that he and Cross had concocted out in the grove of trees.

"Porter, you'll hang back against the south wall of the entrance. Stagger the men at an angle so they have a clear line of fire toward the road as it turns in toward the entrance."

"Understood, Sarge."

"Newman, I'll hit the door first and want you lined up against the left-hand hangar door, facing me. As soon as we're inside, we'll let you know whether to come in. Wait for the signal."

"Will do."

"Colonel Mason, I'd like you to be at the end of Sergeant Newman's squad. While you're with him, whatever he says goes."

"Very good, Sergeant. Weapon out?"

Dunn nodded. Earlier, he had talked privately with Mason about gun safety in a firefight. Mason said he understood the need to not just shoot blindly when there were other Americans in the line of fire. Dunn had expressed in no uncertain terms that Mason must have a clear line of fire before pulling the trigger.

Dunn stood and the others followed.

To Newman and Porter, he said, "I'll give you guys a couple of minutes to go over everything with your men."

The squad leaders nodded and departed. Mason followed Newman.

Dunn stared at Cross. "Man, I hope we get this done safely."

Cross dipped his chin in agreement. "We've been here before."

"Yeah. If I remember it right, that's when you got shot."

Cross shrugged.

They were breaching a door to a manufacturing facility where the Nazis were building their electromagnetic pulse weapon. There was an entire platoon inside and when the door opened, Cross got hit in the side. It hadn't hit anything important, but he was down for a while. Everyone agreed being a U.S. Army Ranger was dangerous business. Of the nine men Dunn had trained with at Achnacarry House in Scotland as a Ranger, only Cross and Wickham were left.

Dunn glanced at Newman and Porter. Both gave him the high sign. He turned around and took off, having the platoon's point position. The line of Rangers marched over the soggy ground a few yards inside the tree line.

When Dunn reached the point where the ground started going up, representing the mountain under which the facility was located, he turned right. He stopped the platoon and he looked at the area in front of him. The entrance tunnel wall rose on his left about forty feet. It seemed massive. He could make out the rear of the white-coated men's car, and the shapes of the three trucks in front of it.

He raised a hand and gave the advance signal. He stepped out into the open and the platoon followed.

The wind had died down quite a bit so the rain was no longer blowing sideways. This made it a little easier to see. The grass along the wall had been tall, but was brown from the colder temperatures and flattened some due to the pounding rain. It made the going tough as Dunn's boots kept getting entwined in the long blades of grass. It reminded him of walking through a hayfield as a boy after the hay had been cut and simply lay on the ground in thick thatches.

He glanced over his shoulder to check on the men. They seemed okay. Perhaps they looked a little like wet dogs. He imagined he looked no better.

He made it to the end of the wall. From here, he had full sight of the car and the three trucks. He rounded the wall's corner and peeked toward the hangar doors. There was no one in sight, which was what he'd expected since the guards had all been busy corralling the prisoners.

He leaned back and spoke to Martelli, who was first in line. "Looks all clear. Pass the word."

Martelli turned around and did that. The message wound its way down the line.

Dunn leaned forward and took a step and stopped abruptly. The personnel door had opened. He yanked himself back and ducked. He peered around the corner. The two white-coated men stepped through the door, talking.

"Shit," Dunn muttered. He waved at his men, who had stopped when he had, motioning them to get flat. Everyone dropped into the wet grass and mud. Dunn did, too. He kept his head up just enough to watch the two Germans.

The shorter of the two was flailing his hands about as he talked. The other man seemed to be listening intently. When they reached the end of the entrance tunnel, they broke into a run to beat the rain. Dunn glanced at the personnel door. Someone had closed it. He wondered whether there was any value to capturing the men. If he was going to do it, he only had a few seconds to decide. They might be able to help Dunn and his men find what they were looking for more quickly, even if it took some persuasion.

As he watched the two Germans run through the rain, Dunn suddenly realized they must be scientists. They reminded him of Dr. Herbert, the lead physicist working on the Nazi atomic bomb who had surrendered to Dunn. He was suddenly angry. Furious at all the despicable things the Nazis had tried to do.

And that made the decision for him.

He rose to his knees and told Martelli to grab two men and follow him.

He jumped to his feet and ran toward the car.

The car doors slammed shut at the same time. A small puff of exhaust gave away that the engine had started. Dunn was still forty yards away when the car drove off. He kept on running.

He climbed into the first truck. Martelli, Goerdt, and Higgins got in on the other side and they scrunched together.

Dunn found the starter button and pressed it.

The engine fired up.

He jammed the gear shift into first and took off.

"Rob, which of these is the windshield wipers switch?"

Goerdt examined the switches and buttons briefly. He pointed at one on Dunn's left. "That one."

Dunn switched on the wipers. He could see the car ahead only a short way. It must have stopped at the main road, and turned left. The road there headed northeast, presumably toward Frankfurt. Dunn increased speed and blew through the stop and got on the same road. He was fifty yards behind. His one advantage was that the Germans would see what they expected: a German truck on the road to Frankfurt. They wouldn't realize they were actually being pursued.

Dunn glanced at his three men. Each wore the same excited look: hunters pursuing prey. It looked like he got his chase after

174   RONN MUNSTERMAN

all. He pictured Cross's 'what the hell' expression. He smiled to himself and sped up.

He closed the gap carefully. He didn't want to seem like a runaway truck to the driver ahead. When he was about twenty yards behind he slowed some more, matching the car's speed of about a hundred kilometers per hour or sixty miles an hour. The road ahead was pretty straight and he began planning where he would force the car off the road. Where there were trees, they lined the road perhaps a yard or two off the pavement. Typical European highway design. The good news was there were lengthy clearings ahead and there was no ditch.

He picked his spot about a half mile ahead.

"Okay, Higgins. I'm going to pull alongside the car. Get in position to aim your weapon right at the driver's face. When he looks at you wave him to stop. If he hesitates at all, fire a long burst right over the car's roof."

"Got it, Sarge."

Higgins turned sideways and raised his Thompson.

Dunn goosed the engine.

The truck overtook the car in a matter of seconds. Plenty of power for a nearly empty vehicle.

Dunn pulled up beside the car.

The driver looked over out of curiosity only to find the huge black hole of a big gun pointed at his face. Higgins smiled and waved at him to stop the car.

The man's face blanched as he realized the man behind the big black hole was American.

Higgins could see the driver's face change as he thought of his various options, which were: stop or run for it. The man's jaw muscle tightened.

"Oh, for shit's sake," Higgins muttered. "He's gonna run."

He lifted the Thompson's barrel.

He squeezed the trigger and fired half of the magazine's thirty rounds in two seconds.

The driver stomped on the brake and the hood dipped.

Dunn did the same thing, but he was already past the car. He glanced at the right outside mirror.

The car was weaving as the brakes worked and the tires tried to find purchase on the sloppy wet pavement.

The car's rear fishtailed around to the right.

The driver overcorrected the slide and the rear end whipped back to the left and kept on going.

The car completed a one hundred eighty degree spin and was sliding backwards toward Dunn's truck.

He stomped on the gas.

The truck lurched forward as if angry at the driver not making up his mind.

Still watching the car in the mirror, Dunn saw it start toward the right. It was going slower, but when it hit the grassy area it must have found some bumps in the ground. The rear end hopped straight up in the air and crashed back down, gouging the mud with the rear bumper.

The car came to a sudden stop and sat there like a felled buffalo.

Dunn stopped the truck and used the mirrors to back up until he was alongside the car.

"Go get 'em!" he shouted. "Put them in the back with you."

Higgins banged the door open and the three Rangers piled out, weapons up.

They approached the car carefully, in case the men inside had weapons.

Goerdt and Martelli ran around to the driver's side while Higgins ran up to the passenger side.

Goerdt bent over to look at the driver, whose face was still white, and whose hands were apparently glued to the steering wheel. Goerdt motioned with his weapon's barrel for the man to get out.

The man shook his head.

"Oh, hell, you're kidding me," Goerdt said, exasperated. He tapped the barrel on the glass. He reached down and grabbed the door handle, yanking open the door.

"Raus!" he shouted. Out!

He stepped back to give the man room.

While the driver climbed out, his hands shaking, Higgins was getting the passenger out.

"Into the truck," Goerdt instructed in German.

The Rangers led the captives to the rear of the truck and helped them climb aboard.

Dunn looked through the rear window in the cab into the cargo area waiting for the men to get settled. Once they were, he drove ahead a ways until he found a farmer's track to turn around in.

He aimed the truck west and charged through the rain.

Chapter 29

Villas of Castel Gandolfo
14 November, 0932 Hours

"Hurry it up, lads!" Saunders shouted. His men were boarding the trucks.

Commander Herriot had received a panicked call—patched through the Guard radio—from the real Pope's assistant. The Pope had inadvertently shown himself to the outside world by standing briefly in front of the windows in his study. Although the assistant had gotten the Pope to step away from the window quickly, there was doubt as to whether he'd been unseen. Not willing to take a risk, Herriot and Saunders decided in just a few seconds that they needed to get back to the Vatican. Herriot had already instructed the Swiss Guard complement at the Vatican, about thirty men, half his force, to move the Pope forthwith to a safe room designed specifically for the purpose of protecting the Pope. The room was located in the bowels of the Vatican's main building, far below the ancient text library.

There were a series of tunnels to navigate through, and which had a hidden entrance unlocked only by a key carried by the Swiss Guard commander on site, which in Herriot's absence, was his vice-commander. Once through the damp tunnels, another hidden door led to stairs to yet more lower levels. Following those steps down two flights led to a gigantic subterranean world, where some of the supports for the building stood like sentinels across the space.

On the far side of the open area was a steel door, whose frame was embedded in the rock walls. Through the door was a well-appointed pair of rooms. One was similar to the Pope's office many floors above. The other was a bedroom.

The Pope currently sat comfortably at his desk reading a passage in the New Testament. Two Swiss Guards stood inside, by the door, and two more were just outside. Others were spread out along the tunnels, and yet more on both sides of the hidden doors. Although those on the outside positioned themselves to not give away the secret door. All were armed with the German MP40 submachine gun and their Berettas. Each man wore a grim expression.

The vice-commander set up a perimeter of Guards outside on St. Peter's Square, close to St. Peter's Basilica's front door. Others were set up along the streets behind the Basilica.

The last of the Commandos and the Swiss Guard at the Villas were inside the trucks. Saunders and Herriot jumped inside the cab of the lead truck.

"Go!" Herriot said, pointing out the windshield. The driver stomped on the gas pedal and the rear tires actually shrieked.

When Herriot received the frantic call, he'd immediately ordered his men and Saunders' to make haste back to the entrance. They'd run the whole distance, including Alfred Welford, who, bless his heart, had picked up the hem of his cassock and run as hard as he could. Being older, he began to lag behind, but Saunders and Barltrop stayed with him, encouraging him onward. When they'd arrived at the entrance, Welford's face was red and he was breathing hard. He refused to bend over, though, and stood next to the Commandos to rest.

"Haven't had to run that hard since the last time our horrible play got run out of town back in twenty-six," he quipped.

Saunders and Barltrop stared at the renowned actor and laughed.

"You're kidding, right?" Saunders asked.

"I wish. It really was a terrible play." He sighed deeply. "Didn't even get late supper." He grinned.

Saunders patted him on the back. "You up for the show down?"

Welford looked at Saunders, and Barltrop. Before their eyes he transformed, drawing himself upright and placing his hands in front of himself. He raised his right hand and gave the Benediction.

"Yes, I'm ready."

"Incredible," Barltrop said. "Good man."

When the convoy reached the outskirts of southeastern Rome, four Rome police cars met them. They took up a position with two leading and two trailing. The convoy sped along the narrow streets of the ancient city, the police cars' sirens wailing. Citizens stopped what they were doing to watch the parade of police cars and big trucks roar by, having no idea what was happening.

Saunders turned his head to Herriot.

"It will happen today."

"You really think they'll try it at the Vatican?"

"Certain of it. Their commander, whoever he is, is pretty angry. We almost fooled him into showing his hand at the wrong place. Only bad luck on our part prevented it."

"You think they were actually watching?" Herriot asked.

"It's what I would have done. It paid off for him."

"I agree with you."

"I have a question. Won't the watcher see us return? You know, what with the coppers and sirens."

"The police will leave us when we pass the Colosseum. We'll go around the back way quietly, the way we left."

Saunders nodded his agreement. He thought about their choices for a few minutes.

"There's only one way to bring this to a conclusion. We have to make it seem easy for him."

"You are correct."

"It's highly risky."

"Again you are correct."

The two men grew silent as they considered what was about to happen.

And what it would mean to the Church if it went wrong.

Chapter 30

12 kilometers southeast of Rome
14 November, 0933 Hours

Another, slower moving, convoy was headed toward the Vatican. *Hauptsturmführer* Werner Möller, like his counterpart Commander Herriot, rode in the lead vehicle. *Hauptscharführer* Horst Sauer was with him.

"I should have known they'd try something like this. A decoy! How dare them," Möller grumbled.

Sauer glanced at his commander and saw a furious man. "Your idea to watch both locations turned out to be quite fortuitous, sir."

"Yes, it did, didn't it? I wonder how they found out we were here."

"It could be they are responding to some other threat. Someone else who's made threats against the Pope. Maybe the communists. The Pope has always spoken out against them."

Möller shook his head. "It's us they're afraid of. I can just feel it."

"Yes, sir." Sauer cleared his throat, unsure whether to ask the obvious question, given the captain's mood. He realized, of course, that it was his responsibility to raise questions, even if it meant getting his ass handed to him occasionally.

"Given they seem to know about our plan and will undoubtedly be taking defensive measures, should we pursue the matter? Or would it be prudent to cancel the operation?"

Möller said nothing for a long time, making Sauer sweat.

Finally, "We will not cancel a mission ordered by our *Führer*, Sergeant Sauer." Möller's expression softened. "I admire you for having the courage to speak up."

"Thank you, *Hauptsturmführer*."

"Are the men ready?"

"Yes, sir. I told them that we were reverting to Plan B. No one needed to ask any questions because we were so thorough during our pre-mission work. Everyone knows what to do."

"Good. I expected nothing less."

The truck entered Rome. The driver began to have his hands full because of traffic and the Italian penchant for crossing the street wherever they were. No one used the actual crosswalks.

Möller had been looking around as they drove through the ancient city. He'd admired the statues and fountains they'd passed. In previous visits to Rome, long before it was lost to the Allies, he'd often traveled around the city to enjoy the aged buildings and artworks around the city. He thought the ancient Romans had been spectacularly skilled at everything, from architecture to politics, to their military. Compared to their predecessors, the modern-day Italians struck him as unworthy. Their military manufacturing factories produced second-rate, maybe third-rate weapons, vehicles, aircraft, and ships. Their military, as a whole, had been a disaster from the beginning when the idiot Mussolini had decided he wanted an empire. He'd selected Ethiopia as a starting point and although he'd eventually prevailed over an army where many Ethiopian men and boys carried nothing but spears, what was the prize? A poor eastern African nation.

It had all gone downhill repeatedly for the Italians, and the Germans had to rescue them. Although he'd never had to work with Italian military, he'd heard the stories of ineptitude and even outright cowardice.

The Colosseum passed by on their right. It was simply marvelous.

The convoy reached a street a few blocks east of St. Peter's Square. Möller sat up and leaned forward, peering out the dusty windshield. He soon found what he was searching for.

He pointed to the right. "There. That alleyway."

"Yes, sir," replied the driver. He slowed the truck and after waiting for a gaggle of pedestrians to get out of the way, turned into the alley. He drove about a hundred meters and stopped. The alley was narrow, but there was plenty of room for the trucks and there would be ample space on both sides for the men to pass by the trucks.

Möller climbed down and Sauer joined him.

The alley was between several four-story apartment buildings. Because it ran north-south, it was in complete shade under the morning sun. Möller's nose wrinkled. The air smelled of Italian cooking and old laundry water, which seemed to be standing in pools along both sides, tossed out from apartments above. He was glad the Italians at least had indoor plumbing, an improvement over the ancient Romans, who were prone to tossing chamber pots' contents out into the streets. Trash, a mixture of paper, old food, and who knew what else, was strewn up and down the alley. He spotted a pack of dogs about fifty meters farther down the alley, various kinds of mixed breeds, from little terriers to big shepherds. Reflexively, he raised his shoes and examined the bottoms of each, happy to have not stepped in dog shit, which was yet another prevalent odor.

"Can you imagine living like this?" Möller asked.

"Never, sir."

Möller shivered in revulsion.

His men hopped down from their trucks and walked around the vehicles to gather in front of Möller's lead truck. They looked like a motley crew of Italian workers. Once again, they carried their MP40s inside a satchel and their Italian Berettas were holstered under their coats.

Möller called for his squad leaders.

When they joined him and Sauer, he said, "Men, plans have changed, but we're prepared. Stick to the plan in place for the Vatican. Remember, each squad enters from a different route and each squad splits up into groups of two or three. Be sure you go to your assigned spot near St. Peter's Basilica. Await my command."

The squad leaders all replied, *"Jawohl, Hauptsturmführer!"*

The platoon of Nazi SS men dispersed slowly from the alley, half going northwest toward the Basilica and the others south toward the center of the square. The last group would change directions and take their positions in front of the Basilica.

Möller and Sauer went northwest a few minutes after the last man disappeared from view. They wound their way along the street, walking side by side. Möller smiled as he passed various Italians, both male and female, trying to appear to be a friendly Italian.

It only took them ten minutes to make it to St. Peter's Square, entering it from the north, passing by the barracks of the Swiss Guard. Möller examined the building as they walked by, smiling to himself. *If they only knew*, he thought. He briefly wondered whether he should have left a few men at the Villa. They could have created a worthy diversion by attacking it. He shrugged to himself. Too late for that. To be honest, he was looking forward to the upcoming frontal attack. The Swiss Guard would have no idea how bad it was about to get.

The square was not crowded. It was a Tuesday after all.

He stopped moving and Sauer stayed with him. They carefully examined the square. Möller wished he could have used a pair of binoculars, but that might have alerted the Swiss Guard. Instead, he watched for his men with his naked eyes. He was pleased to see each squad milling around in its assigned position. They were still grouped in twos and threes to prevent detection.

"Time we split up, Sauer."

"Yes, sir," the master sergeant replied without looking at Möller. He walked away, following the eastern edge of the ellipse.

Möller leisurely headed toward the center of the square, where the Vatican Obelisk was located. When he was about fifty meters from the impressive twenty-five-meter-tall relic of Egypt, he turned right toward the stairs of the Basilica.

Two squads were located at the bottom of the stairs, one on the north and one on the south side of the extraordinarily wide steps. Squad number three was on the top landing to the right of the center door. Their entry point. Number four was just a few meters from the door and would be the first squad inside.

Möller continued his ambling pace. He glanced nonchalantly to his right and after a moment found Sauer, who was almost to the squad on the right at the bottom of the stairs.

Turning back to his direction of travel, he noted the Swiss Guards. Four stood at attention by the front door, except their heads were in constant motion, scanning the few people around. Four other Guards were marching back and forth between the western edge of the ellipse and the stairs. Squad one, on the south, would take care of them.

He passed within a few meters of one of the Guards. The man glanced at him, and quickly decided he was no threat. Möller suppressed a grin. *Ah, how easy*, he thought.

As he placed his right foot on the first step, he glanced at his watch.

Time to capture a Pope.

Chapter 31

2 miles northeast of the Nazi Uranium Facility
14 November, 0946 Hours

Dunn glanced over his shoulder through the window into the cargo area. The German scientists sat huddled next to each other, not talking, their eyes downcast. They looked like defeated men. He wondered what would drive a human being to want to kill other humans with something as terrifying and awful as death by radiation poisoning.

He faced front to keep the truck on the road, but called out, "Rob. Come here."

Goerdt scooted up to the window and knelt, his face filling the window. "Yeah, Sarge?"

Dunn spoke without taking his eyes off the road. "Ask them *why* they're doing this. If they try to lie their way out of it, tell them we know about the ground up uranium-235 and the artillery shells. That we know *everything*."

"You got it, Sarge."

Because of the road noise, Dunn couldn't hear what was being said, which irritated him no end. He glanced quickly over his shoulder. Goerdt was right in the face of the man closest to Dunn and talking away at him in German. Both men were still in the same position as before. Goerdt switched to the other man, but got no response.

He finally gave up and went back to the window. "No luck, Sarge. Not a word from either of them."

"Damn it."

Dunn was surprised by how angry he felt. These two guys were responsible in some way for a plan that could have killed thousands, maybe tens of thousands of Allied soldiers, not to mention unlucky civilians. He felt his heart rate speed up and it seemed like his face was burning hot from flushing. Sons of bitches, that's what they were.

He spotted a farmer's road off to the right just ahead. It looked like it might lead into a grove of trees. A good hiding place. He slowed down and turned onto the side road. About twenty yards along they entered the grove. He found a place where he could turn the truck around and brought it to a stop safely in the grove, facing the main road. He shut off the engine.

"Everybody out except the Germans," he hollered through the window.

He jumped out of the truck and slammed the door shut. Running around to the rear, he met Goerdt, Martelli, and Higgins.

"I'm not going to spend much time doing this, but I'm going to grill these bastards. Rob, give them whatever I say word for word, okay?"

"Yes, Sarge."

Dunn looked at each man for a few seconds, holding their gaze. "Back me up on whatever I say and do. No questions. I'm going to have one shot at this."

The men nodded.

"Rob, Al, go get those guys out. Make 'em kneel in the mud in the rain for a minute."

"Okay," Goerdt said.

He and Martelli climbed back up in the truck. Shortly after, they helped the men get down. The prisoners hadn't been tied up, so they were able to use their hands for balance.

Goerdt told the men to kneel. The taller of the two balked at getting down in the mud, so Goerdt screamed at him in German to get his ass down there. The man looked frightened and knelt.

Dunn watched them for close to a minute, letting them stew. He walked over to the men, and they looked up at the sound of his boots on the wet gravel. He carried his Thompson in one hand, the barrel aiming downward more or less in their direction.

"I'm Sergeant Dunn of the U.S. Army. I have some questions for you."

Goerdt translated quickly.

Neither man spoke, but they watched the business end of the Thompson with fear all over their faces.

"We're going to enter your facility and destroy it and bury your uranium." He waited for Goerdt.

"You," he pointed at the two of them with his weapon, "are going to tell me exactly where the uranium is and where the artillery shells are located."

Their expressions changed. The taller man's face grew more determined, while the small man appeared to be totally terrified.

"Ask them their names."

The tall man resisted, but the short man replied, "Bauer."

Goerdt leaned into the face of the one who refused to speak. He repeated the question.

"Gerber."

Dunn immediately grabbed Bauer by the coat lapels. He made an assumption and said, "Dr. Bauer. Tell me where the stuff is located!"

Bauer tried to cringe away, but Dunn had too tight a grip on his coat. He rattled off something.

"He says, 'I can't, I can't tell you.' "

"Ask him 'why not?' "

Goerdt asked. Bauer replied so softly Goerdt almost didn't catch it. "He says, 'Minister Speer will kill me.' "

Dunn stared at Bauer. It looked like there was only one way to get anywhere. He yanked on the Thompson's charging bolt and placed the black muzzle against Bauer's temple.

"Mr. Speer is not here. I am. This is your last chance."

Bauer just closed his eyes, and said nothing.

Gerber spoke up, which surprised Dunn and Goerdt.

"He says, 'I suppose you're going to torture us?' "

Dunn glared at Gerber. He had no interest nor time for torturing someone.

He smiled at Gerber and shook his head.

"Rob, charge your weapon."

Goerdt immediately did that, and placed the barrel against Gerber's forehead.

Gerber shouted something.

Goerdt said, "He says they are good Germans. They will never betray their country."

Dunn's face turned dark. He leaned close to the two men. He spoke to them and Goerdt translated, "Good Germans? Good Germans? I know a good German and you're nothing like him. Dr. Herbert—"

Bauer looked up quickly and interrupted. "You can't know Dr. Herbert. He's dead! My friend is dead."

Dunn listened as Goerdt translated. He knelt right in front of Bauer.

"Dr. Herbert is alive and well. He's in the United States. He's being a good German."

"But he died in an explosion."

Dunn shook his head. "He was many kilometers away when your Project Dante lab blew up. He was with me."

Bauer studied Dunn's face. "You knew about Project Dante?"

"Yep. I destroyed it."

Dunn looked at the other man, whose face reflected surprise and disbelief.

"You both worked there?"

The two men nodded slowly. Dunn realized he might have found a way to get through.

Bauer asked, "Dr. Herbert is really safe?"

Dunn nodded. "He is safe. Perhaps you'd like to see him again?"

"I would love to see him again."

"All you have to do is tell me what I want to know."

Bauer glanced at Gerber, who nodded. "I will answer your questions."

"Good. We'll go back to the facility first, then you can tell me."

The Rangers helped the men up into the truck.

Dunn jumped in the driver's seat and took off.

When he was able to see the entrance from the road he came to a stop. He raised his binoculars and studied the layout. There were still no guards outside, a welcome surprise. The other two trucks were still parked in the same places.

Dunn picked out the spot where he wanted to park the truck. He was concerned about being seen from inside if he simply put the truck back where it had been.

He drove ahead and turned right onto the facility's road. He lumbered slowly past the parked trucks, which were on his left. He guided the vehicle straight toward the left wall. When he was no more than a yard away, he stopped. He'd positioned the truck so the driver's side was out of view of the personnel door because the wall blocked it. He shut off the engine and climbed down. He ran around to the back and told the Rangers to make sure they stayed on the left side, and for Goerdt to tell the scientists to behave themselves.

When everyone was back on the ground, Dunn led the group along the wall. He eyed the forest ahead of him. Cross stepped out and waved. Dunn gave a thumbs up sign. Cross returned it.

Dunn stopped a few feet from Cross.

"I see you had your chase after all."

"Yep."

"Looks like maybe it paid off. Did you find out what we need to know?"

"I'm about to." Dunn stepped to the side and gestured for the two Germans to approach Cross. They were leery, not knowing who was who, but complied.

Dunn pointed at Cross and said, "David Cross. Dave." He pointed at the short man, "Dr. Bauer, and Dr. Gerber."

Cross took the hint and stepped forward, hand extended and a friendly smile on his face.

The Germans were so surprised that the enemy would offer to shake hands, that they were frozen for a moment. Bauer recovered his wits first and shook hands, giving Cross a tentative smile.

Gerber shook hands next, but didn't smile.

"Rob, tell them: if they continue to help us, I'm offering to take them to England when we leave."

Goerdt nodded and translated the message.

Both men looked from Dunn to Goerdt and back again. Bauer blinked rapidly. He said something.

"He says, 'Would we eventually go to America and see our friend?' "

Dunn nodded. "I think it might be possible."

Upon hearing that from Goerdt, the two men visibly relaxed even more and gave each other a tiny smile.

Bauer whispered something to Gerber.

Goerdt barely caught it. He said, "Bauer just said 'we've escaped Speer, at last.' "

Dunn said, "No more Speer!"

Both Germans smiled.

Bauer's eyes seemed to suddenly light up as he evidently thought of something. He asked Goerdt a rapid-fire question that included 'New York City.'

Goerdt grinned. "Can I see New York City?"

Dunn smiled and nodded. "Sure. I think so."

Bauer almost jumped up and down at Goerdt's response.

Dunn held up a hand, palm outward. "Back to business first."

Hearing the translation, Gerber and Bauer nodded. *"Ja,"* They replied.

Chapter 32

Camp Barton Stacey Hospital
14 November, 0857 Hours, London time

Pamela Dunn walked lightly into one of the ward rooms in the hospital. She stood still, checking the faces of the men lying or sitting up in bed. She spotted Eugene Lindstrom right away, He was by a window on the right, about half way back. It looked like he was reading a magazine. Before Dunn had left, he'd asked her if she wouldn't mind dropping in to visit with Lindstrom. She'd said, 'of course I don't mind.'

Corporal Eugene Lindstrom had been a member of Dunn's squad since late June. He'd been immediately assigned to be Jonesy's spotter. They'd worked well together with Lindstrom quickly able to determine whatever Jonesy might need. He'd become a squad hero recently. On a mission to the Arctic, at one point, he'd had been on guard duty outside the tents while everyone else rested. What he was guarding against was polar bears. The Norwegian Arctic instructor the men had worked with, and who went on the mission with them, had told everyone that polar bears were exceedingly dangerous, and fast, and they loved the taste of humans. One had approached the camp and Lindstrom had heard its giant paws crunching the ice just in time. He fired his weapon into the air which, lucky for him, scared the bear away. He'd thought he was a goner, and the rest of the squad who were all nice and warm in the tents, would end up like pigs in a blanket snacks for the bear.

Later, as they advanced toward a German position, a firefight broke out and he'd taken a round in the thigh. The German round had missed the bone and the femoral artery, so once again he had been lucky. Bob Schneider patched him up. When they made it back to Barton Stacey, he'd gone into the hospital, where he'd been recuperating ever since.

Pamela headed toward Lindstrom. He heard her shoes on the wooden floor and looked up. His eyes lit up and he grinned. Pamela was the most beautiful woman he'd ever seen. And she was kind. No wonder Sarge had fallen for her.

"Hey, Eugene."

"Hi, Mrs. Dunn."

"Pamela," she replied instantly.

"Okay, Mrs. Dunn," he said, grinning.

She grinned back and sat down next to the bed in a guest chair. "How are you, Eugene?"

"I'm great. I can walk without a cane. I've been ready to get back to the boys."

"Have they told you when you get out?"

"Any day. The sooner the better."

"You're looking pretty well fed."

"It turns out I really like the food here. Who would have thought? Some of the other guys don't so I get some of theirs once in a while."

"Ah ha." She lifted a small brown package from her spacious purse and laid it on the bed next to him. "So you probably don't have any need for this?"

He raised an eyebrow. "Is that what I think it is?"

"Depends on what you're thinking."

"Aren't you the cagey one?"

"Better open it, don't you think?"

"I do think." He picked up the package and tore the paper off in a couple of quick moves. It revealed a white cardboard box. He held it up under his nose and sniffed.

His eyes widened and he moaned aloud. "Oh my God." He lowered his voice to a whisper, "Chocolate bar. How'd you manage that?" He knew it was hard for civilians to come by.

"Where do you think?"

"Sarge?"

"Yep."

"Well, thank him for me. And thank you for bringing it to me."

"I will and you're welcome."

Pamela stood and smiled down at the Ranger. "My birthday is coming up soon. Don't tell anyone, but Tom is going to invite the squad plus Colonel Kenton and Captain Adams to a party at the farm. Probably Mac Saunders and his lads, too."

Lindstrom grinned. "Sounds like fun, Mrs. Dunn."

"Pamela."

"Okay, Mrs. Dunn."

She shook her head. "You are as stubborn as he is."

"I'll take that as a compliment."

"Hope you get out soon. See you at the party."

"Bye."

Pamela walked across the ward quite aware that every man was watching her leave.

She went down the hallway a short distance and entered another ward. She spotted Colonel Kenton and walked toward him. A dark haired forty-something, Kenton had good looks and a deep voice. He'd been kind to Pamela when she and Tom had to navigate the army protocol for American soldiers marrying British women. There was supposed to be a sixty day waiting period and an interview by the soldier's commander. He'd waived the waiting period and merely told her he had no need to interview her.

"Hello, Colonel Kenton."

Kenton looked up from the book he was reading and broke into a wide grin.

"Hi Pamela. Please call me Mark."

"Of course, Mark. How are you, sir?"

"Due out any day." He gestured to the chair by his bed. "Please, sit."

"Thank you. That's wonderful. Eugene Lindstrom should be released soon, too."

"Oh, good. I've been a little worried about him. Good man."

"I have something for you from Tom." Once again she opened her purse and pulled out a brown package. She handed it to him.

He grinned and tore the paper off. He held it to his nose just like Lindstrom had done. He closed his eyes and breathed deep.

"Smells better than a steak."

He opened his eyes, which twinkled in delight. "Thank you both. I'd say I'll try and make it last, but I know me better. It'll be gone before lunch."

Pamela laughed.

"So you're feeling back to normal?"

"I am." He shook his head. "The doctor came by yesterday and asked me who the president was. I was so tempted to say Hoover, but was afraid he'd make me stay longer."

Pamela chuckled. "I take it Hoover was FDR's predecessor?"

"Ah. Yes, he was. Had the misfortune of being in office when the crash hit."

"I see. No wonder FDR was elected."

"Oh, it was a sweep. If I remember right, he carried forty-one or -two states. A complete landslide."

"My goodness. How's your son doing?"

"He's had a good semester grade-wise. Seems to like being there. Already looking forward to finals and Christmas break next month."

She smiled. "I'm sure you're quite the proud father."

"Guilty as charged."

She rose to her feet. "I'll let you get back to your book, sir. By the way, Tom wants to have a birthday party bash for me sometime soon. I'd like to invite you in advance. It'll be out at the farm."

Kenton grinned. "Wouldn't miss it for anything."

She leaned over and kissed him on the cheek. "See you soon, then."

As she walked away, Kenton realized he had the same affection for her as he had for Dunn, which was much like a father-son feeling. He'd grown to respect him starting from the time he was a member of his Ranger battalion at Anzio. When Kenton had been put in charge of his current command of special operations Rangers, he'd made sure to bring him along. Since May, they'd worked closely together and he'd begun to think of him as a son rather than just a man in his unit. Perhaps he reminded him of his son, Bobby, who was about six years younger and in his first year at West Point. He realized he often thought of him as a peer rather than a subordinate, but they both made sure they stayed inside the lines of the military hierarchy whenever in front of anyone else.

Dunn was regarded by the rest of the company as the top dog. He was the guy everyone wanted to have on their team. Everyone wanted to be on his squad, but it was tough to get in. It was good to hear that he had taken a mixed platoon, American and British, on the Hitler's Dam mission, and he'd learned from Captain Adams that he had taken Newman's and Porter's squads with him on the current mission. He'd tried to get him to accept a commission, but every time he brought it up, he'd shooed away the idea, saying he needed to stay close to the men. When the best there was wanted something, you nodded your head and gave it to him.

That thought got him to thinking about his current rank, Technical Sergeant, a five-stripe Sergeant. It seemed to him that he had been in that rank since about the middle of July, meaning four months. He smiled to himself. It would be nice that the first thing he did after getting out of the hospital was to promote him to Master Sergeant.

Grinning to himself because of the promotion idea, he glanced around the ward. No one was watching. The beds on either side were empty, for once. He opened the little box and broke off a bite-sized piece of chocolate. He slipped it between his lips and savored the blast of flavor. He lifted his book and resumed reading his Raymond Chandler mystery.

RONN MUNSTERMAN

Chapter 33

In the woods
Just west of the Nazi Uranium Facility's entrance
14 November, 1007 Hours, Berlin time

The rain had slowed, becoming a drizzle. The overcast sky lightened. The wind died down.

Dunn wanted to ask the two Germans standing in front of him again why they'd agreed to do it, but realized the answer was merely a matter of what else could they have done? If they'd opposed it, they'd been sent to a camp or simply shot. He wondered whether they had any moral compunction about what they were planning. The two men were standing close together, probably because they understood they were surrounded by enemy soldiers. Their hair was plastered to their skulls and their white lab coats seemed more gray than white. Their expressions were identical: apprehensive, unsure what was going to happen to them despite what he'd promised.

He stopped his mental gymnastics about the doctors and focused. "Dr. Bauer, describe the inside of the facility for me?"

Goerdt acted as the translator, since he'd been working with the men already.

Cross, Newman, and Porter stood close so they could hear for themselves and save time for Dunn.

Bauer spoke for quite a while, stopping when it was necessary for Goerdt to catch up. In the end, Dunn felt like he had a good idea of the layout, and more importantly where the uranium stockpile and artillery shells were located, plus how the German soldiers were deployed.

Dunn had one more question. "The guards at the entrance. Will they recognize you and Dr. Gerber and just let you in?"

Goerdt translated.

"*Ja,*" came the answer.

"Excellent." He turned to his squad leaders and Cross. "Here's how we're going to do this."

He laid it all out for everyone and finished with, "Anyone have any questions?"

No one did.

To Newman and Porter, he said, "Make sure your walkie-talkie is set to the right frequency." He gave the number. Both men nodded that they were okay.

The SCR-536 was a five pound handheld radio that came with built-in batteries and it was water proof.

"Let's get going," Dunn said.

A few minutes later, the platoon was bunched up at the end of the wall, with Dunn at the front with the scientists and Colonel Mason.

Dunn knelt and peeked around the edge of the wall. The hangar doors were still closed, as was the personnel door, which looked puny. The only window was in the personnel door at head height.

In total, the width of the two hangar doors was about thirty yards, plenty wide for any wingspans of the German twin-engine bombers.

Dunn glanced behind him at Cross and nodded.

Cross and the rest of the squad, except Goerdt, went around Dunn in the hunched over combat run. Cross hugged the wall, although the squad was inside the entrance opening. It only took a few steps to reach the left hangar door. He turned right and followed along it until he was about ten feet from the personnel door. He knelt and the men behind him did, too. They had their weapons at the ready.

Newman's squad moved up behind Dunn and Porter's followed.

Dunn looked at Goerdt. "Tell the doctors we're ready to go to the door. Make sure they stick to the plan."

Goerdt nodded and explained what Dunn said.

Gerber and Bauer nodded. Both looked like they were about to throw up.

"Tell them to relax. Everything will go fine if they stay focused. Tell them it's like an experiment where they have to be precise."

Goerdt raised an eyebrow at the analogy.

As he translated once again, the scientists' expressions changed as they nodded their understanding.

Goerdt looked at Dunn. "Nice analogy, Sarge. Seemed to work."

Dunn grunted. "Hope so. Send the tall one."

Goerdt pulled Gerber forward and told him it was time.

Gerber walked around Dunn and headed for the personnel door. He walked at a good clip, evidently overcoming most of his nervousness. As he approached the door he gave Cross and the other American soldiers a sidelong glance, but as he'd been told, he didn't turn his head.

Cross nodded at him encouragingly.

When Gerber reached the door, he stopped and knocked loudly.

A few seconds passed and the door opened inward. Dunn caught side of a German helmet over Gerber's left shoulder.

Gerber stepped through the door.

Dunn pulled back and said to Goerdt, "Send Bauer."

The little scientist started walking.

Dunn watched.

The plan was for Cross to wait until Bauer was halfway to the door.

Before that happened, everything went to shit.

RONN MUNSTERMAN

Chapter 34

North of St. Peter's Square
Vatican City
14 November, 1008 Hours

"We have one chance at this, Commander," Saunders said quietly. "The SS commander has his men in position and from the looks of it, they're going to launch the attack any moment."

Saunders and Commander Herriot had their men to the north of St. Peter's Basilica's façade, just outside the area of the ellipse. The morning sun gave them plenty of shadows, which would be useful.

"Do you think the plan will work?" Herriot asked, showing some nervousness for the first time.

"Yeah. It'll work. He'll have no choice. We know for a fact his spy has lost all sight of the Pope. When we dangle Mr. Welford in front of him, he'll have no choice but to follow the white coat he can see."

"I hope you're right," Herriot replied.

"Not to worry, Commander. I am. Most days."

Saunders looked at the Swiss Guard members lined up in their dual-column protective cordon around Alfred Welford, in full Pope's regalia. At the front of the cordon, the vice-commander stood next to a lone trumpeter. He would be the Guards' call to action for the SS men, hopefully triggering their interest in the decoy Pope. They were standing under the portico that curved around the north side of the square. Saunders was standing next to one of the pillars supporting the portico, which placed him about eighty-five yards from the Basilica's front steps, where the SS were located. He was also about a hundred yards from the Guards' barracks. Between the barracks and his position was a warren of side streets that wrapped around the north side of the square. These were most commonly used by Vatican employees, especially the Swiss Guard.

Earlier, Saunders and Herriot had fortified the front door where it appeared the SS would make their entrance. Multiple heavy pieces of furniture were piled in front of the doors. They knew they wouldn't stop the SS forever, thus the need for the decoy on the outside. They had to keep the SS out. Too much damage to the priceless building and property inside would take place otherwise. All staff had been hastily sent to safety in the bowels of the building.

Saunders, standing in the shadow of a building, raised his binoculars. The SS men stood out because in spite of their Italian clothing, they'd forgotten a couple of things. They moved like soldiers, and every single one of them was carrying a satchel. Who carried a satchel to the Vatican? No one, especially ones that were identical. He'd already decided which of the men was the SS leader. All he'd had to watch for was a man to whom others paid deference. They wouldn't be able to help themselves. It was ingrained in their being, as it was in all soldiers. Two men stood near the leader listening to something he was saying.

The leader looked around the stairs leading into the Basilica. Saunders knew he was doing a last check of his troops' positions.

"It's going to start. Get the men moving," he said.

Herriot turned around and looked at his vice-commander. He gave the high sign.

The vice commander said something to the trumpeter, who immediately marched forward to stand on the surface of the square. He was about ten yards from Saunders, who drew back even farther into the shadows.

The trumpeter began playing a fanfare, which rang and echoed across the square.

All of the people stopped what they were doing and stared in his direction, trying to see if maybe the Pope was making a surprise visit.

Saunders watched the SS commander. The man was intently staring at the trumpeter.

The vice-commander waited thirty seconds, and started the cordon moving toward the trumpeter. Welford, the Pope, was fourth in line behind him.

SS *Hauptsturmführer* Werner Möller stared in surprise as the Swiss Guard trumpeter played some kind of rousing fanfare. Whatever it was, it certainly wasn't Richard Wagner, the *Führer's* favorite composer. The presence of a trumpeter, in and of itself, was quite unusual and his alarm bells were ringing. The Swiss Guard cordon suddenly came into view. He turned toward his men who were spread out close to the Basilica. He lifted his hat from his head and wiped his forehead with his hand. The signal to redeploy to the north.

He started walking toward the cordon. As he passed Sergeant Sauer, the man fell in step with him.

The Pope came into view, smiling and waving to the few people around the north side of the ellipse.

Möller broke into a run. Behind him, his men ran toward the Pope. As they ran, they were opening their satchels and withdrawing their MP40s.

Herriot put a whistle to his lips and blew a double-note. Lots of things happened as a result of the sharp sounds.

The Swiss Guard cordon reversed course and ran. Two Guards next to Welford grabbed his arms on each side and helped him along. The men who had been at the rear of the cordon stood stationary. As the front half with the Pope ran past, the rear Guards formed a line crossing the path, weapons up.

Herriot and Saunders turned north and ran along the portico toward the street by the barracks.

The SS was committed and were in full chase. When they were about twenty yards from the Guards in line formation, the Guards turned and ran after the Pope, who was already in the street.

Möller couldn't give the order to fire because the Pope might be hit, even though he had reached a street outside the square. He kept running, and Sauer was right beside him. His men were catching up and formed up on both sides of the SS commander.

All of the civilians in the square had at first stood stock still when it suddenly seemed that everyone was running away, including the Pope, a sight no one had ever seen before. Some of the people spotted the SS men revealing their weapons and they scrambled in the opposite direction. Some of them helpfully screamed, "They have guns!" as they ran. In short order, it was pandemonium in the ellipse, with the group of civilians running in one direction while the cordon and the SS men went in the other. From above, it looked like two large flocks of birds wheeling away from each other.

Möller and the front of his platoon reached the outer edge of the square. He could still see the tail end of the cordon, which had run to the right to go down another street. He and his men dashed through the north portion of the portico and into the street. When they made it to the next street on the right, Möller ran around the corner. He entered the street, which was quite narrow, perhaps only three meters.

About a half block ahead, the cordon had stopped. Some of the Guards were bending over. Möller altered his path to get a clearer view of what was happening. It looked like the Pope had stumbled on the stone street and fallen. Möller dug deep and sped up. His prey was almost within reach.

The Pope made it to his feet and the cordon began moving forward again, but at a slower pace.

The SS platoon was fully in the street and pursuing their target, which was tantalizingly close. Möller felt he could smell the fear coming from the Pope and his famous Swiss Guards. *Not so infallible, eh?* he thought to himself.

From his position in a second floor window, Saunders watched the careless SS platoon run pell-mell down the street as they chased who they thought, incorrectly, was the Pope. His walkie-talkie chirped to life with a single click.

Möller spotted the Pope, who was stumbling through a doorway only thirty meters ahead. The cordon disappeared, but he knew which door. Almost there!

Saunders raised his walkie-talkie, pressed the button, and said, "Fire!"

Saunders' squad was on the Germans' right and Massie's squad was across the street. Blazing fire erupted from both sides. The MP40s, which could fire five hundred rounds a minute, created a cacophony of sound that echoed in the narrow street.

Men behind the SS commander began falling to the stone roadway in bloody messes. He shouted a command in German.

He and the man next to him ran to the nearest door and tried to enter. It was locked. He kicked it once with his boot, but the door didn't budge. He pointed to the street's entrance behind them, some seventy yards away. The only possible escape. They started running in that direction, firing their own MP40s upwards.

Half of the platoon was down, either dead or seriously wounded. The other half was shooting back, raking the windows and the stones around the openings. A pause suddenly silenced everything. The German commander waved at his men, who were in front of him, to go to the street's exit.

The platoon wheeled around.

Commander Herriot and a squad of Swiss Guards suddenly appeared in windows that had been closed when the Germans first went by. They had a great angle on the retreating Germans, from the enemy's front. They opened fire.

Saunders' and Massie's squad joined in.

The SS platoon, or what was left of it, began to disintegrate as man after man collapsed to the ground in a bloody heap.

Möller watched his men die in front of him. He stopped running. He dropped his weapon and held up his hands. He yelled, "Drop your weapons, men! Surrender!"

About ten men, one fourth of his entire platoon, immediately threw their weapons on the ground and dropped to their knees with their hands in the air.

Saunders yelled into his walkie-talkie, "Cease Fire! Cease Fire! Massie hold position. Commander Herriot, down into the street. Be alert and careful. Check bodies and weapons."

He turned to his men in the room with him. "Let's go gather up the bad guys, lads. Steve, lead the way."

In a short time, Saunders and Barltrop were walking carefully along the blood-soaked street. As the alert squads advanced, they stopped and checked every German lying on the ground. Those still living were disengaged from their weapons.

Gilbert, whose squad had been at the far end of the street came into view. Their job would have been to keep the SS trapped in the street, completing the killing zone of the ambush.

Saunders reached the SS commander first. He was on his knees facing the opposite direction, so Saunders walked around in front of him. He motioned with his MP40 for the man to rise. When the commander stood, Saunders looked pointedly at the holster on the man's right hip. He held out his hand.

The commander, using his left hand, removed the weapon from the holster and held it out to the Swiss Guard in front of him, butt first.

Saunders tucked it in his own belt.

"What's your name?"

The commander stared at Saunders in surprise.

"British? You're British?" he asked in clear, but accented English.

"Aye," Saunders replied with a grin, his red handlebar mustache twitching in delight.

The commander looked around the ambush site. His jaw muscles tightened. When he turned back to Saunders, his eyes were dark and angry.

Saunders sensed the man was considering rushing him. To forestall more killing, he said, "I wouldn't recommend that, sir. Your men will be well treated. Your wounded will receive medical care. Shall we attend to that?"

The commander's face relaxed. "Captain Werner Möller."

"Sergeant Major Malcolm Saunders."

"Commandos, are you not?"

Saunders nodded.

"Your men have performed admirably."

Saunders shrugged. "You were careless, Captain. Rushing into a blind street without checking it first."

Möller's lips compressed. "I'm trying to be honorable with you."

Saunders laughed, a rumble from deep down inside.

"Honorable? Fook you, Captain Möller. You were trying to kidnap the Pope."

Möller drew himself up and was about to reply.

"Shut it! Or I'll knock that smug face right off your head."

Commander Herriot arrived just then, his men behind him, all wearing grim expressions and hate in their eyes.

"Is this the commander?"

"Aye, Commander. It's him. Captain Möller."

"Step aside, Sergeant."

Saunders nodded and stepped to his left.

Herriot took his place and stared at Möller with fury in his eyes. He pulled his Beretta from the holster and aimed it between Möller's eyes.

Möller's expression turned to one of deep fear, but he said calmly, "You cannot shoot me. I am a prisoner of war. You must turn me over to the Allies."

Herriot answered by clicking the hammer back.

Möller licked his lips and glanced at Saunders.

"Don't look at me for help. I'm here at his command."

Möller looked at Herriot, which was difficult with the Beretta in the way.

Herriot jammed the gun forward into Möller's forehead.

"You have committed a grave sin. You attempted to harm the Pope. I should kill you right here."

"You cannot."

"You have forgotten where you are, Captain," sneered Herriot. "This is the Vatican, not Italy. I am the Swiss Guard Commander. I can do whatever I please with you."

"Your Pope will never forgive you."

"*My* Pope will never know what happened to you. You'll just be another dead Nazi caught in the ambush."

Möller's face drained of all color.

Herriot smiled. He pulled back the weapon and released the hammer carefully while aiming in the air. He holstered his weapon.

"That's the reaction I was waiting for. You are an SS man, yes?"

Möller straightened his shoulders with pride. *"Ja!"*

Herriot glanced at Saunders who looked skyward and began whistling tunelessly.

Herriot took a step forward and short punched Möller in the chin. His head snapped back and he took a faltering step and sat down hard on his butt.

Saunders looked down at the Nazi, then at Herriot with an incredulous expression. "Oh, dear, what happened to the poor man? Did he fall down?"

Herriot shook his head and laughed. "Let's take them to the cells, shall we?"

"Oh, aye. Let's."

Neither man offered a hand to Möller as he got to his feet slowly and unsteadily.

Chapter 35

Nazi Uranium Facility's entrance
14 November, 1012 Hours

The German sentry stepped through the personnel door. Perhaps to get some fresh air. Whatever it was he wanted to do, it was the last thing he ever did. He turned his head to the right. His eyes about bugged out at the sight of Americans right at his feet.

He tried to grab for a whistle that was attached to his uniform tunic by a long silver chain.

Cross fired his Thompson and a single .45 caliber slug punched through the man's forehead, exiting in a horrible mess out the back, through the helmet. The sentry fell over backward like a chopped pine. The remnants of his head, and his shoulders conveniently blocked the door, keeping it open.

Dr. Bauer took one look at the gore in front of him and collapsed in a dead faint.

Cross jumped up and ran to the personnel door. The squad ran behind him.

A shadow thrown from the lights inside crossed the ground in front of the door from left to right. Cross knew someone was taking a position on the right of the door, which was hinged on the left. Cross stayed perfectly still.

The barrel of an MP40 appeared, aimed at the trucks.

Cross leaned forward and fired another single shot. A thud came from inside.

Cross pulled back and glanced over his shoulder at Dunn.

Dunn waved for him to back up. He had the better angle. As soon as his friend moved out of the way, Dunn fired a long burst through the door.

Cross leaned into the doorway and peeked behind the door through the gap on the hinge side. Seeing no one there, or on the other side, he darted through the door to the right. He dove to the floor and raised his weapon, swinging it from side to side as he looked for targets to acquire. Seeing none in the gigantic space, he was at the same time shocked and relieved.

"Get inside!" he shouted.

Martelli was first. He ran around the door to the left and knelt, taking up a firing position. The rest of the squad entered, each man going the opposite way from the one his predecessor took.

Dunn ran straight to the door. Colonel Mason followed. Newman's and Porter's squads came next. Dunn bypassed the German doctor, who was lying on his back. His eyes were closed, but he was breathing. He stopped long enough to catch Porter's eye. He gave him some hand signals for Porter to leave a man with the doctor, and to get him awake, and inside the facility to join Dunn. Porter acknowledged the complex signal.

Dunn started running again and reached the personnel door along with Newman.

"I'll go first," he told Newman, who nodded.

Dunn peeked in and was able to see his men, some to the right and some to the left. He combat ran through the door and took a knee next to Cross, who had risen to a kneeling position. From here, Dunn surveyed the facility. The main tunnel they'd just entered was the width of the dual hangar doors, thirty yards. It ran straight west under the mountain for at least a quarter of a mile, 440 yards, the same length as a high school track laid out in a straight line. Along the center line above the tunnel, bright lights were hung about every ten feet shedding brilliant light everywhere. On the floor, in the center was what would have been the main assembly line for the bombers. It was in essence a pair of rails raised above the floor about three feet.

A chain was between the rails and ran across support wheels. At the front end of the assembly line, which was about twenty-five yards from him, a machine was hooked to a sprocket whose purpose was to spin, pulling the chain forward. There would have to be a matching one at the opposite end to retrieve the chain. A pit formed of poured concrete lay underneath the rails so workers could stand below and work on the plane as it passed overhead. No planes or partial planes were on the line.

Along both sides of the tunnel, many German transport trucks were parked, their canvas tops in place. They faced the hangar doors. He did a quick count: a dozen, half on each side.

The walls were relatively smooth, but were rock, not concrete, except around the doors where an inset of concrete had been placed to frame the doors. Being a cave, it was cool, he figured around fifty degrees, a little warmer than it was outside in the rain and wind. The air was remarkably fresh. The Germans must have built some excellent fresh air tunnels fitted with heavy duty fans to pull in the fresh air and exhaust the stale air.

He rose slowly to his feet. It was then he saw the crumpled form of Dr. Gerber, the tall scientist. He was lying on his side a few feet away. Dunn ran over and checked for a pulse and found one. He rolled the man over gently and found a bloody knot on the right side of his head. Dunn surmised the second guard had figured Gerber was a plant and was helping someone try to enter the facility. Dunn thought the man had been lucky not to have been shot on the spot.

Gerber moaned and tried to sit up. Dunn spotted Schneider, the squad's resident expert in first aid. He waved the big man over. Schneider knelt beside the patient and started working on him, speaking soft comforting German words.

Newman's and Porter's squads were inside. Porter's men took a position just inside the door facing out for defense. Porter pulled the dead guard out of the doorway and closed the personnel door. He took a position behind the window, where he could see outside clearly.

Dunn jogged over to the lead truck on the left, keeping his eyes on the wall on his right. Bauer had said that side was where the offshoot rooms were located, three of them. A couple were enormous storerooms and the other was where smaller assembly parts were put together prior to being added to the aircraft on the main assembly line.

The uranium-235 was stored in the second room, which was where the workers were grinding the uranium into a fine metal powder. The first room was where other workers were packing the 105 mm shells with the lethal powder.

Dunn walked over to where Gerber, who was on his feet and looking better after Schneider's help, and Bauer were standing. Schneider was packing away his first aid kit.

To both men he directed a question. "Where do the workers come from?"

Schneider stood and translated without being asked.

The scientists looked at their feet and wouldn't meet the Ranger's eyes.

He refused to let them off the hook that easy and pressed them several times to answer the question. The last time, he'd shouted at them, "Answer the damned question!"

Schneider did a good job translating with the same emotion as Dunn.

Finally, Bauer cooked up enough courage to look at Dunn. "The workers are all from Flossenbürg Concentration Camp. *Herr* Speer told us—he's the one who arranged it all—it's almost three hundred kilometers east of Frankfurt, near the Czech border."

Bauer looked away quickly, not wanting to talk about it anymore.

"You're using prisoners for labor?" Dunn hadn't heard about that before.

Bauer nodded reluctantly. "All over Europe. For years. We needed the manpower."

"What would have happened to these men after they finished their work?"

Bauer shrugged. "Those that survive might go back to Flossenbürg."

"Those that survive? What the hell does that mean?" Dunn's face turned red and the irises of his eyes flashed black.

"They *are* working with dangerous material after all, Sergeant Dunn," Gerber said. It came across quite smug, which pushed Dunn over the edge. He grabbed Gerber by the lapels of his white coat and yanked him closer. Gerber was smart enough not to fight back.

"You haven't protected the workers at all, have you? They're all going to get sick and die a horrible death. You disgust me."

"We have, too, protected the workers!" Bauer shouted. "As best as we could with protective gear and masks. But they are in close proximity to the uranium. We don't know how it will affect them."

Dunn shoved Gerber so hard the man stumbled backwards and fell down on his butt. Dunn frowned, and pointed at Schneider. The Ranger helped the German get up.

Dunn walked away shaking his head. He didn't have time for any more bullshit from the two Germans.

He easily spotted the openings for each of the rooms on the opposite side of the main tunnel. Each one had heavy metal double doors on them. All were closed. Of course.

The first order of business was to see what was in the trucks. Ordinarily, he would search for the German soldiers. He'd seen an entire squad enter the hangar doors earlier. However, Bauer had told him exactly where that squad was located, as well as that of the other squad already inside. At the moment, they did not present a problem.

He ran behind the first truck in line and pulled back the canvas flap, exposing the cargo area.

"Shit!" He slapped the canvas closed as if it had burned him. He jumped back several feet.

Colonel Mason, who had been standing close to Cross while Dunn had run off to explore, had been watching Dunn carefully. He tapped Cross gently on the left arm. Cross turned toward him.

"Yes, sir?"

"I think Sergeant Dunn has found something. I should go check it out with my Geiger counter."

Mason had the forethought to bring along the army's version of the radiation detector, the Model 247A, made by the Victoreen

Instrument Company specifically for the military. It was a fourteen pound gadget that naturally came in one color: a baked-on green enamel. The dial showing the quantity of radiation present was on the top front of the device. It was surrounded by a red enamel seal. The dial had three areas going from left to right: green, yellow, and red. The handle was attached to the back of the unit, but rose up and over toward the front, reaching almost to the dial itself. Calibrating knobs were set under the handle.

"Okay, sir. Do you need some help with it?"

"Could you help me by lifting it out of my pack?"

"Ayup."

Cross moved behind the doctor and unhooked the flap covering the main part of the backpack. He reached in with both hands and got a good grip on the handle. He lifted it out carefully and set it on the floor. He closed the pack's flap, but left it unhooked.

He picked up the device by the handle, but got his other hand underneath so he could pass it to Mason in a way that the doctor could easily grasp the handle.

Mason accepted the machine and turned it on, pointing it toward the truck Dunn had hopped away from. The device took a minute to warm up. When it was operational, the dial's needle moved slightly to the right. The device clicked slowly, sounding like a metronome set for a slow song.

"Is something there?" Cross asked, nervously.

"Just a tiny reaction, but that is probably because we're some distance from that truck. You stay here, please."

"Yes, sir."

Mason strode quickly toward the truck, his head down as he watched the dial and listened to the clicks. By the time he was ten feet from the vehicle, the dial had moved farther to the right, but fortunately stayed in the green zone. The clicking had sped up, but was still relatively slow. He joined Dunn at about five feet from the back of the truck. The dial moved again, but stayed in the center of the green zone.

"We're okay out here, Sergeant Dunn."

Dunn looked relieved. "So I don't need to check my film badge?"

"No. I'll use the counter first at the doorways when they are opened. That'll give us a pretty good idea of what's in store for us, and whether we can enter at all."

"Okay. I'm sure glad you're here with us, sir."

Mason gave Dunn a little smile. "Me, too."

RONN MUNSTERMAN

Chapter 36

Main tunnel
Nazi Uranium Facility
14 November, 1015 Hours

Dunn stared at all the trucks. Some or all were loaded with the lethal artillery shells. Mason was beside him.

"Come on, sir," the Ranger said.

He took off running toward Cross, signaling to get his squad and Newman's ready to go. Mason ran awkwardly alongside Dunn carrying the Geiger counter in both hands.

By the time he reached his squad, everyone was on their feet, including Newman's squad.

Dunn motioned for the two squads to gather around in front of him. Dunn reviewed the plan of attack quickly, reminding everyone not to take any chances with the uranium. He told them it was time to get Colonel Mason's special gear out and put it on, which they did quickly. Colonel Mason had arranged for full protective gear, which included a portion that pulled up over the head, leaving the face uncovered. The whole thing was the army's olive drab color. It even had the American flag sewn on the right shoulder like the Rangers' combat uniform. Next was a rebreather style mask that had a variety of material inside the dual filters that stuck out at an angle from each man's face. The eye covers were clear Plexiglas. Dunn had been insistent on that. He didn't want his men's ability to see clearly interfered with. Since the masks' purpose was to keep the men from breathing in the uranium powder, the nose filters were sufficient. Last were protective gloves that were thin enough for the men to work their weapons. They had removed their equipment belts and packs, and put them back on over the protective clothing.

The men were properly clothed and had their masks on, and their helmets back in place.

Dunn looked at them and had to fight back a laugh. The masks and helmets gave them a macabre look, as if they were skeletons instead of men.

"One last reminder, men: do not shoot the workers unless they are armed and aim a weapon at you. German soldiers are the priority. Keep your distance from them. We don't want to devolve into hand-to-hand combat. It takes too long and could increase our risk of getting exposed to the uranium." Dunn's voice was muffled by his own double-filter mask.

Dunn told Porter to stand guard at the hangar doors with his squad.

He gave the order to form each squad into two lines about ten feet apart. He was first in his squad and Newman in his. He nodded at Newman. The squads advanced toward the door behind which the shells were being packed. It was located about ten yards past the end of the last truck on the right side. He led his squad straight toward the left side of the doors. When he got there he examined them. They appeared to be heavy and thick, and covered with one inch diameter rivets to hold it all together.

Dunn motioned for Mason to step up next to him.

Mason flipped on the device. He'd turned it off to conserve battery power. After it powered up, the dial jumped to the right, but stayed in the green.

"We're okay, right here."

Newman was in front of the right door. There was a large lever, perhaps a foot long, like something you might find on a bank vault door. Dunn's squad changed positions so they had unobstructed fire lanes toward the place where the two doors would separate as the right door was opened.

Newman glanced at Dunn, who nodded.

Newman pushed down on the lever. It moved smoothly and when he glanced over at Dunn, Newman's eyes wore an expression of surprise mixed with relief. Dunn nodded at him encouragingly. The three hinges supporting the door, which were each a foot long, were on the outside which meant the door would swing open outwardly.

Newman pulled on the handle, but the door didn't budge. Thinking he'd felt relief too soon, he slung his Thompson over his right shoulder, and put both hands on the handle. He leaned backward to use his body weight as an extra helper. He pulled. The door began to move. He backpedaled in small stutter-steps, making sure to keep a good grip on the handle, and his body leaning backward. He continued pulling until a nice three-foot gap was there for Dunn's squad. The door turned out to be six inches thick.

Colonel Mason aimed the Geiger counter inside. The needle hopped all the way into the yellow zone.

"It's more dangerous in that room, Sergeant. Don't touch anything in there."

Dunn nodded.

What Dunn saw first was disheartening and frightening at the same time. About forty prisoners were busy using equipment along a series of low and long workbenches. As Bauer had told him, all were wearing protective jumpsuits with a head cover, masks and gloves. He realized that the Germans would have known that the workers wouldn't have been able to finish one day's worth of work without the protective gear. They would have become deathly ill from radiation poisoning, probably within hours. And therefore useless to the Nazis.

Small wood crates sat on the benches. One man would dip a small metal cup into the crate and then pour powder inside the cone shape of the artillery projectile, which was already seated in the huge 105 mm brass shell. The next man would pick up the round and carefully set it in front of himself. He picked up a small cone-shaped fuse and gently screwed it into place. He used some sort of rubber gripping device to tighten the fuse completely. Next he picked up the completed round, and put it inside a large crate behind him. Each crate was designed to hold fifty rounds, packed with straw to keep them secure.

"God almighty," Dunn muttered to himself.

Where were the guards? This puzzled Dunn. He edged closer and peered around the door that was still closed. There they were. Ten German soldiers were on the left, lined up facing the men working on the shells. They wore the same protective gear as the workers. They had their MP40s' slings over their right shoulders and the weapon at the ready at waist height, aimed at the men working. Dunn questioned the wisdom of that and began to worry about a firefight inside this particular room. A single errant shot could possibly kill everyone in the room, including the Americans.

He motioned for Newman to close the door.

Newman raised his eyebrows, but complied. One of his men jumped in beside him to help push the heavy door closed. As the door neared the closed position, Newman and his man leaned backward to slow the door, so it wouldn't make a bang. It crept back into the closed position and Newman lifted the handle gently until it *snicked.*

"What's up, Sarge," Newman asked.

"Change of plans already. We can't go in there and start shooting. Might set off one of those doctored rounds. Too dangerous."

"We have to entice the guards to come out of there. All of them," Dunn said to Cross.

"Want to use one of the German doctors? Maybe they could talk the soldiers into coming out here."

"I think they might just send one guy to see what the hell the doctor wants. We're going to have to be the bait. It'll all depend on what their orders are and how disciplined they are. I understand why they didn't come running when we shot those other guards. Sounds can't go through that steel door."

Cross glanced at the door and nodded. "Ayup, makes sense. So what's next?"

Dunn looked around quickly. He pointed at the last truck in the line not too far away.

"Go see if maybe that truck is empty. If it is, get in and drive it over here. Keep it about ten feet from the door with the nose stopped in the center of the two doors."

"Will do."

Cross ran over to the rear of the last truck and pulled back the canvas. He peeked inside and let go of the canvas. Looking at an expectant Dunn, he gave a thumbs up.

Dunn nodded. Good, he thought, as he waved at Cross to go ahead.

Cross ran around to the driver's side and climbed aboard. Moments later, the deep rumble of the engine started up. Cross backed it up a few feet to get more clearance from the rear of the truck in front. He turned the wheel sharply to the right and drove around in a half circle. Soon he had guided the truck into the exact spot Dunn wanted. He shut off the engine and hopped out.

Dunn walked over to his sniper. "Hey, Jonesy, I need you under that truck with your Colt .45. I think the slower muzzle velocity will keep us out of trouble." Dunn withdrew his own Colt and handed it over. "In fact, take mine, too. That'll give you fourteen, plus you can put two more in the chambers. If I can't draw all ten of the soldiers out here, you take out any who stay inside. I'd say body shots to help cut down the chance of a bullet having too much energy left and go bouncing around in there with all those shells. Avoid shots to the helmet."

Jonesy took the weapon. He immediately checked that the safety was on, and racked the slide to seat a round. He ejected the magazine and swapped it for a full one on his belt. The weapon had eight rounds. He repeated the process for his own .45.

"All set, Sarge."

Jonesy moved away from the squad and crawled underneath the truck, positioning himself to the right of the front right tire, which would become his cover. Dunn gave instructions to the men. Newman would open the same door and that would start the engagement. Or so Dunn hoped.

The two squads got into position. Dunn asked Colonel Mason to take the two German doctors to the far side of the assembly line and get out of sight.

Dunn waited until everyone was in position, and nodded again to Newman. Since he'd done it before, he knew how much force was needed, and it was easy for the squad leader to swing the door all the way open until it was flush against the stone wall. He took up his position, which was behind the rear of the truck parked in front of the door. His men were lined up behind him, ready to jump out from behind the truck into angled clear lines of fire. Dunn's men were located behind the assembly line structure, kneeling and ready to fire.

Dunn, who had been standing to the left of the opening turned to his right and walked out half way toward the truck. He double checked everyone.

He took a deep breath.

And stepped toward the open doorway.

Chapter 37

Main tunnel
Nazi Uranium Facility
14 November, 1024 Hours

Dunn checked on the guards. They were intently watching the workers, perhaps out of some sort of fear of something going wrong and dying a terrifying death. Assuming they'd even been told everything about it.

He raised his Thompson and aimed it at the empty space deeper in the tunnel. He fired two bursts of three rounds while watching the guards for their reactions. To their credit, all of them snapped their heads around and spotted Dunn. Their bodies rotated and some stepped forward to get a clear shot. Dunn bolted to the safety behind the left hand door. MP40 rounds from several weapons slammed into the sheet metal of the truck. He continued running around the front of the truck and headed for the safety of the assembly line with his men. Sounds of running boot falls came from inside the room.

The leader of the German squad made a beeline for the door. All but three of his men followed. He aimed to his left so he would arrive to that side of the opening, which would give him a better angle to see where the American soldier had gone. He didn't take time to try figuring out *why* there was an American soldier in a top secret German installation. All that mattered was the fact that he *was* there.

He leaned against the stone wall on the inside of the room. He peered out in the direction the enemy had run. He waved at one of his men and pointed toward the front of the truck. That soldier bent down and ran quickly through the door.

Newman, whose weapon was up and ready, didn't fire when the first German popped through the door. The man was looking in one direction: the front of the truck. He reached the bumper and knelt. He peeked around the radiator grill and tried to spot the American.

Jonesy waited.

Dunn saw the German at the front of the truck. He stood and fired a two-shot burst. The German ducked back to safety. He missed the soldier, but the man found him when he resumed his peeking position. The German fired and Dunn ducked and ran deeper into the tunnel, bullets whining behind him, ricocheting off the assembly line rails.

The German squad leader had seen enough. He waved at the men near him and pointed. He charged through the door first. He ran alongside the door, and the stone wall going deeper as Dunn had been seen doing.

Newman and Cross continued to wait. This was the crucial moment. Would all or most of the enemy soldiers come out?

That answer came quickly as five more Germans sprinted through the open door, following their leader along the wall.

Newman fired first, followed by his men. A couple of the trailing Germans pitched over face first onto the floor and lay unmoving.

Cross fired at the squad leader who was several yards ahead of everyone else. The man ducked and spun around firing blindly in Cross's general direction.

Dunn fired a burst that took the leader in the chest. It drove him into the wall where he slid slowly down to the floor, a messy red streak painting itself on the wall.

The rest of Dunn's squad fired bursts at the remaining Germans, who fell after being struck by at least a dozen rounds each.

Jonesy aimed for the farthest target and squeezed off one round. It struck the German in the right side of the chest and went through his right lung, his heart and lodged in the humerus bone in his upper left arm. He fell straight down. The other two guards dropped to the floor. There was no place for cover. Because the MP40 had a long magazine, the two men had to position their heads about a foot off the ground.

That presented a huge target for Jonesy. He aimed at the closer man's throat, the small indentation at the base. He fired. The round tore through the man's throat, followed a line down his chest, cutting the aorta in half. The bullet spent its energy against the first thoracic disc, slicing the spinal cord.

The remaining soldier got off a long burst that struck the wheel just to Jonesy's left.

Jonesy stayed put and sighted on the last man. The man appeared to panic and started to get up to run for cover.

Jonesy fired.

The round struck the soldier in the center of his left thigh and he screamed and fell down, facing toward Jonesy's right. Jonesy fired once more. This time the bullet entered the enemy's right side, plowed through the right lung, pierced the main heart muscle and stopped against the ribcage.

Jonesy smiled to himself. He hadn't needed Dunn's Colt after all. He scooted backwards until he was clear of the left side of the truck. He rose carefully to his feet, looking down into the tunnel. He saw all seven of the Germans who had run out of the room were down. "Excellent," he muttered to himself.

Dunn climbed over the assembly line and waved at Jonesy.

Newman moved to the open door and peeked in.

All of the workers had stopped moving and were staring at him. He quickly scanned them, but none were carrying any kind of weapons. He stepped inside the room after first checking along the right and left interior walls to be sure no Germans were lying in wait for a careless American.

He turned his body so the workers could see the American flag on his right shoulder. Some of them waved and a few others solemnly gave him a salute. He stood at attention and returned a sharp salute. They started walking toward him. Dunn had given him specific instructions about this. He held up his hand in the universal stop sign. The men appeared confused, so he gestured that they should sit down where they were.

A few picked up on his meaning and they turned to speak to the others. Soon, all were seated, some cross legged, others stretched out and lay down on their sides or backs.

Dunn whistled and his squad, and Newman's all ran to join him. Colonel Mason brought Gerber and Bauer along with him.

"Great job, everyone."

Jonesy stepped forward and handed Dunn his Colt .45. Dunn noticed it felt loaded by its weight. He raised an eyebrow. "Didn't need it, huh?"

Jonesy grinned and shook his head. "Four shots."

"Wow, damn, Jonesy. You've impressed me."

"My dream every day, Sarge."

The group burst into laughter.

Dunn shook his head. He held up his hands. "Knock it off, you knuckleheads. We're not done here."

A few "Okay, Sarge" replies came from the group.

"Next on the list is the grinding area. They might still be at it and we want to get the workers out of here. We'll start out the same way. Opening the door slowly and taking a look to see what we're up against. The other German squad is in that room, so we'll have to put them down. This time, there are going to be two sets of doors. According to Dr. Bauer, the second set will be about twenty-five yards down the tunnel.

"Our approach to this one is different. We can fire into the room if needed, because the uranium and the powder are not explosive. We'll try to limit civilian casualties, but I'm afraid that's a secondary concern. The guards must go down and we must have control of the whole facility. Let's go."

Cross moved the squad to the left of the door so they stretched out along the wall, while Newman's second in command placed his squad to the right.

Dunn stood just to the left of the door. Newman pressed the door handle down and pulled. A crack appeared and Dunn tried to look in. Light came through, but he needed more space.

RONN MUNSTERMAN

Newman kept tugging the door open. Dunn looked again. The tunnel was there just as Bauer had said. It was dimly lit, with only a few lights strung across the ceiling.

When Newman got the door open about three feet, he stopped its motion. Dunn ran through the door and his squad followed. He led them down the right side of the tunnel. Newman and his men came next going down the left side running to catch up with Dunn. In no time, the squads made it to the next set of heavy metal doors.

Dunn examined the doors. At first they appeared to be the same as the others, but he found a rectangular recess at eye level. It looked exactly like the sliding hatch he'd seen in movies about Chicago's speakeasies. Because he was on the right this time, he put his hand on the handle and pushed down. He was half surprised when it moved. He pulled until the door was open about an inch. A whirring sound came from inside. He pointed at Schneider, who was third in line.

Schneider took his place on the handle, while Dunn slid to the left so he could look in the room. After the big man pulled the door open another foot, Dunn peered inside. The room was enormous. The ceiling was about thirty feet high. Lights hung on long wires. On the left side stacked about six feet high were crates. Dunn assumed those were the raw uranium. On the opposite side were ten workers, each manning a grinding machine. The men fed chunks of the uranium into a hopper, much like a wood chipper. Fine dust spewed out from the other side into small wooden crates. Like the men in the packing room, the workers wore protective gear.

The German guards stood against the far wall, about fifty feet away. It seemed they wanted to be as far from the powder as possible. Like the other guards, they wore masks and protective equipment. Their eyes were on the workers.

It would be a simple ambush, but it would carry some risk.

Chapter 38

Outside the uranium grinding room
Nazi Uranium Facility
14 November, 1031 Hours

Dunn nodded to Schneider and held up two fingers, indicating to open the door another two feet. He checked on the guards. Still looking the wrong way. To Newman, he signaled ten and that the enemy soldiers were straight ahead fifty feet. Newman mouthed 'okay.' Next Dunn signaled he wanted five of Newman's men to breech the door and hit the floor firing. The rest of the squad would wait until Schneider pulled the door open another few feet. Dunn's squad would still be behind the cover of the door and join in after a few seconds, if it wasn't already all over.

Dunn peered into the room again. To his shock, one of the Germans was walking toward the door, his head tilted in the sign of someone who's curious about something not being right. That something, of course, was the open door. He was about half way across the room.

Well shit, Dunn thought. He was wishing he'd decided on the Sten with its built in suppressor. He leaned flat against the left door, motioning to Newman to back off. He held up a finger, and made two fingers walk across a palm.

Newman nodded.

He handed Newman his Thompson and pulled out his combat knife with his right hand. Over the grinding machines, he was finally able to make out the sounds of the German's boots. He took a deep breath and let it out slowly.

The boots were just a few feet away.

A left boot appeared in the opening.

Dunn readied his left hand.

The German's masked face and helmet appeared just a couple of feet from Dunn's face. The masked face turned to Dunn.

The soldier was handicapped because he carried his weapon right handed. The only way to shoot Dunn was to step to the left and rotate.

Dunn's left hand flicked out like a striking snake and grabbed the front of the soldier's protective clothing. He yanked the man into the side of the closed door. At the same time, he drove his knife into the solar plexus with an upward thrust. He twisted the knife as he'd been trained. He let go of the knife and grabbed the soldier's clothing with his right hand. He pulled the man the rest of the way through the door and dragged him a few feet. Dropping the dead soldier, he wiped his bloody hand on the man's clothing.

Kneeling, Dunn peeked around the corner of the door. Half of the Germans were running toward him. He reached back with a hand and Newman, anticipating Dunn's needs, slapped the Thompson into it. Dunn leaned out just enough to take aim.

Newman leaned over Dunn.

Dunn fired.

Newman fired.

Together they raked .45 caliber slugs across the running enemy soldiers. All five went down.

Dunn and Newman altered their aim to the four remaining soldiers, who had dropped prone and fired.

Dunn and Newman ducked back as 9mm rounds peppered the heavy metal doors. A few zinged through the opening and back up the tunnel.

Dunn dropped prone and inched out. He fired a short burst, striking one of the soldiers on the right.

The workers had all dropped what they were doing and scattered to the far side of the room away from the Germans. They hit the floor and covered their heads with their hands.

Newman leaned back into the line of fire and squeezed off a long burst.

Schneider switched his Thompson to his left hand and fired from behind the right door. Martelli dropped to a knee and maneuvered into a shooting position in front of Schneider. He fired.

Dunn and Newman changed magazines and resumed firing.

The three Germans took a large number of rounds and ceased firing. And living.

Newman stepped back. Dunn jumped to his feet.

He leaned in and double checked the enemy soldiers. They seemed dead. Dunn pulled back. He tapped Newman, Schneider, and Martelli on their shoulders. He pointed with two fingers for Martelli and Schneider to go in to the left, while Newman and he went right.

He raised three fingers and did a countdown.

He dashed through the door and hit the floor. Newman was right behind him. Schneider and Martelli flopped down on the left.

None of the Germans reacted. Dunn and Newman scrambled to their feet and ran across the room toward the Germans, making sure not to cross in front of Schneider's and Martelli's line of fire. Dunn reached the enemy soldiers first and he checked each one quickly. He stood up and gave the 'all clear' signal.

He tapped Newman and pointed toward the door. The two ran across and exited the room. Schneider and Martelli had already jumped up and stepped outside.

"Colonel Mason?"

Mason had been at the tail end of Dunn's squad. He joined Dunn. Without being asked, he aimed the Geiger counter inside the room. He'd turned it on during the firefight.

The needle jumped into the yellow zone.

"As I expected. It's a lot hotter than the other room. We can't spend much time in there. No more than five minutes."

"What about those prisoners? They have protective gear on."

Mason shook his head sadly. "If they don't get treatment, they'll probably die within a couple of weeks."

Dunn looked over at the prisoners, who had risen to their feet and were staring at the door.

"But if they *did* get treatment they could survive?"

"Yes. Probably ninety percent of them, maybe more."

"What about the ones in the other room?"

"I'd guess the same for them."

"Oh, man."

Mason looked at Dunn with a new perspective. "Are you really thinking of trying to save those men?"

Dunn gave the colonel a grim look. There was pain in his eyes. "There's no other choice I can make, is there?"

"Oh, okay. I see." Mason hadn't expected to find so much compassion in a Ranger. A man who spent his days and nights killing human beings. "What we have to do is get those men outside in the rain with their gear on. They need to stand in the rain for two minutes. Then they need to move to another spot and remove the gear."

"Okay. I'll give you Goerdt, who can translate for you. I'll get some other men to help you corral them all. I assume we shouldn't touch them while they're wearing the gear?"

"You're correct. No touching. The clothing itself won't radiate, but you can't touch it because uranium particles are bound to be on it."

Dunn called for Goerdt to join them and gave him a quick rundown.

"Give me your explosives pack."

Goerdt wiggled out of his pack and handed it over. He slung his Thompson over his shoulder and walked a few feet inside the room. He raised a hand and waved at the prisoners to come toward him. They didn't hesitate.

Schneider pulled the door open the rest of the way.

Dunn ordered all of his men to stand against the left wall of the tunnel.

Goerdt held up a hand to stop the prisoners when they were a few feet away. He started to explain in German what they were going to do, but could tell right away they didn't seem to understand him.

"Sprechen Sie Deutsch?" he asked.

All he got were blank stares.

"Oh, boy," he muttered.

He waved at them and turned around walking out the door. He glanced over his shoulder. They were following meekly.

Colonel Mason joined Goerdt. He led them up the tunnel and toward the hangar doors.

Dunn gathered his men and they discussed briefly where to place the charges. They had two goals: seal the room, but also disperse much of the uranium so the room would become completely irradiated. That was just in case the Germans tried to excavate the uranium again.

Dunn sent Higgins and Barker to go get the explosives Porter and his men were carrying. He said to use the truck as it would fit inside the tunnel leading to the grinding room. While they were gone, Dunn sent the two squads inside and they began setting the charges. The charges inside would go first, and a couple of minutes later, the ones that would collapse the doorframe and the rocks around it would explode.

Dunn kept close track of the time.

Higgins and Barker arrived. Higgins had backed the truck the entire length of the tunnel.

The men finished their tasks and ran out of the room. Dunn check his watch as he ran along. Just over three minutes. He did a mental *whew* of relief. Not more than five minutes, Colonel Mason had directed.

He and Newman closed the door with an enormous clang and slammed the handle into its locked position. He got both squads crammed into the truck. With Higgins driving, they departed. When they entered the main tunnel, Dunn had Higgins stop.

Several of Newman's men clambered down and set charges to collapse the outer doorframe and rocks around it.

Once that was accomplished, they were off again toward the first room.

Chapter 39

Main tunnel
Nazi Uranium Facility
14 November, 1050 Hours

When Higgins stopped the truck in front of the first room, the one where the shells were being filled and armed, the two squads aboard untangled themselves and got out. Dunn reminded them all not to touch anything and to keep their masks and gear on. The men nodded, an odd movement with the masks on, and ran into the room.

Colonel Mason and Goerdt arrived with the ten workers from the other room.

"Colonel, if you'd stay with these men, I'll go get the others," Goerdt said.

"That's fine."

Goerdt ran inside the room and stopped near the workers, who for the entire time since the firefight, had been sitting on the floor. They all stared at the American Ranger.

"Sprechen Sie Deutsch?" he asked.

A small man in the middle of the pack raised his hand nervously.

Goerdt waved for the man to join him.

The worker rose unsteadily and walked over to Goerdt. He kept his eyes downcast.

In German, Goerdt said, "Everything will be all right. I need your help telling the men to come with me. We have to go outside in the rain to help wash the powder off of you. Do you understand all of this?"

"I do. Yes, I'll help."

"What's your name?"

"Arno."

"Okay, Arno, what language is it you all speak?"

"Czech."

Goerdt nodded. "Okay. Let's get the men going. It's important we do this quickly."

The man turned and rattled off something in Czech. One of the men closest to him asked a question.

Arno turned and repeated it. "What's going to happen to us?"

"You understand you've been exposed to something dangerous?"

"Yes."

"We want to take you with us back to England so doctors can treat you and keep you healthy."

"England?"

"It's your only chance."

Arno raised his eyes and met Goerdt's gaze.

"I understand." He turned and explained it to the men. They started talking at the same time. Goerdt held up his hand and shook his head.

"Come on, Arno. We have to go!"

Arno shushed the group and waved for them to follow.

Goerdt led the men into the main tunnel, where they gathered up the other ten. Goerdt guided them to the door and outside. He was relieved to see that it was raining pretty hard, and hoped it kept it up long enough. He ushered the men out into the rain, and told Arno what he wanted them to do, which was to simply stand in the rain with their gear on until he told them to take it all off. After two minutes, he moved the men to another spot, closer to the trucks and told Arno to have them get their protective gear and shoes off and throw them to the side. When that was done, to Arno he said, "Tell them to wash their faces and all exposed skin with the rain water."

The Czech passed on the instructions. Soon, fifty men were washing away, wearing only their striped prisoner uniforms.

Back inside the facility, Dunn called for Porter to come join him.

"Yeah, Sarge? Everything go okay? Everybody all right?" Porter knew he and his men had an important job, but he couldn't help feeling left out of the main action. Not that he would ever let the incredible Tom Dunn know that.

"It did. And everybody's okay, no casualties."

"That's swell, Sarge."

Dunn put a hand on Porter's shoulder and stared at him intently. "I know you're disappointed to have been put on guard duty. Just wanted to say thank you."

Porter was surprised, but shrugged, hoping he'd hidden his surprise. "Whatever you need done, Sarge."

"Yep. I know. But I still appreciate it. So, here's what I need. Leave a couple of your men at the door. Have the rest check all of these trucks. The ones that are loaded with crates, put one satchel of explosives in each one. Right on top of the nearest crate. Don't touch the crates. We'll use the extra oomph of the shells to maybe bring this whole place down. The explosives are in the truck we used."

Porter's face lit up at the chance for his men to contribute. "Will do, Sarge!" He started toward the hangar doors.

Dunn stopped him. "Hey, Porter!"

Porter swung around.

"Tell you what, I'll take over at the door in a couple of minutes. Use all your guys."

Porter smiled. "Thanks, Sarge."

Dunn walked over to the door to the first room and glanced inside. Newman's, and his, men were busy laying charges around the crates of shells. Martelli and Higgins were placing some around the door, on the inside of the room. Dunn shook his head. This was going to be one of the biggest explosions they'd ever set off, not counting the six thousand pound bomb they used to destroy Hitler's Dam and the nuclear blast at the Nazis' atomic bomb lab.

Colonel Mason was standing in the center of the room looking down at his Geiger counter, which he'd set on the floor facing the small crates of uranium stacked against the left wall. He had a notepad out and was writing in it.

"Hey, Doc!"

Mason looked up.

"Everything all right?"

"Yes. I'm just recording some readings. We're still in the green here."

Dunn gave him a thumbs up and left the room. Porter's men ran past him about half way to the hangar doors. Even with their masks on, he could see excitement in their eyes. He smiled to himself.

When he got to the door he looked out and saw the amazing sight of a bunch of grown men washing themselves off in the cold rain.

Goerdt told Arno that it was time to stop and to go back inside to try and warm up. They led the group past Dunn, who nodded at the men. Goerdt led the men to the left and invited them to sit down.

He stepped over to Dunn.

"Good job, Rob."

"Thanks."

"Did you fill them in?"

"Yep. Can't tell for sure, but they seemed excited by the news of going to England."

"I better get on the radio. One C-54 is not enough. Can you track down Bob?"

"Sure."

Dunn walked away from the personnel door toward the first room.

He didn't hear a car drive up and stop near the entrance.

The Nazi Minister of Armaments, Albert Speer, stepped inside the facility and stopped abruptly. Not fifty feet away he saw an American. Or at least it appeared to be one, based on the helmet and the Thompson submachine gun. The apparition was wearing protective gear and a breathing mask. How did they know about the uranium? That was the only explanation for the specialized gear. To his left he saw all of his workers sitting on the floor without their protective gear on. They looked to be soaking wet. Someone had taken the precaution of washing the men to get the uranium powder off their gear. What was happening?

Who was this soldier? He had to be a Commando, or in this case, an American Ranger! Fury erupted from him. Rangers had made his life a living hell. They'd stopped the magnetic pulse weapon program, stolen V2 rocket engines from under his nose, stolen untold millions of Reichmarks worth of gold and jewels from Himmler's doomed Arctic expedition, and completely destroyed Hitler's Dam and the power station attached to it. Damn them all! "You bastards!" he shouted in German, forgetting that he was unarmed.

Dunn glanced over at the noise at the front door. He was surprised to see Albert Speer standing there all by himself. Had the idiot returned to check on the workers' progress?

Dunn turned to face the Minister and raised his Thompson. He expected Speer to raise his hands in surrender, but was surprised when the man spun around and ran out the personnel door, slamming it closed behind him.

"Oh, for . . . damn it!"

Dunn took off at a run. By the time he reached the door, Speer's car was speeding away, already almost to the main road back to Frankfurt. It was at least five hundred yards away. No possibility of a shot with a Thompson. It would have been easy for Jonesy and his Springfield. A pissed off Dunn lowered his weapon and watched as the car disappeared in the gloom.

Cross ran outside to join him.

"What happened?"

"Oh, I had that son of a bitch Speer in my sights and let him get away. I wanted to capture him. I think he understood that, and knew I wouldn't actually shoot him. Damn it anyhow! That would have been so damn fantastic. What a catch he'd have been."

Cross patted Dunn on the back. "Ayup, that is a shame. I don't know how we'll ever live this failure down. You know, maybe it is time for me to move on and have my own squad. Who knows, maybe we'll catch Speer."

Dunn looked at his friend like he was about to punch his lights out. "Don't overdo it, chum."

Cross raised his hands slightly with the palms up and gave Dunn a "who me?" expression.

Dunn punched Cross in the arm.

"Asshole."

"Ayup. So are you going to tell Colonel Kenton? Or would you rather I took the heat?"

"You're all heart, Dave."

"Ayup. Just tryin' to be helpful is all, my friend."

Dunn sighed. "Yeah, and with friends like you . . ."

Cross chuckled.

The two best friends walked back inside to wrap up everything needed to blow up the uranium and seal it forever under thousands of tons of rocks.

And escape.

Chapter 40

Main tunnel
Nazi Uranium Facility
14 November, 1112 Hours

Of the dozen trucks in the facility, four were empty. Dunn had Higgins check the fuel gauges in those four. Thanks to German planning and efficiency, they were all nearly full. He'd need them to transport the workers to the airfield. He'd been able to contact Captain Adams, who probably used General Hopkins' name to get a second C-54 ordered to go with the one Dunn already had requisitioned. It would take the planes two hours to get there. They'd be escorted by at least one flight of four P-51 Mustangs. Dunn didn't know if it would be Captain Norman Miller again. Miller had flown escort for Dunn a few times, most recently on the dam raid.

Dunn checked his watch. The first charges would go off in five minutes. The men were outside, loaded on the trucks. They'd discarded their protective gear and the masks just outside the facility. He took one more look around, and left through the personnel door, which he pulled shut behind him. He took a couple of steps and turned to look at what he'd just done. Closing the tiny door when 1,500 pounds of plastic explosives and who knew how much in artillery shells was going to explode. He laughed out loud as he ran to the lead truck, which Higgins was driving. He climbed into the cab.

"Hit it, Chuck!"

Higgins goosed the gas pedal and the truck leaped forward. At the intersection with the main road, he slowed and turned right. The convoy of seven trucks was strung out over almost a hundred yards.

"Okay, stop here."

Higgins stopped the truck, not bothering to pull off the road.

Dunn turned to face the facility and raised his watch. One minute. He opened the door and stepped outside in the rain. He glanced to his right and grinned. His men in all three trucks had rolled up the canvas on the right side so they could watch the fireworks.

Cross leaned out and waved at him. "Hey, all we need is popcorn!"

Dunn chuckled.

Dunn started a countdown, "Okay, guys. Ten . . . nine . . ."

At zero, a disappointing *whump* came from the facility.

He stared at the hangar doors.

Another, slightly louder *whump* came.

That was the second set in the grinding room. A third explosion went off in the artillery shell preparation room. Dunn felt that one through his boots.

A fourth massive explosion was the plastic explosives in the loaded trucks.

A deep rumbling sound emanated from the facility.

The overpressure hit the hangar doors. They flew out from underneath the entrance's overhang and clanged and clattered along the roadway leading to the facility, turning end over end.

Dunn heard someone, possibly Jonesy, say, "Wow!"

Smoke bellowed out through the entrance, obscuring all view of it. Not even the rain could dampen the clouds of roiling smoke.

A deafening crack shot through the air. Dunn felt his chest vibrate. It seemed that the ground shook beneath him and he grabbed onto the truck for support.

The hillside over the entrance and main tunnel vibrated side to side.

Then it collapsed in on itself. The plume of dust and smoke soared into the rainy air.

"Holy shit!" Dunn shouted.

He heard cheering. He leaned out and saw that the workers had also raised their canvas. They were hollering in Czech and were shaking their fists at the facility's remains.

Dunn nodded to himself. A good day. Stopped the Nazis and saved fifty men from an agonizing death. Or at least he hoped so.

He took one last look and climbed in the truck.

"Go, Chuck."

It was six miles to the airfield.

He hoped Speer hadn't stopped and called someone.

"There's the airfield, Sarge," Higgins said.

Dunn opened his eyes. He'd dozed off for a few minutes. They'd crested a hill. The airfield sat below them.

"Stop up here."

As Higgins stopped the truck, Dunn lifted his binoculars.

When the Allies had reached air supremacy by destroying much of the Luftwaffe and its ability to defend Germany, the Germans had reacted by combining squadrons and abandoning airfields all over Europe. They dotted the landscape like dandelions did the lawn in the spring. Alan Finch, while working for MI5, had noticed this and come up with the idea of using these airfields as landing zones for Commandos and Rangers, as well as their escape routes. Dunn had learned from the man's genius and had successfully used the idea himself several times.

However, for the first time, it appeared there might be a problem with using the airfield.

Three fighters were parked on the tarmac. He thought they were Me-109s.

Did Speer make contact and request help? Or was this just bad luck? A coincidence?

"Oh, hell."

"What is it, Sarge?"

"German fighters at the airfield."

"What do we do?"

Dunn checked his watch. "Well, it's still about an hour and a half before our rides show up."

Dunn shifted the focus of his glasses from the planes to the main building. It looked like some lights were on.

He lowered the glasses and studied the road. It went downhill fairly straight, and toward the airfield. At the bottom of the hill, it curved a little to the east and, in essence, went around the back side of the field, behind the buildings and the hangars.

An idea occurred to him. "Hold it here, Chuck. Gonna let everyone know what we're gonna do."

"Sure thing, Sarge."

Dunn turned to the window in the back of the cab and called for Cross. When his friend put his face in the window, Dunn lifted his walkie-talkie to his lips and called for Newman and Porter. When they acknowledged him, he laid out what was in front of them and what they were going to do about it. He spoke loud enough for Cross and Higgins to hear. He gave each squad an assignment and after they acknowledged, he signed off.

He pointed downhill. "Off we go."

Higgins drove as fast as was safe on a wet downhill road. When he reached the bottom of the hill, he sped up some more. As they neared the airfield, He slowed to a crawl. The main road continued on southward, but there was a road leading to the airfield building, and hangars, of which there were six. The hangars were stretched out in a line going south from the building. He stopped the truck about fifty yards from the building.

Dunn eyed the back of it. There were no windows or doors on the east or south sides, the two he had a clear view of.

"Stay with the truck, Higgins."

"Right, Sarge."

Dunn opened the door and jumped down. He waved at Cross, who was peering out from underneath his truck's canvas. Dunn had placed the two German scientists in his truck, along with the doctor, Colonel Mason, so he instructed Cross to leave Schneider with the Germans and the doctor. Soon, Cross and the squad members started appearing around the right side of the vehicle. Newman and Porter and their squads disembarked from their vehicles. Two of Porter's men and two of Newman's were driving the trucks carrying the Czechs, and would stay in place.

As soon as the entire platoon was gathered, Dunn pointed to the north side of the building and nodded at Newman. Newman and his men ran bent over toward the northeast corner of the building, where they would wait for Dunn's word over the walkie-talkies.

Dunn checked that his men and Porter's were ready. Satisfied they were, he nodded to Cross, who had point for the advance to the building. Cross took off. Dunn took the second spot. His squad trailed him, followed by Porter and his remaining seven men.

Cross reached the southeast corner and stopped. He stared ahead in the gloom of the rainy and cloudy day. He could see the leftmost Messerschmitt, but not the other two. No one was moving around. He started up again, gliding along the side of the wooden structure. At the southwest corner, he stopped again and took a knee. Leaning forward, he peeked around the edge to the right. No one. He looked left down the line of hangars. Clear. He pulled back and turned to Dunn.

"No one in sight anywhere. They're bound to be in this building. There's a window on each side of the door about halfway from the corner to the door. The door doesn't have a window in it."

Dunn nodded and lifted his walkie-talkie. He spoke quietly to Newman, giving him the go ahead to come around the front.

Cross and Dunn waited until Dunn's walkie-talkie clicked once. Newman was in place.

Dunn patted Cross on the back. He clicked his radio once for Newman.

Cross stayed low and advanced toward the door. Newman popped around the other corner and headed toward him.

Dunn and Cross had discussed whether to peek through a window and decided it would be worth it if they could get the interior's layout and perhaps where the enemy was located. Cross reached the window and stopped. Everyone else halted, including Newman.

He removed his helmet and the rain got his face and hair wet in seconds. He slowly lifted his head at the right corner of the window. He situated himself so only his left eye would be visible. The interior was just one large room the size of the building. Some desks were spread around and a table sat in the center.

He ducked down slowly, not wanting to catch someone's attention by a blur of unexpected motion.

He wiped a hand over his head and face, clearing off the beads of water. He shook his hand to flip the water away. He plopped his helmet back on and turned to Dunn.

He spoke in a low voice. "Six men around a table in the center of the room. They're drinking coffee and playing cards. Three pilots. Three maintenance guys, I would guess. No one else in sight. One large room. The way the table is set up, only one guy is facing the door.

"Could just take 'em out with a grenade, unless you're worried about the noise."

"We are pretty far from anywhere." Dunn thought it over. A grenade would kill or wound all of the Germans. They could clean up by shooting anyone left alive, or use a knife. In some ways, Dunn didn't care one way or the other. Enemy combatants had ceased being people to him a long time ago. However, these were pilots and they might have information useful to the Air Corps planners.

He sighed.

Cross raised an eyebrow and whispered, "What? You want to capture them?"

Dunn suppressed a chuckle. How well his friend knew him if he could discern a decision by a sigh. He wondered if he was that easy for Pamela to read. Probably easier for her.

"Yep."

"Okay."

Cross turned around and gave a signal to Newman, who replied in sign that he understood.

Cross advanced passing under the window. When he and Newman reached the stoop in front of the door, Cross stood and put his hand on the door knob, which was on the right. This meant the door would swing open outwardly to the left, blocking Newman.

Newman rose to his feet and moved to a position just off the stoop, facing the door, weapon raised.

Cross checked over his shoulder. Dunn nodded.

Cross turned the doorknob and threw open the door. It swung all the way on its hinges and slammed against the opposite wall. He dashed inside toward the left, followed by Dunn and Goerdt.

The three Rangers formed a line, weapons aimed, before the Germans could react to the suddenness of the door slamming open.

"Hände hoch! Hände hoch!" Goerdt shouted.

Martelli, Schneider, and Barker ran into the building toward the right.

The Germans were facing seven Rangers and their Thompson .45s.

All of the Germans raised their hands, their faces wearing shock.

Dunn told Goerdt to get the Germans under control and outside. He went out the door where Newman was waiting.

"Roy. Would you send some of your guys back to drive the first three trucks up here?"

"Sure, Sarge. Be glad to."

"Let the other drivers know to follow."

"Will do."

Newman ran to the corner of the building to tell his men.

Dunn ran over to Porter, whose squad had remained at the corner.

"Don, take your squad and clear each of the hangars. Take note of any vehicles and let me know."

"Will do, Sarge."

Porter passed the word to his men and they ran to the first hangar.

Chapter 41

Swiss Guard mess hall
The Vatican
14 November, 1203 Hours

Saunders and his platoon of Commandos joined the Swiss Guard complement for a farewell lunch. They wore their usual uniforms instead of that of the Swiss Guard's tricolor. The barracks dining hall was large, long, and wide. Saunders guessed it could seat a hundred and fifty men. As it was, minus the half of the Guards who had to remain on duty, there were over sixty men ready for lunch.

Saunders and Barltrop were asked to sit at the head table with Commander Herriot and his vice commander, David Surbeck. The decoy Pope, Alfred Welford, wearing civilian clothing instead of the white cassock, joined them. The Commandos and Swiss Guards were all sitting together rather than in separate groups. Most of the Guards spoke English so conversation seemed to be no problem as the room buzzed with voices.

The eleven SS soldiers who were still alive at the end of the ambush had been taken to the Vatican's jail and locked in separate cells. The leader, Werner Möller, had been grilled for about an hour. Saunders had watched it through a two-way mirror. Herriot had been precise in his questioning and carefully returned to previous questions, but asked them in a different way. He'd given up nothing, which hadn't surprised Saunders or Herriot. He'd been tossed into his own cell without another word being said to him.

Saunders took a bite of his roast chicken, marveling at the burst of flavor from the Italian cook's spices. Also on his plate were fried spicy potatoes mixed with red and yellow peppers, and fresh green beans. To drink was a wonderful white wine.

"This is an excellent meal, Commander. Thank you for providing it for the men."

Herriot finished chewing a bite and said, "It's the least I could do for you. You have done us a great service."

"It was our honor, sir. So what else has happened? What about the mess in the street?"

"That's being handled by the Rome police. They were appalled that the Germans had been so brazen as to try and kidnap the Pope. They were quite angry, as will be the Italian public shortly when the radio stations break in with the news.

"The Vatican's public relations office is taking care of the press release concerning the event in St. Peter's Square. I heard they'd been ordered by the Pope himself to be truthful."

Herriot looked away briefly and cleared his throat nervously.

"I am embarrassed to tell you that they are going to play up the tremendous work carried out by the Swiss Guard. Your contributions will be left out."

Saunders smiled. "It's all right, Commander. We don't expect public recognition. That's not why we do what we do."

Herriot smiled gratefully at Saunders' tact. "Nevertheless, I, my men, and the Pope are extremely thankful you were here. I honestly don't believe we could have withstood the SS without you. However, the Vatican was . . . concerned that including your participation would cause people to conclude that the Swiss Guard was incapable of protecting the Pope. The Vatican could not allow that embarrassment for the men who would lay down their lives for the Pope."

"I fully understand, sir."

"I submitted a request to the Pope for an immediate increase to the Swiss Guard, effectively doubling our size. Would you believe I got an approval with his signature within an hour?"

Saunders chuckled. "Pretty good idea to ask when something bad just happened."

"I know I should be embarrassed to admit to the timing, but somehow, I'm just not."

"You do what you have to do."

"Yes. That's right. Are you planning to fly home tonight or tomorrow?"

"I'm giving the men a sixteen-hour pass. We'll leave at eight in the morning."

Herriot nodded with a smile. "That's good of you."

Saunders leaned closer and lowered his voice. "Oh, it's not really for them, sir. I love architecture and I want to tour Rome."

Herriot burst into laughter and the room grew silent, staring at the head table.

"Sergeant Saunders," he said quietly, "you are an honest man to a fault."

"Aye, I suppose so."

Saunders leaned forward so he could see Welford. "Mr. Welford, that was quite a good pratfall you made in the street. Perfectly done. It gave the SS a chance to think they could catch you."

Welford grinned. "A useful skill from my more youthful days, Sergeant."

"Indeed." Saunders leaned back, grinning.

Herriot reached below the table and retrieved a small canvas bag. He stood and said, "Gentlemen!"

The room grew quiet again.

"Swiss Guard, attention!"

All of the Guards stood.

Herriot right-faced to Saunders.

"Hand . . . salute!"

All of the Guards snapped a salute toward the head table.

Saunders and Barltrop jumped to their feet at attention. They returned the salutes.

The Guards dropped their salutes and sat down.

Herriot opened the bag and pulled out a brass plaque on a wood background frame.

"Sergeant Saunders, this is for you and your men from grateful brothers in arms."

He held the plaque up so the room could see it for a moment. He turned it back so he could read:

"To the British Commandos on this fourteenth day of November in the year of our Lord nineteen forty-four, we give thanks. Your contributions to the Pope's safety are known to us and will never be forgotten.

"The Swiss Guard.

"Acriter et Fideliter

"Fiercely and Faithfully."

He handed the plaque to Saunders.

The big redhead was silent for some time. He felt a lump rise in his throat, a rarity. At first he thought he wasn't going to be able to speak, but he took a breath and it seemed to help get his emotions under control. For reasons he could not explain, this moment seemed to be a culmination of all he and his men had done in the war as an elite Commando unit, all they had suffered through, and all that was yet to come.

Saunders held out his hand and as Herriot shook it, said, "Thank you, Commander Herriot, for this. We are honored to have served alongside men such as you and your incredible men."

Saunders turned to the room and held up the plaque so his men could see it again. He set it down and raised his wine glass.

"Commandos, rise and give a hip, hip, hoorah to our brothers in arms, the Swiss Guards!"

The British Commandos jumped to their feet, raising their glasses.

At the top of their lungs they shouted, "Hip, hip, hoorah!" Each man clinked his glass with the nearest Guard.

After the men sat down, the room began buzzing again as British and Swiss soldiers celebrated a job well done.

Saunders took his seat and said to Barltrop, "This is quite the sight, isn't it?"

"It truly is," Barltrop replied.

Herriot, who had remained standing, picked up an envelope from next to his plate. He turned to Alfred Welford.

"Mr. Welford. I have here a letter for you from His Holy Father. He personally asked me to read it aloud, if that's agreeable with you."

Welford smiled and nodded. "Certainly, my good man."

Herriot opened the envelope and removed a single sheet of heavy stationary folded in half. He flipped open the letter.

Before he could utter a word, the door to the mess hall opened and three cardinals stepped through.

Herriot froze in place, staring at them. This had never happened before.

When the white gowned Pope stepped inside the mess hall, Herriot muttered, "Oh."

All of the men in the room jumped to their feet at attention.

The Pope walked quickly toward the head table. He stepped around to the back side and stopped next to Herriot. Herriot immediately dropped to a knee and bowed his head.

Pope Pius XII said in Italian accented English, "Rise, my son. No need to kneel for me today of all days."

Herriot stood.

The Pope turned to face the room, standing between Herriot and Saunders. The Pope smiled at Welford, who stared back wide eyed.

The Pope took the letter from Herriot and held it out so he could read it.

"To my perfect look-alike, Mr. Welford of Great Britain. Thank you from the bottom of my heart for your willingness to die in my place. Your courage is a shining example of what it means to be an Englishman.

"Signed, Pope Pius the Twelfth."

The Pope handed the letter to the astounded Welford.

"Thank you, Holy Father."

The Pope looked out at the men standing before him. "To the British Commandos, thank you for coming all this way to save this unworthy Italian's life. Your courage will not be forgotten. To the Swiss Guard I say, thank you for your continued protection. Your service, dedication, and loyalty are deeply appreciated."

He raised his right hand and blessed the men in the room. He looked at Saunders and said, "Thank you."

Saunders managed to get out "You're welcome, Holy Father," before the Pope turned and walked away. In a moment, he disappeared through the door, the cardinals trailing him.

Saunders turned to Herriot, who still seemed frozen by the Pope's sudden appearance.

"I take it that doesn't usually happen."

Herriot shook his head to clear it and looked at Saunders. "Not in the four hundred and thirty-eight years we've existed."

"Well, lad, I'd say you've something to tell your grandkids, eh?"

"Yes. Yes, I suppose I do."

A few hours later, Saunders sent his men on their way into the streets of Rome. He stopped at a small store and bought an English-Italian dictionary, a notebook, and a pencil. He hailed a taxi and, after looking up a phrase, told the driver to take him to the Colosseum, his first stop of many.

Chapter 42

German airfield
6 miles south of the Nazi Uranium Facility
14 November, 1308 Hours

Bob Schneider tapped Dunn on the shoulder. "Hey, Sarge. Good news. Got a call from one of the C-54 pilots. They're five minutes out. He wanted to know about the condition of the runway, so I told him 'wet,' which seemed to be what he wanted to know."

"Great. Thanks, Bob."

Dunn looked around the hangar, the second one in the line. After Porter and his men had checked all of the hangars, the report was that all were empty, except the first one, which had a German car in it. Presumably it belonged to the three maintenance men. Dunn had ordered all trucks and everyone, from Rangers to workers inside the hangar to stay out of view. A nice byproduct of that decision was that everyone was staying dry and were out of the wind. Dunn situated the workers with Colonel Mason in the southeast corner. The six airfield captives and the two white-coated scientists were under guard by four of

Newman's squad. Mason had checked all of the Rangers' film badges and reported good news: no one had received a dangerous exposure to the uranium-235.

After seeing everyone, Dunn felt a little like a traveler picking up hitchhikers all the way along his trip. He was sitting with his back to the north wall, resting. Wickham and Kelly stopped by.

"Found a few full jerry cans. Should be enough to blow up and burn those planes out there," Wickham said in his Brit-Tex accent. "Should be a right good show."

"Our planes are five minutes out. May as well go ahead and take care of the one-oh-nines. Wait." Dunn held up a finger.

"Bob, did you tell the pilot about the enemy planes and that we were taking care of them?"

"I did."

Dunn turned to Wickham. "Off you go then."

After Wickham and Kelly left to go start some fireworks courtesy of German aircraft, Dunn slowly got to his feet. He felt tired. Worn out, actually. He'd be ready for a few days off. He hoped they would get them. It suddenly dawned on him that Pamela's birthday was coming up soon. He already had a surprise gift for her that he was sure she would love. Her mother had immediately agreed to help with the party. It would be a large gathering. His squad and Saunders', Colonel Kenton and Captain Adams, and Colonel Jenkins and Lieutenant Mallory. Was it going to be around twenty-five people? Wow. It would be at the Hardwickes' farm, south of Andover. It was November in England. The weather would be an additional invitee. Would it bring a nice present, a clear sunshine-filled day, or a day like this, cold and rainy and windy?

He made his way over to the personnel door built next to the hangar door. He peered into the gloom through the window. He tried to estimate how low the cloud ceiling was, but couldn't get a bead on it. Nothing to act as a reference for comparison. He hoped the pilots could find them and they could board without trouble, for once, and just get the hell out of this miserable place.

Higgins and temporary replacement Frank Barker had been assigned to stand watch over the road in both directions, north and south. The only vantage point available was the roof of the airfield's main building, which was flat. Higgins had a walkie-talkie with him and he checked in with Dunn every ten minutes. Dunn recalled that it was about fifty miles to Frankfurt. Had Speer, after just barely escaping, made it to Frankfurt and called in some help? When would they arrive? *Probably about now*, he thought grimly. *I sure the hell hope not. Give us a damn break just once, would you?* He wasn't sure if that was a prayer, but if it was, it might not have pleased the Lord, what with the 'damn' in it. *Sorry, about that, God. But if you could help us out this time, I'd be very grateful.*

As if in answer to his prayer, he heard the first rumbling sounds of big aircraft engines. A lot of them. He pushed the door open, stepped through, and looked up. A small overhang kept him dry. The sounds were coming from the north, with the wind, which had changed directions from earlier. He kept his eyes on the bottom of the gray and white clouds there.

Suddenly, a silver P-51 Mustang popped out through the clouds leaving a trail of rotating wisps behind him from his propeller. The plane was headed southeast. The pilot dove to about fifty feet off the ground. Dunn ran out waving his arms. As the pilot roared by, Dunn could clearly see he was looking right at him. The plane's name was *Sweet Mabel II*, so it was Captain Norman Miller providing escort again. Miller waggled his wings and flew back up inside the clouds.

A few minutes passed. A massive C-54 appeared under the clouds lined up right on the runway, probably helped by Miller's flyby. It seemed to be moving so slowly that it was just hanging in the sky. It swept past Dunn and touched down rolling to the far end of the runway. Dunn had measured the runway in the old recon photos that were available and made sure the planes would have ample run off space. He'd also ensured it was wide enough for a turnaround so they could take off against the wind, pilots' preferred method to help get air moving over the wings faster.

The second plane landed and joined the other, leaving plenty of space for each to complete their 180 degree turnabout. Four Mustangs appeared. They flew slowly across the length of the airfield. Dunn guessed their altitude at maybe five hundred feet. It was amazing the pilots had found the airfield in this soup.

Dunn ran back to the hangar and poked his head in through the door.

"Let's go everyone. Time to get aboard."

He used his walkie-talkie to get Higgins and Barker back.

The workers all climbed back inside the trucks they'd arrived in. The Rangers and the German prisoners boarded last.

Dunn did a quick check to make sure no one was left behind. He looked northward at where Wickham and Kelly were getting ready to destroy the enemy planes. Big Wickham was standing on a wing, next to the open cockpit. He had a jerry can in his hand. Something white dangled from it. He lit his lighter and held it below the white thing, which caught fire. He took a step back and tossed the fuel-filled can toward the cockpit. He didn't wait and jumped off the wing.

The cockpit erupted in flames.

Kelly did the same with the middle plane and it turned into a torch.

Wickham had one to go. As soon as it was burning, he and Kelly ran for Dunn's truck. They clambered up into the back.

Higgins floored the gas pedal as soon as someone pounded on the back of the cab.

At the end of the runway, the planes had turned around and were ready. The trucks got onto the tarmac and raced toward their escape planes. The fifty workers would fill one of the planes, the first of the two. Colonel Mason would fly in the same plane to keep an eye on them for the two hour and twenty minute flight. Rob Goerdt joined the doctor in case he needed a translator.

The Rangers ran aboard the second plane. Dunn pushed the prisoners into seats at the rear. Best to keep them far from the cockpit. As his platoon settled in, Dunn assigned six of Newman's men to guard the Germans.

Dunn ran forward and stuck his head in the cockpit.

The pilot and copilot glanced over their shoulders at him.

"Tom Dunn. Thank you, guys. You did a hell of a job finding us!"

The pilot tipped his head to his partner. "All his doing, Sergeant Dunn."

"Thank you, Lieutenant."

"Glad to help out."

The pilot was listening to his headset. "Lead aircraft says they're ready for takeoff. Give the go?"

"You bet! Let's get out of here," Dunn said happily.

Dunn watched the lead plane start rolling. It seemed so slow, he wondered if it was really moving. But of course it was. As soon as the lead plane rotated over its main gear, Dunn's pilot pushed the throttles forward. The plane ahead soared skyward. Within a minute, it was into the clouds. The pilot and copilot pulled back on their wheels and the plane's nose lifted.

Dunn looked out the right window and gasped. A convoy of six German trucks was heading for the airfield. A German staff car led the convoy. Dunn was one hundred percent certain Albert Speer was in that car. The lead truck stopped and some soldiers jumped out, raising their rifles.

The plane disappeared in the murky world of the clouds and their safety.

Dunn didn't mention the convoy to the pilots. He left the cockpit and found a window seat next to Cross. He climbed past his friend and sat down, taking off his dripping helmet. He let it fall to the floor.

"We made it by about two minutes, Dave."

Cross rolled his head and looked at Dunn.

"Speer got help?"

"Sure did."

"Too bad for him." Cross turned away and closed his eyes. His breathing slowed almost immediately and Dunn knew his friend was already out cold.

Not a bad idea, he thought. Just when he was about to fall asleep, something woke him up. Oh, yeah, one more thing to do.

Lord, thanks for hearing my prayer today. I really appreciate it.

RONN MUNSTERMAN

Chapter 43

Colonel Mark Kenton's office
Camp Barton Stacey
14 November, 1650 Hours, London time

Colonel Mark Kenton entered his office for the first time since the plane crash. He stood quietly and examined his desk, which was completely cleared of paper. Only the black phone was there, and a black ash tray. The map table to his left seemed to be in the right place. The guest chairs were lined up neatly in front of the desk. The window shades were open allowing the weak light from a cloudy day to come into the office. He walked briskly to his chair and pulled it back. Sitting down, he opened his middle drawer and pulled out his favorite pen, a gold-topped Parker fountain pen. He smiled. He loved quality pens and Captain Adams always made sure it was there for him. That meant, of course, that Adams had come in sometime earlier and tidied up. He couldn't imagine asshole Cole, as he'd grown to think of him, would leave it in such pristine condition.

Still wearing a cast on his right forearm from hand to elbow, he carefully unscrewed the pen's top and set it down. He pulled a blank paper from the same middle drawer with his left hand. He grasped the pen in his right hand the best he could with the cast. He signed his name.

"Oh hell." It was a mess. He tried again. After four tries, it almost looked normal. He shook his head at the difficulties of everyday things. He threw the paper away in the trash can behind him and set the pen on the desk for later.

He opened the bottom right drawer and pulled out all of the folders. He stacked them neatly on the right side of the desk, where he often placed them just before he perused each one looking for the mission that had to be done. He pulled a pack of Lucky Strikes from the middle drawer. They were unopened, so he knew Adams had struck again. He smiled. He tore off the cellophane, ripped open the package, and tapped out a cigarette. He stuck his hand in his pants pocket and grabbed his Zippo. He lit his cigarette and puffed away contentedly.

Motion caught his eye at the door. Captain Adams and Dunn were there. Adams carried a slim folder in one hand.

Kenton waved them in with a smile.

Dunn grinned when he saw Kenton sitting at his old desk, smoking as he often did. Things were back to normal. He needed it. He stepped through the door and snapped off a salute. Kenton returned it being careful not to bonk himself in the head with his cast, and waved at the chairs.

Dunn and Adams sat down.

"Welcome back, Colonel," Dunn said.

"Thanks, Tom. Glad to be back."

"Feeling all right?"

"Yes. Seem to be back to normal. Headaches gone. Only four more weeks of wearing the cast."

"Glad to hear it, sir."

Kenton leaned forward, holding out his pack of cigarettes. Dunn and Adams each took one and lit them with Dunn's own black speckled Zippo.

"How'd the mission go? I appreciate the phone call from Hampstead Airbase letting me know it was successful. General

Hopkins sends his thanks. He's already letting the brass know the early results."

"As I mentioned, a complete success, sir. Blew up the entire facility, burying all of the uranium and the shells they'd already prepared. We brought back two physicists who were responsible for running this bizarre program. Sent them off for interrogation.

"We also, uh, freed fifty Czech workers who'd been brought there from a concentration camp in eastern Germany. And they'd been exposed to the uranium even though the Germans put them in some protective gear. Colonel Mason said they'd die if they didn't get treatment."

"And that's when you contacted Captain Adams for a second plane?"

"Yes, sir."

"Highly unusual, Tom."

"Yes, sir. But you should have seen them. Emaciated already from the camp. Poisoned by radiation on top of that. They deserved better."

"You did the right thing. Where are they?"

"Colonel Mason arranged for them to be sent to a specialized hospital where they could get the treatment for radiation poisoning."

"What did he say their prognosis was?"

Dunn's lips compressed briefly, showing how unhappy he was. "He said, that in all honesty, ninety percent of them could survive, perhaps more."

"You did all you could. A lot more than anyone else would have, I have to say."

"I know, sir, but still . . ."

"You can't save everyone."

"No, sir." Dunn looked down, clearly upset.

"Let's not forget the sixty-two POWs you rescued in Italy back in August," Adams said. "Plus getting Colonel Rogers out of the Gestapo's hands before he could give away information on the invasion of southern France."

Dunn and his men had broken into a POW camp and had indeed rescued all of the British soldiers there, and an American intelligence officer who had been shot down over Italy on a recon flight.

"And let's not forget, either, that you saved an entire Italian village from destruction and death. How many people was it, Tom?" Kenton asked.

Dunn raised his head and gazed at the two officers in turn. He held up his hands and smiled. "Okay, enough. I get it. Thank you both very much."

He frowned. "You know, I almost got Albert Speer."

"The Minister of Armaments was there?" Adams asked.

"Yes, sir. Had him in my sights, but wanted to capture him, so I didn't shoot. Son of a bitch got away. He got a couple of platoons of soldiers and was headed right for the airfield as we took off. I just know it was him in the lead car. One thing, though. You should have seen his face when he saw *me*. Looked fit to be tied. That was worth something. Probably hates me by now."

"Well, that's quite an endorsement if I ever heard one. Pissing off Speer, and by extension, Hitler. Sounds like an excellent day to me," Adams said, grinning.

Dunn laughed at the 'by extension' remark. "True." He glanced at the pile of folders on the desk. "Anything in there for me, sir?"

Kenton shook his head. "I haven't read these. And even if I had, no. I want you and your men, plus Newman's and Porter's to take a couple of days off."

Dunn grinned at Kenton. The colonel always had the men's welfare at heart. Perhaps now was the time.

"Sir? The men lost a weekend, well actually just one day, due to some problems during a short notice inspection. Could we tack on an extra day?"

Kenton glanced at Adams, who nodded.

"This was another of Cole's doings?"

"Yes, sir."

"I'm thinking about a week should do it instead. Spend time with Pamela. Take her to London. Whatever you want to do."

"An entire week, sir?" Dunn asked, surprised.

"Yes. An entire week. Off the base. Everyone. Especially you."

Dunn held up his hands in surrender. "Yes, sir. I'll arrange that. By the way, Pamela's birthday is coming up. I'm planning a birthday party out at her folks' farm. She and I would love it if you could both come."

"Yes. She mentioned it when she visited me. I'll be there, and so will Captain Adams. When is the party?"

"Her birthday is next Monday, the twentieth. I was thinking everyone could show up around sixteen hundred."

"We'll be there."

"That's great, thank you both."

Kenton smiled. "I heard Lindstrom might be getting out."

"Oh, yeah. Yes, sir. He's due to come to the barracks tonight. The doctors gave him his release to duty."

Dunn looked from each officer to the other. "Uh, Colonel, any word on Colonel Cole's final outcome?"

Adams laughed out loud. It took a little while for him to get it to stop. "Sorry, sir. I've just never heard of a better comeuppance for a more deserving asshole, pardon my French. General Hopkins walked him to the plane taking him stateside himself."

"Good riddance," Dunn said. "Oh, sorry."

Kenton laughed lightly. "Don't be sorry, Tom. We're well rid of the worst officer I've ever met, and believe me, I've met more than a few. I'm glad you were able to withstand his bullshit."

"Yes, sir. Thank you. Anything else you need from me? I'll have the after-action report for you tomorrow morning."

"That'll be fine. No, nothing else."

Dunn stood.

Kenton held up a hand. "Wait, Captain Adams, there is one more thing, isn't there?"

"Oh, I'm afraid so, sir. It's not the greatest news."

"I thought as much."

"I worry that Sergeant Dunn might suffer permanently from this."

Dunn looked from one officer to the other. Both had dead-serious expressions on their faces.

"What?" he asked.

Adams handed the folder to Kenton, who laid it on the desk and flipped it open.

With his Parker fountain pen, he signed his name on the bottom of the sheet of paper. He stood and said, "Tom, I'm sorry,

I don't know quite how to tell you this, but you're going to have to do some sewing. Captain Adams, if you please."

Adams stood and held out his hand to Dunn, who glanced down.

"Congratulations, Master Sergeant Dunn!" Adams and Kenton said together.

Dunn took the proffered six stripes in surprise.

"You guys. Jeez, way to mess with a guy."

Kenton and Adams laughed.

"Too much fun, Tom."

Dunn smiled at the officers. "Thank you, both of you. I appreciate this."

"It's well earned. And since you won't accept a commission, this is what I can do for you."

"Thank you again."

"Go on and get out of here. Say thank you to the men."

"I will do, sir." He shook hands with both officers, stepped back and saluted. After Kenton returned the salute he left.

Kenton stared at the open door for a moment, and turned his gaze to his longtime aide.

"One of a kind."

Adams smiled. "He is definitely that, sir. We're lucky to have him."

"Yes. Very."

Chapter 44

Colonel Rupert Jenkins' office
Camp Barton Stacey
15 November, 1723 Hours, the next evening

Colonel Jenkins examined Saunders and Barltrop carefully.

"You two appear to be well rested."

"Yes, sir. Slept a full night in Rome and some more on the plane ride home," Saunders replied.

"Quite a result there, I must say," Jenkins said. He was rarely impressed enough to say something.

Saunders nodded. "Thank you, sir. The best we could have gotten, I believe."

"How was it working with the Swiss Guard?"

"I'm impressed by their knowledge and skills. Top notch fighters. Herriot had his head together and stayed calm, at least on the outside. His men would do anything for him."

"As would yours."

"Aye, yes, sir."

"Nothing useful from the SS character?"

"No. Tight as can be. Last I knew, he was still locked up in the Vatican jail. A miserable place, I must say. Cold, damp, older than everything. To be honest, even though Herriot said he was turning the SS men over to the Allies, I think they're going to stay right where they are. Probably forever. Herriot was particularly affronted that someone would even consider kidnapping the Holy Father."

"Bread and water, then?"

Barltrop laughed. "More likely to be those little communion wafers, just to make a point."

Lieutenant Mallory, Jenkins' aide laughed so hard, he snorted.

When everyone looked at him with amusement on their faces, he said, "I'm Catholic. I'm imagining eating those wafers every day for the rest of my life."

"Sounds like 'cruel and unusual' to me," Jenkins said. "But fitting. Tell me about the Pope's vacation villa."

Saunders shook his head. "Stunning, is the word that comes to mind, sir. As cared after as the grounds of Buckingham Palace itself. I'd love to go back someday, take Sadie there."

"You just want to see the Colosseum again," Barltrop quipped.

"Aye, that, too. My God what architects they were."

A silence fell on the group for a bit.

Saunders broke it up. "Mr. Welford was glad to touch English soil again. Although he was extremely pleased to have received a personal note of thanks from the Pope. Oh, and you should have seen Herriot's face when the Pope popped in at lunch to thank everyone. I thought he was gonna faint there for a minute."

"Indeed," Jenkins murmured. "I hope Mr. Welford is sitting down when he opens a letter that was hand delivered to his flat today. A thank you from the King."

Saunders nodded. "Excellent, sir. He was brave beyond words, especially when we knew the SS was right behind us. He held himself together very well. Would have been a hell of a soldier."

Jenkins smiled. "You didn't know?"

"Know what, sir?"

"He was a Sergeant Major, like you, in the Great War. Earned no less than a Victoria Cross."

Saunders sat nonplussed for a moment. "He never said."

"Never do, do they?" Jenkins said.

"No, sir. Never do. Explains a lot about his behavior."

"Indeed." Jenkins looked at his watch. "Why don't you lads get on? I have enough to pass up the line."

Neither Commando needed to be told twice to hit the road.

After salutes and "good nights," the two men were outside. They jumped in a staff car with Barltrop driving. He headed for the camp's gate.

"Your flat?"

"Aye."

Saunders thudded up the stairs to his second floor flat. When he reached the landing in front of the door, Sadie opened it. She ran into his waiting arms and he twirled her in the tight space. He set her down gently and kissed her.

"I'm so bloody happy to see you, darling," he said.

"You, too, Mac."

She took his hand, and led him into the flat. She pushed him toward the new sofa they'd bought recently and said, "Have a sit down. I'll put a pot on."

"Right."

Saunders sat. He pulled off his beret and laid it carefully on the arm of the sofa. He leaned back and stretched out his legs, crossing one boot over the other.

Sadie made some clanking sounds in the kitchen and returned soon after. She sat down next to him, facing him with one leg curled underneath her. She took his big hands in her small ones.

Saunders' brow knitted. "Everything okay?"

"Oh, my darling, yes. It's all okay."

Saunders searched her beautiful face, peering into her brown eyes. "What is it?"

"We need to think of some baby names, Mac."

"Baby names? What . . .?" His eyes grew wide. He looked down at her tummy and back up to her face. "Are you . . .?"

"Yes! I'm pregnant. I found out today!"

"Oh my God, Sadie!" Saunders leaned over and pulled her close and kissed her gently. They held each other for a while, her head on his massive shoulder.

"When are you due?"

"Fourth of the seventh."

"No. You're kidding!"

"No, not kidding. Why? What is it?"

"If our baby is born on the fourth of July, I'll never, ever hear the end of it from Tom Dunn."

"Really? He'd make a big deal out of it?"

"Aye, really. You have no idea."

"Well, maybe baby will be late. Most first ones are, you know."

"God, I hope so."

They hugged and kissed some more.

The tea kettle whistled.

No one moved to turn it off.

Chapter 45

Pamela's 23rd Birthday Party
The Hardwicke Farm
5 miles south of Andover
20 November, 1614 Hours, 5 days later

England can be kind to you on certain days. This was one of them. A warm front had moved in Sunday night and Monday morning brought warmer air, sunshine, few clouds, and a feeling of hope. By four in the afternoon it had reached an incredible fifty-four degrees.

Parked in the Hardwicke barnyard were two trucks, one each for Dunn's and Saunders' men, a couple of jeeps, one for Colonel Kenton and Captain Adams, and one for Dunn so he could run any last minute errands, and a British staff car for Colonel Jenkins and Lieutenant Mallory, and another for Saunders and Sadie. All of the vehicles were tucked in close to the barn on the north side, so the sunset wouldn't be blocked for the party-goers.

Mrs. Hardwicke had taken on the job of cooking for so many people. When Pamela had tried to help, her mother shooed her out of the kitchen.

Dunn and Cross had arrived early and had created, with the help of Pamela's dad, picnic tables out of wood planks and sawhorses. Dunn had finagled a bunch of wooden folding chairs from the camp mess hall. The tables were in the center and south portion of the barnyard, running east-west so everyone would have a clear line of sight to the valley to the west and the sunset, which Dunn promised would be spectacular today.

A reinforced table was set up on which several kegs of beer sat. Dunn had hired a bartender from the Star & Garter and purchased the kegs of British ale. There was tea, too, of course, but who cared?

Dunn and Cross made a head table for Pamela and Dunn, and the Hardwickes, and a smaller table to the side for Pamela's presents.

All of the soldiers wore their dress uniforms, although it was likely that later, the ties might accidentally come undone, as well as the top shirt button.

Dunn and Pamela circulated amongst the guests together. First to visit was Colonel Kenton.

"Colonel, it sure is good to see you here," Dunn said.

Kenton turned and lifted his beer glass. "Happy birthday, Pamela."

"Thank you, Colonel," Pamela replied with a wide smile.

"And thank you, Tom. It's so good to be out of the hospital."

"I bet."

"Thank you for promoting Tom," Pamela said.

Kenton smiled. "You're welcome. He's earned every bit of it."

Pamela put a hand on his left arm. "Thanks for coming today."

"My pleasure."

Dunn looked over the crowd and spotted Colonel Jenkins. He nodded in that direction for Pamela's benefit.

"See you later, sir."

"Yep."

They approached Jenkins, who was standing with his hands behind his back facing the valley. The sunlight played on his face. Dunn thought he was enjoying it.

"Colonel Jenkins?"

The British Commander turned slightly. His face broke into an uncommon grin when he saw Pamela. "Mrs. Dunn! Don't you just look radiant today?"

Pamela smiled at the compliment. She took his hand and stepped forward. She kissed him on the cheek.

"Thank you, sir."

Jenkins seemed surprised by the kindness and his eyes became wet, but he kept his gaze on Pamela. "Happy birthday, my dear." He looked at Dunn and smiled.

Dunn was surprised. He'd never, ever been the recipient of a Jenkins' smile, especially at Commando School.

"You make a lovely couple. I'm truly happy for you both."

Dunn was frozen by the unexpectedly kind words.

Pamela came to the rescue, "How very kind, sir. Thank you. We feel very blessed."

Jenkins nodded and offered his hand to Dunn.

Dunn finally recovered and shook hands. "Thank you, Colonel."

Jenkins nodded again and turned back to enjoy the sunshine.

Dunn and Pamela moved away. When they were out of earshot, he said, "I've never seen him like that."

She glanced over at her husband. "Well, he's unmarried, right?"

"Uh, yeah, I think so."

"I suspect he was thinking about someone in the past. Someone he let get away, or maybe he chose the army over her."

Dunn stopped walking in surprise. "What? How . . . how could you possibly figure that out?"

She smiled and patted him on the arm. "Oh, Tom. Really? You have to ask that?"

"But . . . no, I guess I don't. You do always seem to understand people better than I ever will. You have a gift, I think."

"Yes, I do. And don't you forget it."

Dunn laughed. "How could I possibly?"

Pamela giggled. It continued a little longer than usual and Dunn said quickly, "Watch out. You're gonna snort."

Pamela drew in a deep breath, her face turned pink, and she began to snort. She buried her face in his shoulder until they stopped. When she finished, she pulled back, her eyes wet from laughter crying. Dunn gave her his handkerchief and she dabbed her eyes.

"Oh, dear. It's been awhile."

"Snorting may be dangerous for your health."

"Knock it off, buster, you're not helping."

Dunn gave a fake snort.

"Who's next?" she asked.

"Saunders' men, Steve first."

They made their way over to the group of Commandos, who were gathered not far from the beer table, big surprise there.

Barltrop spotted them coming and he quickly set his beer down and snapped to attention. "Lads! Ten . . . Shun!"

Each Commando set his glass down and faced Dunn and Pamela, snapping to attention.

Dunn smiled at Barltrop and raised a hand. "No need for that, Steve."

Barltrop ignored Dunn and stared at Pamela with his blue eyes, which suddenly crinkled as he broke into a huge grin. At the top of his voice, he shouted, "At ease! Happy birthday, Pamela! On behalf of the squad!"

"Thank you, Steve." She looked at each of the British soldiers in turn and gave them a warm smile. "Thank you, all of you. Very much. I'm so glad you came."

"Our pleasure, Mum!" Barltrop shouted.

Pamela stepped forward and pecked him on the cheek. "How's Kathy? And don't shout it at me."

"She's fine, Pamela. Saw her over the weekend."

"Set a date yet?"

Barltrop blushed. "We're getting there, I think."

"Good. Tell her 'hello' for me."

"I will do."

The couple made their way over to Dunn's men, who were standing in a clump near their tables. Schneider saw them first and he said something Dunn couldn't hear. The men stopped talking and turned to face the couple with grins on their faces.

Dunn shook hands with each man, and introduced Pamela to Higgins and Kelly, the only two she hadn't met before.

Everyone wished Pamela a happy birthday.

Dunn stopped at Eugene Lindstrom.

"How's the leg, Eugene?"

"It feels pretty good, Sarge. Not weak anymore."

"It's good to have you back."

"I'm glad to be back. I heard I missed some pretty cool stuff."

"You did."

Both men knew that was as far as they could go in front of Pamela.

Dunn shook hands with the man from Eugene, Oregon.

He turned to move on, but Pamela tugged at his arm. "Wait, Tom."

He turned back, puzzled.

Pamela waved at the men to gather close around her. When they did, she said, "Boys, I just want you to know how much I appreciate what you're doing. I know how courageous you all are. I also want to, to—" She looked down trying to regain her composure.

Dunn put his arm around her shoulders.

She looked up again. Tears were running down her cheeks. "I want you to know I also am very grateful to you every time you bring my Tom back to me."

The men, evidently all thinking the same thing, stepped forward. Each man gave Pamela a gentle hug and moved aside for the next man. When the last man, Dave Cross, stepped away, Pamela murmured, "Oh my goodness. Thank you, boys."

Dunn guided Pamela away and she spent a few minutes working on her composure.

"You okay, Honey?" Dunn asked.

"Yes, I'm okay. You have wonderful men."

"I do. I'm very lucky. Are you ready to say 'hi' to Mac and Sadie?"

"I really am."

Saunders and Sadie were standing a little farther west than Jenkins had been, admiring the sunset. He had moved away.

"Hi guys," Dunn called from a few feet away.

The British couple turned around and wore great smiles. Everyone hugged everyone else. Close friends happy to be together.

"You look beautiful, Pamela," Sadie said.

Pamela was wearing a robin-egg blue dress that highlighted her Arctic-ice blue eyes. Her hair was brushed and coiled around her face.

"Thanks, Sadie. You do, too."

Sadie wore a pink dress. Her brown hair was brushed long and down to her shoulders.

Sadie looked up at Saunders with a question on her face.

He grinned, the tips of his red handlebar mustache twitching. "Shall we tell them?"

She nodded and turned to Pamela. "I'm pregnant!"

Pamela squealed in delight and hugged Sadie for a long time. "I'm so happy for you."

"Thanks. I just found out the other day."

"When are you due?"

Saunders moaned.

Dunn raised an eyebrow at that.

Sadie giggled. "Fourth of July!"

Dunn stared at Saunders, who wore a wary expression. He started to say something, but stopped himself. He simply winked at Saunders.

Saunders gave a visible sigh of relief.

"Congratulations, Mac," Dunn said. He offered his hand.

Saunders took it and said, "Thank you, mate."

"You hoping for a boy or a girl?" Dunn asked.

"Either or. Healthy is all I pray for."

"Good for you."

Saunders glanced at Dunn's left arm. He grinned, his handlebar mustache twitching again.

"Got yourself promoted, I see. Congratulations, Master Sergeant."

"Ah, thanks, Mac."

"Took you long enough to catch up, mate."

"Yeah, well, here we are at last. First one to officer loses."

"Aye. Not happening. Ever."

Dunn looked at his watch. "I'd say it's time for dinner. Shall we?" He offered his arm to Pamela and she slid her hand through the crook.

The two couples walked toward the tables.

After dinner, Dunn rose to his feet. He clinked a knife against his beer glass. The guests stopped talking and looked his way.

"Ladies and gentlemen. Thank you for coming to help celebrate Pamela's birthday. It means a lot to us to see you all here."

The guests all shouted, "Hear, hear!"

"It's time for the cake and candle blowing out ceremony. And of course the Birthday Song. Feel free to sing it whichever way you want, British or American."

Mr. and Mrs. Hardwicke quickly lit the candles on the cake.

The guests cheered. They sang the Happy Birthday Song, some the British way, some the American way.

Pamela closed her eyes briefly, making her wish. She leaned forward and blew out all the candles in one breath, no stragglers.

Mr. and Mrs. Hardwicke cut the cake. Sadie, Saunders, and Cross all jumped up to help distribute the pieces.

Dunn leaned close to Pamela. "Time for presents, dear." He pointed at the brimming table of gifts.

"Oh boy," she said.

Dunn brought over a few at a time and Pamela opened them. For each one, she thanked the giver.

When there was one box left, he picked it up and set it down in front of her gently. It was small, about the size of three cigarette packs stacked together. He sat down and looked at her expectantly.

She pried the top off and set it aside. When she peered inside, she gasped. She dug in, pulled out a small bottle, and held it up triumphantly. Unscrewing the lid, she placed the bottle under her nose and breathed in the wonderful fragrant aroma.

"Oh my God. Tom, where did you find this? I didn't think it was available anymore."

Dunn got a mischievous look on his face. "You're right. Couldn't find it here. Hotel gift shop in Washington, D.C."

"You're a sly one. How'd you sneak it past me?"

"Put it in a clean pair of socks. Made sure I packed and unpacked my own suitcase."

"Well done, buster."

Dunn grinned.

***

Later, in bed, Pamela lay with her head on Dunn's left shoulder and an arm draped over his chest.

"Was it a happy birthday, dear?"

"The absolute best ever. You truly surprised me with the perfume. You're quite a lot more sneaky than I thought."

"Thank you, I think."

He stroked her left arm gently.

"What'd you wish for?"

"A couple of things. War's end. And a healthy baby, like Mac said."

Dunn nodded. "Both excellent wishes."

They lay there quietly for a few *minutes, basking in the comfort of each other.

"I confess, there was one other wish, Tom"

"Yeah, what was it?"

"For you to take me home tonight, dear."

Dunn, not being dumber than a rock, knew exactly what that meant. He slid out from underneath her and leaned over.

He kissed her deep and long and the lovemaking began.

RONN MUNSTERMAN

Author's Notes

Hello, readers! I hope you enjoyed adventure number ten with Dunn, Saunders, and cast. When I do the research for these books, which as I always say, I love doing, I never know what it is that will catch my eye and become a book. Sometimes, I'm not even thinking about the book when an idea shows up, knocking. However the story idea comes, it usually doesn't take me long to accept it as *the* idea. Sometimes the idea comes fully formed and I already know the start and the end. Sometimes not.

(Note: you'll find the links for bolded text in another section following the Author's Notes.)

For this book, I was reading a list of **WWII operations**. Dunn's main story line is based on a top secret mission that the U.S. Army was going to implement. They were concerned that the Nazis, who were growing more and more desperate in Europe, would stoop to spreading ground up uranium across the beaches of Normandy (**Operation Peppermint**). Obviously, the Nazis didn't, but I loved the idea of Dunn having to stop them from doing that on the front line in eastern France.

Saunders' mission is based on a German top secret mission that was also never implemented (*Operation Rabat*). The **Pontifical Swiss Guard**, who protect the Pope and the **Vatican** is a fascinating subject. As Commander Herriot tells Saunders, they have an incredible history dating back to 1506. Commander Herriot is fictional, but the information he gives Saunders about the Swiss Guard is true.

Pope Pius XII gets a mixed review from historians. Some believe he did many things right in a difficult time, and others think he didn't criticize the Nazis enough publicly. I leave it to you to read more about it and decide for yourself. The picture on the Wikipedia page about him is the one I used to describe him. The Pope's vacation home, the **Villas of Castel Gandolfo**, is truly beautiful and the gardens are spectacular. It became a museum in 2016. Saunders, who you'll recall, loves architecture, was beside himself with all of the ancient structures in Rome. I used Google maps to see exactly how St. Peter's Square was laid out and could even see the Swiss Guards' barracks. The **Archbishop of Westminster, Bernard Griffin** was a real person, as was Pope Pius XII. I wrote the scenes with both of these men from a point of respect and hope it carried through for you. Saunders' love of architecture, if you haven't guessed, comes from me. It all fascinates me. Here are the **Colosseum** and the **Vatican obelisk**.

Our enemy in Italy, Colonel Werner Möller, was a member of the Nazi SS **Einsatzgruppen**, who were responsible untold numbers of deaths.

Albert Speer seems to have quite a problem with our hero, Sgt. Dunn. Seems fitting, and unlikely to stop. The **White Hart Pub** is real and dates back to the 17th century. My treatment of its interior is all fiction. **Radiation sickness** (poisoning) is dreadful. The symptoms Colonel Mason describes are from the Mayo Clinic's page on it. The cave where the Nazis were creating their radiation bombs (think of the modern term "dirty bomb") is fictional, but is loosely based on photos of underground manufacturing sites the Germans used.

Pamela's news that she can become a nurse in Iowa by taking a test (with her British credentials) is accurate for that time. Sadie's news was fun to write and when I did the math and saw she would be due in July, naturally it would have to be on the Fourth! While Dunn was kind to Saunders at Pamela's birthday party by not saying anything, you know as well as I do that it'll come up again.

Dunn's promotion to Master Sergeant was probably overdue, but we got there.

As things worsened for the Nazis, they really did become desperate and looked at all kinds of "super" weapons. To say I'm fascinated by these ideas is probably an understatement since many of the books deal with that subject. To give Dunn and

Saunders impossible missions is just an everyday occurrence for them, and I love them. Thank you, readers, for appearing to love them, too.

For the next book, number eleven, I have the big idea (came from online research again) for Dunn. As of today, I have plans for Gertrude that will give her more pages and an interesting, and hopefully very surprising story line.

RM
Iowa
August 2018

Please consider following me on my blog and or Twitter to get up-to-date info on what's happening with upcoming books.

www.ronnmunsterman.com
http://ronnonwriting.blogspot.com/
https://twitter.com/RonnMunsterman
@ronnmunsterman

The Sgt. Dunn Photo Gallery for each
book: http://www.pinterest.com/ronn_munsterman/

Links for the Author's Notes

WWII operations
https://en.wikipedia.org/wiki/List_of_World_War_II_military_operations

Operation Peppermint
https://en.wikipedia.org/wiki/Operation_Peppermint

Pontifical Swiss Guard
https://en.wikipedia.org/wiki/Pontifical_Swiss_Guard

Vatican
https://en.wikipedia.org/wiki/Vatican_City

Pope Pius XII
https://en.wikipedia.org/wiki/Pope_Pius_XII

Villas of Castel Gandolfo
https://en.wikipedia.org/wiki/Papal_Palace_of_Castel_Gandolfo

Archbishop of Westminster, Bernard Griffin
https://en.wikipedia.org/wiki/Bernard_Griffin

Colosseum
https://www.history.com/topics/ancient-history/colosseum

Vatican obelisk
http://www.obelisks.org/en/vaticano.htm

Einsatzgruppen
https://en.wikipedia.org/wiki/Einsatzgruppen

Albert Speer
https://en.wikipedia.org/wiki/Albert_Speer

White Hart Pub
https://www.whitehartandoverpub.co.uk/

Radiation sickness
https://www.mayoclinic.org/diseases-conditions/radiation-sickness/symptoms-causes/syc-20377058

About the Author

Ronn Munsterman is the author of the Sgt. Dunn novels. His lifelong fascination with World War II history led to the writing of the books.

He loves baseball, and as a native of Kansas City, Missouri, has rooted for the Royals since their beginning in 1969. He and his family jumped for joy when the 2015 Royals won the World Series. Other interests include reading, some more or less selective television watching, movies, listening to music, and playing and coaching chess.

Munsterman is a volunteer chess coach each school year for elementary- through high school-aged students, and also provides private lessons. He authored a book on teaching chess: *Chess Handbook for Parents and Coaches.*

He lives in Iowa with his wife, and enjoys spending time with the family.

Munsterman is currently busy at work on the next Sgt. Dunn novel.

RONN MUNSTERMAN

Made in the USA
Coppell, TX
04 May 2023

16429763R00184